WHAT WE DO
in the
LIGHT

STYLO FANTÔME

Published by BattleAxe Productions
Copyright © 2019
Stylo Fantôme

Cover Design:
Najla Qamber Designs
najlaqamberdesigns.com
Copyright © 2019

Interior Design/Formatting by Champagne Book Design

DEDICATION

For the ladies at Give Me Books
This book was cursed and I was awful
You were amazing and gracious and encouraging
You made me feel better when I felt the worst
I cannot thank you enough for all you do for me

WHAT WE DO
in the
LIGHT

Day to Night, #2

1

*G*od, those hands.

      Running over her body. Flitting across her breasts—he loved her breasts. Not overly large, but ample and perky on her slender frame.

    She let out a deep sigh as the hands smoothed down her sides. She rolled her head forward and looked down her front. His mouth was against her stomach, all she could see were his riotous blond waves of hair. She managed to lift her own hand and gently comb her fingers through the strands.

    I almost love his hair more than his hands. Almost.

    She sighed again as one of those hands found its way between her legs. The sigh turned into a throaty moan, and she bit down on her bottom lip as two fingers gently probed inside her body. She let her eyes drift back shut and just concentrated on feeling.

    Feeling everything. Every moment. Every breath. It was the best with him. The worst. The worst and the best. Always.

    I want this to go on for always …

Something slammed into the back of Valentine O'Dell's head, startling her awake. She lifted her head just in time to narrowly avoid getting hit again—a backpack was dangling haphazardly in front of her face while the owner swung it about in an attempt to get it on.

"Excuse you," she grumbled, rubbing at the back of her head before smoothing her hand around her top knot, making sure the backpack hadn't dislodged it.

"There is no excuse for you."

Ah, that explains it.

Harper Kittering spun around, her backpack now firmly in place. She didn't look directly at Valentine—she never did, anymore—but it was clear who her comment was directed at; they were the only ones left in the classroom.

"I do love our little chats, Harper," Val sighed as she climbed to her feet.

"You were *snoring*," the blonde bombshell sneered. "I guess being a homewrecking slut is really exhausting, huh?"

"You have no idea," Val laughed. "But for the millionth time, you and Ari were broken up, and he and I are no longer involved, so I still have no clue as to why you're angry at me."

"I'm angry because if it weren't for you, he and I would be back together. I'm angry because I got overlooked for some piece of trash. I'm angry because you're disgusting and sitting next to you is bad enough—knowing we shared a guy, it makes me want to vomit."

Valentine didn't have the energy for this; Harper had said it right, Val was exhausted. It had been a rough couple weeks.

A rough couple years.

"If it makes you feel better, it makes me want to puke, too. Did you change your mind about working together?"

Harper was the cause of many of Valentine's problems. They'd been assigned to work on a very important class project together—that was how Valentine had met Harper's ex, Aaron Sharapov. They'd been working at Harper's apartment when Ari had shown up, though unbeknownst to everyone, he'd shown up in order to break up with Harper.

Mistake number one—meeting Ari.

Harper had never been a very good partner. She was incredibly snobby, her father was some big, important politician there in Chicago, the deputy mayor, or something or other. Her and Ari's family had been friends for years, their relationship had been planned since their infancy. Harper hadn't handled the break up very well.

Mistake number two—not realizing what a crazy bitch she is.

By the time Harper had found out that her classmate and partner was boning her ex-boyfriend, Valentine and Ari had ended. *Badly.* But that hadn't mattered to Harper. She was angry and finally had someone to direct all her anger at, and she hadn't let up for one moment. She would make Valentine pay for the end of her relationship, regardless of the fact that Val had almost nothing to do with it.

It was mostly little things. Spreading rumors and lies at the design university they both attended. Making fun of her with her little friends. Shoving her in the halls, knocking her paperwork out of her hands, hitting her with her bag. There had even been a somewhat serious incident in the school parking lot—a white Mercedes, an SUV type of vehicle, had swerved dangerously close to Valentine when she'd been on her bike. She'd fallen over and rolled down into a shallow ditch. She hadn't seen the driver, but she'd heard a very familiar cackle as it had driven away.

How long can this go on for? Surely she'll lose interest at some point.

Of course Valentine could fight back. Tell a teacher or file some sort of report, something. But in all honesty, she was scared. Between problems with her grandmother and working all her crazy hours, Val was already on academic probation—if she got a bad grade in this management class, she could kiss school goodbye. Her grade in the class was almost entirely dependent on her group project with Harper. So as awful as the woman was, Valentine couldn't afford to get rid of her. Not yet.

"You will *never* set foot in my apartment again. I had the locks changed," Harper informed her. Valentine barked out a laugh.

"Which am I, Harper—a slut, or a thief?"

"The two aren't mutually exclusive."

Touché. I'm almost impressed.

"Well, I have no plans to rob you any time soon. We could meet at my—"

"Do not even suggest it. I probably have lice just from sitting so close to you."

"Okay, we could meet at Starbucks. A pizza joint. The library. The park. *Anywhere*. I can't do this whole project on my own," Val said. Harper smirked at her.

"I guess you should've thought about that before you fucked my boyfriend. *Bye*."

And with that, Harper whirled around, flicking her hair over her shoulder as she went. The blonde strands whipped across Valentine's face.

"You need this grade, too, Harper!" she called after her.

"*You* need this grade," Harper snapped, pausing just long enough to lean back in the doorway. "I, on the other hand, actually have a father to help take care of things like that for me."

As she stomped away, Valentine stared after her. Had Harper just really made a crack about Val's dead dad?

Incredible.

She didn't have time to dwell on it, though. She had to be at her club by nine, and it was already five. That was barely enough time to bike across town to visit her grandmother before having to head home to get ready for work. So she pushed Harper out of her mind, and she quickly made her way down to her rickety bike.

Twenty minutes later, she was pulling her helmet off and walking down a different hallway. Even though she'd been visiting almost every day for over a week now, it still felt strange to her. Alien. The smell of antiseptic. The loud voices. She didn't think she'd ever get used to it.

Probably because I shouldn't have to. I shouldn't be here at all.

Barely a week after her grandmother had been admitted to the hospital for her second stroke, Valentine had received a call from her doctor. Apparently, the Illinois Department of Human Services was accusing her of elder neglect. Or really, *someone* had accused her of it, and now IDHS was investigating her.

It had been a devastating blow. She'd still been reeling from the implosion of her relationship with Ari—then to be denied any sort of relationship with her grandmother? It had almost broken her. While the investigation was ongoing, Gam-Gam wasn't allowed to go home. So she'd been transferred to a skilled nursing facility.

Before moving to Chicago, Valentine had thought of all "old folks home" as just that—a retirement home for old people. But it turned out there were all sorts of different kinds, with different classifications. A skilled nursing facility was almost like a miniature hospital, and it was built to house patients with intense medical conditions, and many were also equipped to house patients with memory problems.

Gam-Gam was all of the above.

"Hello?" Valentine drummed her fingers against the counter as she walked up to the first floor nurse's station.

A nurse finally popped up, and Val informed her that she was there to see Eugenia Parker—her grandmother. She wasn't allowed to see her unsupervised. It humiliated her, killed her, to have to ask permission to see the person she'd been taking care of for the last six months. The person she'd loved since she'd been born.

But getting angry didn't make things any easier. So she did what she always did—she gritted her teeth and she played by the rules. She was kind and polite, and she turned in every piece of evidence she could find to prove she'd never abused her grandmother. She showed up to every meeting, returned every phone call, and always walked on egg shells, paranoid one of the social workers would find out about her real job.

Is it like this with children? Can a person be an escort and still be allowed take care of their sickly grandmother? Better to keep it quiet, just in case.

She followed the short nurse down another hall. They chatted as they went, saying hi to other patients along the way, then they both fell silent as they approached Gam-Gam's room.

"She's been doing well today," the nurse said, leading the way into the dimly lit room.

"She has?" Valentine replied, folllowing close behind.

There was a tv mounted on the wall, a reclining chair under it, a small sink and cabinet built into the wall next to her, and in the middle of it all, a narrow hospital bed. Laying in the center of it was her grandmother, looking sickly and frail. She was breathing heavy in her sleep, her eyes squeezed shut tightly.

"Yes," the nurse continued as she walked across the room and opened the blinds. "She talked about you and your sister and your mother, and she remembered which table was hers for lunch."

"That's awesome. I wish …" Valentine sighed as she sank into the recliner. "I used to spend afternoons with her, at home. We'd talk about my mom and sister, too."

The nurse smiled sweetly at her. Everyone knew Valentine's situation, and thankfully, they all seemed to be on her side. If only IDHS would hurry up with their investigation. Gam-Gam's insurance only covered so many days in a nursing facility, and she'd already used up a lot of them. In the not too distant future, Valentine would have to start paying out of pocket, and as good as she was doing at the club, she didn't think she could manage an additional $9,000 a month on top of everything else she already had to pay for.

"Would you like me to wake her?"

Val glanced back at the nurse, then shook her head before looking at her grandma again.

"No, let's let her sleep. I'll come tomorrow and—"

"Is that you, Patricia?"

Once upon a time, Eugenia Parker'd had a deep, somewhat booming voice. Loud, bawdy. Always laughing, always directing the conversation. Now it was frail sounding, and scratchy. Val stood up and hurried to the chair at the side of the bed, smiling as her grandmother slowly blinked her eyes.

"Hi, Gam-Gam, it's me, Valentine," she said. Patricia was Valentine's mother's name, and Gam-Gam often mistook her for her anymore. She'd struggled with her memory before being hospitalized, but afterwards, it had gotten so much worse. Valentine was still hoping there'd be improvements.

"I was waiting for you," her grandma said through a yawn.

"You were? I was waiting for you!" Val teased. The nurse winked at her, then quietly shuffled into the hall. She was supposed to wait in the room, technically, but most of them didn't bother anymore. It was obvious to anyone that Val would never hurt her grandmother.

"Were you? I'm sorry I'm late," her grandma said, struggling to sit up in bed. Valentine helped her get into a more comfortable position, then they both sat back.

"What were you waiting for me for?" Val asked. Her grandma thought hard for a second.

"We were going to go on a walk," she said, shocking Valentine.

"You want to go for a walk? That's awesome, I'll see if we can find a chair," Val said excitedly, and she started to stand up.

"Yes, with you and your boyfriend."

Valentine froze mid-stand.

"Me and ... who?"

"I like tall men," Gam-Gam sighed. "I'm tall, so I'm glad he's tall."

Valentine stared at her grandmother. Ari was tall, over six foot.

"You want to go on a walk with Ari?" she double-checked, though she'd be surprised if her grandmother recognized the name.

"I'm too old to walk," Gam-Gam grumbled. Valentine smiled and sat back down.

"We don't have to."

"Good. I'll tell him when he comes."

Her smile disappeared.

"Tell him when ... who? Who comes?" she asked. Her grandmother yawned again, then snuggled deeper into the pillows behind her.

"The boyfriend," she sighed. "The tall one. I'll tell him when he comes that we don't want to walk. He's a nice young man."

"He's ..." Valentine struggled for a moment, but couldn't bring herself to agree.

The only time she ever met Ari, we were out on a walk. She must be just remembering that time, for some reason, and thinking it happened recently. At least she's remembering, though.

"I like him. You know who else I like? My granddaughter, Valentine. She's very smart."

Val held onto her smile, but she couldn't stop her eyes from swimming with tears.

"You think so?" she asked in a shaky voice. "Sometimes I wonder."

"Not me," her grandmother was fading back into sleep, but her voice still held tinges of pride in it. "I know so. My sweet Valentine, so smart. So pretty. She's a good girl. I'm glad she found a nice boy. I wish she'd visit me."

And then she was asleep, and Valentine was crying, and she had the sudden realization that there was a very distinct possibility that it might never, ever get better for the two of them.

Story of my life.

2

Ari Sharapov wasn't addicted to the gym, like some men he knew. Being a lawyer could be a very stressful job, so a lot of his friends took out their stress on their bodies, or on punching bags. Not him.

He did like to stay in shape, though, and he was a Sharapov, so he had a membership to an exclusive country club. He didn't golf, and he only played tennis occasionally, but he did make use of the gym a couple times a week.

Though since blowing things up with Valentine, and then finding himself unable to get in touch with her, "a couple times a week" had turned into almost every day.

One, two, three, four ...

He counted push-ups in the back of his head while his mind wandered. Where was she, what was she doing. He'd been banned from her club, and he'd yet to be able to catch her outside her house. The one time he'd gone banging on her door in the middle of the night, her roommate had threatened to call the cops on him. Valentine's school would tell him that she was attending classes regularly, but wouldn't tell him which classes she was taking. He was completely frozen out of her life, and Ari was not a man accustomed to being kept out of anything.

... thirteen, fourteen, fifteen, sixteen ...

He couldn't stand being at home. She'd spent so much time there towards the end, it felt like part of it belonged to her now. Sometimes Ari thought of moving out, but then he worried that if she did ever come looking for him, she wouldn't know where to find him.

... twenty, twenty-one, twenty-two, twenty-three ...

And he hated being at work, because it just reminded him of what a fuck-up he was; he was still struggling with his two worlds. Working for his father, wanting to be the kind of man she'd want; achieving all his life long goals, changing his life long goals.

... thirty-one, thirty-two, thirty-three, thirty-four, thirty-god, fuck this, fuck her, fuck. I used to be fucking normal person, what happened to me? A nice pair of tits in a dark club, and suddenly I'm fucked.

Ari collapsed onto the ground, then rolled over onto his back, draping his arm over his eyes. It was all a lie. The first time he'd met Valentine, he'd been intrigued, but it was the second time that had caused him to become obsessed. Seeing her sitting there in her ratty cardigan, no make-up, her hair a rat's nest on her head. Such a chameleon, and from that moment on, she'd never stopped surprising him.

He chuckled at that thought, realizing just how true it was—it had been three weeks since he'd laid eyes on her, and yet she was still surprising him. With her tenacity, with her anger, with her ingenuity. How could it be so hard to get ahold of her?

Because you're going about it the wrong way. You're attacking the fortress from the front door—maybe see if someone's left the back door open.

Ari's arm dropped to the ground and he stared up at the ceiling, feeling like an idiot. Of course, he'd never felt this way about a woman before, so he figured he was entitled to a lot of idiocy.

If he couldn't get to Valentine on his own, and he couldn't get her to come to him, then he'd have to get someone to act on his behalf. Someone to bring her *to* him. But who? Not the goth-y little roommate, she would never turn against Valentine, she seemed to idolize her. Same with the giant bouncer at her club. Ari needed someone ... more corrupt.

WHAT WE DO IN THE LIGHT

He needed someone he could buy.

He needed Marco DelVecchio, her boss, the owner of the nightclub she worked at—the same nightclub Ari was now banned from for life.

"Holy shit," he chuckled. "I really am an idiot."

He hurried off the ground and began to stride towards the locker room, almost barreling over some other members. He ignored them and the showers, changing right back into his clothing before leaving the club.

Even though he was still technically on his lunch break, Ari went straight back to his office and locked his door behind him, instructing one of the receptionists not to let anyone through. He combed through a bunch of files, pulling out folders, then sat hunched over his desk, sifting through all the paperwork.

When Ari had first ever paid for Valentine's time, part of the deal had been that he would help the club's owner, Marco DelVecchio, with some of his legal problems. DelVecchio had a lot of fingers in a lot of different pies around Chicago. His club Caché was the newest at only eight years old, and also the most lucrative. But he also owned several legitimate night clubs, had a large stake in a casino, and several pay-day loan businesses.

The pay-day loans were the problem. Shady businesses in the best of circumstances, Del ran them like he was a loan shark. Lots of questionable practices and tactics took place, and it was obvious to Ari they were also used to funnel laundered money. There had been multiple complaints, and now it looked like the IRS—and possibly the FBI—were on the brink of shutting Del down.

And if the FBI got involved with one business, it was very likely they would dig into his other businesses. Caché was registered as a night club, that's how they got their liquor and business license. But Ari knew from personal experience that a lot of the events that took place within Caché's walls weren't strictly legal. All it would take was one surprise inspection, one legitimate raid, and the place would be shut down for good.

Ari was pretty sure Del wouldn't like that one bit.

DelVecchio had stopped talking to him at the same time as Valentine, clearly valuing his employee more than the potential legal help he could get, which really spoke highly to his character. But the pay-day loan businesses would give Ari a foot in the door. He wasn't a Sharapov for nothing—he had contacts in both the IRS and the FBI offices there in Chicago, as well in the Gaming Commission, Liquor Control Commission, and multiple other agencies.

So he started making phone calls, and he didn't stop until he'd called in enough favors, and offered more in return, to get what he wanted.

"Rose!" he hollered when he finally unlocked and opened his door. She worked in the secretarial pool and handled all his phone when he wasn't available. She stood up in her cubicle, her coppery bangs just barely visible over the wall.

"Yes, Mr. Sharapov?"

"I've gotta step out," he said, going back into his office. He could hear her footsteps approaching, so he kept talking. "I won't be back today. Take any messages for me, okay? I'm expecting a call from an Agent Brewer."

"Yes, sir," she said, hovering in his doorway while he put on his blazer and his overcoat. "Anything else?

Ari thought for a second, then grabbed his briefcase and car keys.

"Yes. Don't tell my father about any of this, don't mention Agent Brewer or the FBI, got it?" he said, then he gave her a hard stare. He knew he was an intimidating man, and had no problems using it to his advantage. She swallowed thickly, but kept a straight face and nodded.

"Got it. I won't tell senior Mr. Sharapov anything."

He gave her a tight smile, then brushed past her as he walked into the hallway, leaving her to shut and lock the door behind him. He liked that Rose liked working for him, but he liked it even more that she *didn't* like his father.

He made quick time driving through town, and though it had

been weeks since he'd been there, Ari found his way to Caché easily enough. He parked near the alley behind it, then walked up to the back door. After ringing the bell, he stood back and glared up at the security camera. A couple moments later, the door swung open, and the giant bouncer Serge stepped outside.

"Ari, my man," he said, yawning and stretching. He was only wearing a white tank top and a pair of wrinkly jeans. "Didn't expect to see you around here again."

"Hello, Serge," Ari said. "Your boss here?"

"It's his home, ain't it?"

"Wanna get him for me?"

"Not particularly."

Ari had come prepared for this moment. He knew the large man would love nothing more than to beat him up—Serge acted like Valentine was his baby sister and was always at the ready to defend her honor. So Ari pulled an envelope out from his inside pocket, and he handed it over to the bouncer.

"Then give this to him. I'll wait."

"And why should I do this?" Serge grumbled, looking over the blank envelope.

"Because it's not about her," Ari retorted. "This is about Del, and it's about Caché, and it's about him potentially losing the whole thing."

Serge looked doubtful, but he eventually turned around and stomped back inside. The door slammed shut behind him. Ari folded his arms and leaned against the railing, waiting for his return.

He didn't have to wait long.

"You're a lucky guy," the giant grunted when he opened the door again, this time holding it wide so Ari could pass through. "I don't think I've ever seen Del entertain someone after he's cut them off."

"I'm a *smart* guy—big difference."

"Can't be too smart if you were stupid enough to piss off Val."

Fair point.

Once upstairs, Ari was made to wait in the garish office for almost fifteen minutes. It was infuriating; he was used to getting his own way, used to being doted upon and respected. Two months ago, he simply would've walked away after the first five minutes and left Del to have his world collapse around him.

Now, though, that world involved Valentine, and Ari wanted— *needed*—to get back in it. So that meant he needed Del.

"You must have brass balls, kid," Del sighed when he finally walked in the room. Ari stood up and held out his hand, but the club owner ignored it. "Valentine ain't here. As much as I love her, I learned a long time ago not to take in strays."

"I'm not here for her," Ari assured him, but Del just laughed.

"Sure, you're not. You got five minutes, lawyer man, so make 'em count."

"You're about to be the subject of an investigation from the IRS and the FBI."

That wiped the smug smirk off Del's face. He stared at Ari hard for a moment, obviously trying to read whether or not he was lying. Ari stared right back, his own smirk firmly in place.

"So your little note said. Just how did you come upon this piece of information?" Del asked.

"*You* gave it to me," Ari replied. "It was with all the other paperwork you sent me a month or so ago."

"I don't know about any raids, so you must be bullshitting."

"Cook Pay Day Loan, ring any bells?"

"Sure."

"The Better Business Bureau has logged a substantial amount of complaints against it," Ari said. "And there are several pending civil suits. The IRS has been flagged."

"*Shit*," Del hissed, glancing away. He thought for a second, then looked back at him. "But still, it's nothing that hasn't happened before, nothing I can't handle."

"It's different this time," Ari shook his head. "They're connecting the dots, they're going to investigate *all* your businesses, including Caché."

"Says who?"

"Says me."

"And who the fuck are you?" Del laughed, leaning back in his chair. "Those guys don't answer to you."

"They do this time."

The entire atmosphere in the room changed. Del the silly caricature of a business owner was gone, and Marco DelVecchio the seasoned business owner was present. His eyes narrowed into slits, and then he gave a sly smile.

"See? I told you. This *is* about her," he spoke softly. Ari nodded.

"Isn't everything?"

"So I'm assuming that since you know so much about my predicament, you know how to get me out of it?" Del asked.

"Yes. I've been very busy today, making a lot of phone calls."

"Shining a lot of light on my little situation here, you mean," Del growled.

"Yes. But I also have the power to move it back into the shadows," Ari assured him. "I'm a powerful man with a lot of powerful connections—I can make this go away, but it'll cost me."

"Which means it'll cost *me*. How much?" Del demanded.

"I want my membership reinstated," Ari said.

There was a long silence. Del finally looked around the room awkwardly.

"And …?" he asked, holding up his hands. Ari shook his head.

"And that's it. Well, and a guarantee that it will never be revoked."

"You're gonna make this massive legal problem just evaporate, and all you're gonna ask for in exchange is *membership?*" Del checked. Ari grinned at him.

"What can I say? Something about having that shiny gold DVC card in my wallet just makes me feel special."

Del snorted.

"Just because you get to come waltzing back in here, that don't mean you get to harass my staff," he said. "I can't make Valentine like you, and I wouldn't even if I could, not for any price. You upset her, and I don't care, I'll have Serge rip your fucking head off."

"I won't upset her," Ari said. "Or at least I'll try my best not to."

"But you *are* gonna harass her."

"No more than is necessary."

"*Necessary?*"

"Valentine ..." Ari sighed. "She has somewhat of a stubborn streak, you may have noticed."

"Oh yeah."

"There's too many places for her to run away to and hide from me. She can't run away when she's here. I just want her to listen to me. Then I'll leave her alone."

"Sure you will," Del grunted. "But you know what? Go ahead. Harass her. Kick her in the ass a little. Anything to stop her moping and attitude. Maybe getting some closure will get her back to normal."

Ari ran those words over in his head for a moment while DelVecchio rooted around in his drawers.

"She hasn't been normal?" he asked. Del snorted again.

"What do you fucking think? You stomped on her heart, kid, and ever since she's been caught somewhere between pissed off and depressed. It hasn't been pleasant. And on top of all *your* bullshit, she gotta deal with that bullshit with her grandma."

"The stroke."

"The stroke was the easy part," Del said, sitting upright with one of the gold membership cards in his hand. The lamp light reflected off it, flashing in Ari's eyes while Del inserted it into a card reader. "You didn't hear?"

"Del, I'm blackmailing you in order to get back in the club, all just so I can finally speak to her. I haven't heard *anything* in three weeks. What's going on with her grandmother?"

"Some asshole got social services or whatever involved, it was all

WHAT WE DO IN THE LIGHT

anonymous. They took her grandma away, put her in a home, told Val she was neglectful or something. She's been having to fight it. Tough cookie, our little Vally-wally."

Valentine? Neglectful of her grandmother? Ari had never seen a person more dedicated to a parental figure than Val was with Gam-Gam. Who would ever accuse her of neglect? Why? It was insane.

And she's been dealing with it all on her own, because that's how she's always done things. Because she thinks I'm the fucking devil.

"You don't know who called social services?" Ari checked. Del shrugged as the card reader popped out the gold card. He grabbed it and held it out over the desk.

"She has no clue. And I was serious," Del stated, pulling the card back at the last moment before Ari could take it. "You hurt her again, and I will put a period to your existence. Got me?"

"Understood," Ari nodded, then he snatched the card and quickly slid it into his inside pocket. "So long as you allow me to go about my business like any other member."

"Sure, sure. Now get out of here, I'm a busy man. Not all of us have *Daddy* paying our bills," Del sneered. The insult slid right off Ari—his father may have had a great deal of control over his life, but he certainly didn't pay his way. Ari worked hard for his money, so he didn't care what other people thought. He climbed to his feet and straightened out his jacket.

"Is she working this weekend?" he asked.

He was surprised when Del didn't respond, and even more so when he looked up to find the older man watching him carefully. A slow smile spread across his face, and Ari wasn't sure whether he should feel wary or intrigued.

"Yeah. Yeah, she's working this weekend. Tell you what—you wanna get some guaranteed one-on-one time with Saint Valentine *and* stay in my good graces? Come check her out tomorrow night."

"What's happening tomorrow?" Ari asked. Del held his arms open wide and his smile turned into a grin.

17

"C'mon, Ari! This is Caché! It would be easier to ask what *isn't* happening on a Friday night," he chuckled. "Be here around ... let's say eleven. That should be late enough."

"Late enough for what? Is there—"

"Kid, get the fuck outta here before I call Serge back in. I got a busy day planned," Del growled, and as if to emphasize his point, he spun away and picked up his phone.

Ari contemplated hanging the phone up, but decided he didn't really care. There must have been some sort of party, or event, happening that Friday. Wasn't it St. Patrick's Day? Or possibly nothing at all was happening—maybe Del was closing the club for a private party, and he'd have a good laugh watching Ari stand outside the door while no one answered the bell. Anything was possible, really.

So Ari simply turned and walked out of the office. Serge was actually waiting for him, and he led him back downstairs and out the rear exit. Ari's membership may have been reinstated, but apparently he wasn't going to be allowed all access to the club just yet.

Is she here? Right now? Hiding from me?

"You and bossman worked out some kind of deal, I expect," Serge grumbled as they walked down the stairs to the alley.

"Yeah. I'll be coming in the front door from now on," Ari informed him. The bouncer laughed loudly.

"Good luck with that. Big Lou will ..." Serge's voice died away when Ari flashed his membership card. He glared at the gold and at the lawyer before finally speaking again. "Val's gonna be fuckin' pissed."

"I don't really care—she's not the owner," Ari countered. "And neither are you. So I'd appreciate it if you kept your *boss's private dealings* private—especially from her."

"I don't gotta do fuck all for you," Serge said. Ari shrugged.

"Maybe not. But this isn't about her—this is between Del and I, and it's about allowing people like you and Valentine to keep their jobs," Ari snapped. He was about to say more, but then stopped himself. Aggressive and heavy-handed were his go-to responses, but they'd never worked particularly well on Valentine. They didn't seem to be working well, now. So he took a deep breath and calmed down. "Look. I'm not coming to create problems, alright? I'm not coming to hurt her. I promise. So just … do me a favor this one time, and don't talk to her about me, alright? At least give me until tomorrow night. *Please.*"

God, it killed him. To have to say "please", as if he had to beg Serge.

Ari missed Valentine and felt guilty about the way things had ended between them, but sometimes—just sometimes—he kind of wanted to strangle her for putting him in these positions.

"Alright," Serge finally growled. "Till tomorrow. But after that, I ain't promising shit."

"You're a peach, Serge," Ari chuckled, then gave a small salute as he finally headed off down the alley.

Finally, headway. It had cost him a lot in personal favors—it wouldn't be much fun when they were called in, but that was okay. By that point in time, Valentine would be paying him back in her own way, too.

Just gotta stay the course.

3

She couldn't pinpoint why, but Valentine had a weird feeling about the night.

Of course, the entire club was done up in green, and she was wearing a sequined pair of emerald booty shorts with matching suspenders, but that really wasn't too far out of the normal for Caché—it was St. Patrick's Day.

Valentine had never been there for St. Patrick's Day before, and apparently it was a big deal at the night club. They held a Leprechaun Auction for charity, and apparently it was the stuff of legends. She didn't particularly feel like getting auctioned off to the highest bidder, but she'd called in sick for St. Valentine's Day—and that was *after* Del had planned an entire event around her. Guilt kept her from bailing on this holiday, too. Half the proceeds went to charity, and Del had promised to give her ten percent of whatever her final bid was, so she agreed to be the anchor for the event. The most popular hostess at Caché was guaranteed to fetch a high price, so how could she say no? She'd probably done stranger things during her time working for Del.

Yet still, Val had a weird feeling.

She was crawling up a ladder so she could sit on the swing in the giant gold bird cage—but that was also pretty par for the course, she'd been on the swing lots of times. She sat still on the thin seat while Serge clipped a thin belt around her waist. It was in turn secured with heavy duty, thin wires to the cage, ensuring that if she fell, she wouldn't go far. Then Serge was gone, and the ladder was pulled away. The cage was hoisted away from the floor until it was floating in the middle of the room.

In the room next door, she could hear bawdy laughter. Could hear shouts of excitement and groans of disappointment as people won—and lost—bids. Charice's voice came in above it all, introducing each new staff member as they were put up on the auction block. Apparently, Charice still held the record bid—over fifteen thousand dollars! Winning bids got a week of service from the participating "leprechauns". Two years ago, Serge had been bought by a ladies' book club, and they'd made him wear a thong and serve them mai tais. Angel had to clean a guy's house for a week straight. So who knew what Valentine had in store for her. It was all new to her, and she was a little nervous about the kind of people that would be bidding on her, but that *still* wasn't what had her feeling weird.

There was just *something* in the air that she couldn't put her finger on …

"Everything's fine over there?" Val asked, nodding at the closed doors separating them from the auction. Serge nodded as he handed over the ladder to another person to take away.

"Going smooth—gonna be a record high this year, I think," he said.

"What's the highest bid so far?"

"I think Angel went for around eleven grand or so. Never seen a green angel before," he chuckled. Valentine frowned.

"Wow, eleven? Del said he expects me to top sixteen," she mumbled, then she reached behind her and pulled a handled mirror out from the back of her shorts.

She gave her look a once over. She'd contemplated wearing an orange wig for the event, but that had just seemed like too much. She'd stuck with the shorts and suspenders, pairing them with a tight mesh top and a black sparkly bra, as well as a mini-top hat, which she'd pinned to the top of her head at a jaunty angle. She'd found some black tap shoes in a thrift shop, which she'd removed the taps from and then spray painted green. Rounding out the look were her fishnets, which she'd liberally covered in green rhinestones.

I look like a slutty extra from the Wizard of Oz.

She hadn't been willing to wear the wig, but she hadn't wanted to go out with just plain old hair—this was *Saint* Valentine people were expecting. So Valentine had spent almost the whole day with her hair in tight rollers, then Charice had helped to unfurl them and somewhat tease them. Her thick, brunette hair normally hung to the center of her shoulder blades—now it was a riotous mass of curls that were so thick, her hair barely brushed her shoulders. She'd used a lot of bronzer, making her tan skin pop against the bright green. Dark, smoky shadow on her eyes and dark matte gloss on her lips, and she was the sexiest leprechaun she'd ever seen.

But was it sixteen thousand dollars worth of sexy? She didn't really think so.

Maybe I should've worn the wig. Or just pasties ...

"Between your tits and your reputation, I think you'll get a lot of bids," Serge assured her. She snorted and tossed down the mirror to him.

"Does Del really give half the money to charity?" she asked, glancing down at said tits and adjusting them in her bra.

"Yup," Serge nodded. "All to some hospital organization for kids. Guy's a softy."

"That he is. And the whole auction thingy—we really have to do whatever the people who buy us say?" she checked.

"It's not so bad, Vally, I promise. You'll probably get a banker or something, he'll want you to wear a maid outfit and clean. Or he'll make you nanny his kids, or drive him around. Anything you don't wanna do, tell 'em to fuck off. They give you any shit, you call me, those are the rules," he instructed. She smiled and nodded.

"Will do. You're the best, Serge."

"Yeah, yeah, just remember that later," he grumbled, rubbing at the back of his neck.

"What?"

But before Serge could explain, there was a sharp whistle from the other room. She glanced at the closed doors for a moment, and when she looked back down, Serge was gone. She frowned, then took a deep breath when the lights around her dimmed. Several small spot lights came on, all pointing at her on her perch. The crowd from the other room had grown quiet, and then she heard Del's voice over the microphone.

"Hell of a night, people, it's been a hell of a night! Who knew a bunch of bastards like you could raise so much money for charity? But now we've reached the end of the rainbow, and we all know what's waiting there, right?" Del sounded excited.

"A pot of gold!" the crowd shouted back.

"And Caché's very own *real* leprechaun!" he yelled. "Now, of course, I can't just let this magical creature go! Do you know what it takes to snag a leprechaun!? So if you want her, you gotta impress *me* with those bids! Ladies and gentlemen, our final auction of the evening, is none other than ..."

Valentine pasted a naughty smile on her face and pumped her legs, starting a gentle swing. When the double doors across from her slid open, large gold confetti started falling from the ceiling above her. They caught the spotlights and shined, twinkling like gold coins as they fell to the floor. She swayed to and fro, delicately swinging her legs, giving flashes of thigh as she moved back, lots of cleavage as she came forward.

The crowd surged into the room, hooting and hollering. Since she'd started at Caché, Valentine had been somewhat of an instant favorite. But in the past couple weeks, her reputation had grown in leaps and bounds, thanks to all her hard work. All the club regulars knew exactly who she was, and immediately fists full of money were held in the air, with random prices being shouted out. But Del put an end to it as he and Charice moved onto a small stage off to the side of the cage.

"I said 'impress me'," he barked. "Not act like wild fucking animals! You'll scare her away! Now—the bidding will start at ten thousand dollars. Remember, this is for charity, you bunch of bastards, and this is a real live saint, so don't insult us!"

"Who's got ten thousand dollars?" Charice boomed over her microphone, and Val's jaw almost dropped. Surely that was too high of a bid to start with, considering Angel's bids had only got up to—

"*Ten!*" a man shouted from the back of the crowd, holding up a green paddle with a number on it.

"Ten-five!" another yelled, waving his paddle wildly from under Val.

"Eleven," a woman added her bid before winking at Valentine.

"I'm embarrassed at these offers! This is *Saint Valentine*, for fuck's sake!" Del shouted. "You all know her, you all love her, and here's your chance to get her to yourself for a week, and *eleven grand* is the highest we got so far!?"

"I've got more money than that under my left titty," Charice snorted. "And here I thought we had *real* men and women here—I must have been mistaken."

The bidding commenced in a frenzy, the amount quickly racking up to sixteen thousand dollars, just as Del had predicted it would, and even got as high as eighteen thousand. Valentine managed to keep her composure, laughing and smiling and flirt from her perch, all the while reminding herself that this was for charity, *and* for herself.

After eighteen, though, it came down to a bidding war between two clients she regularly spent a lot of time with lately. They were going in increments of a hundred dollars, and while the amount was still staggering, she couldn't help starting to feel a little embarrassed. Was it going to get down to fifty dollar increments? What next, ten, five? She swallowed a yawn and leaned far back on the swing, holding her legs straight out in front of her. She hoped one of them caved soon so she could—

"*Twenty thousand dollars.*"

Valentine almost fell off the swing. The last highest bid had only been nineteen thousand one hundred—someone had just blown her clients out of the water. Everyone went nuts, roaring and cheering. She sat upright, smiling big, and scanned the crowd for the new bidder. But everyone was moving, hands were in the air, she couldn't tell who had the winning the paddle.

"Finally, someone with a *real* set of balls!" Charice shouted, gesturing grandly across the room. "Anyone going to be *man enough* to challenge him?"

And then something extraordinary happened.

"Yeah," Del piped up, and Valentine's jaw dropped when he reached into his jacket and pulled out what looked like a checkbook. "Yeah, I think *I'm* man enough. I got twenty-one thousand right here for my little Vally-wally."

"*A first in the history of Caché!*" Charice yelled, and again the crowd erupted. "Signore DelVecchio himself has the highest bid! Do we have a challenger?"

"*Twenty-two thousand.*"

Valentine had been too busy gawking at Del, so she once again missed who the mystery bidder was; it was too loud in there to clearly hear him. She craned her neck around to look, but Del was bidding once again.

"Yeah? *Chump change.* Twenty-three thousand."

This was insanity. Was Del really trying to bid on her? She *already* worked for him. She stared at him in shock, but then it hit her. He wasn't trying to bid on her—he was trying to *drive up the bid*. But why? Twenty thousand had already been an amazing bid, the highest ever in the auction's history. Was he crazy!? He was going to scare away the bidder!

*... unless this is all a ruse because he **already knows** the bidder will take the bait and offer more. Oh god ...*

"*Twenty-five thousand dollars,*" came the counter bid, and this time, Valentine heard the voice clearly. Maybe because a hush had fallen over the crowd. Or maybe because she now knew who to listen for—though she had been hoping she was wrong. "And that's my *final* offer."

Valentine held her breath as Ari Sharapov finally made his way through the center of the crowd, staring at her every step of the way.

*Please, please, don't let it be true. Outbid him, Del. If you sold me out, I don't know what I'll have left. Please, **please** outbid him.*

"Twenty-five thousand dollars," Del seemed to mull the price over. He stared down at his checkbook, then glanced at Charice. Looked across the crowd. Ignored Valentine completely, and finally settled back on Ari, who had turned to glare at him. "Well … I still say it's not nearly enough for St. Valentine, but since no one else here has the cajones …"

There was another pregnant pause, and Valentine stared at the crowd below her, praying someone would raise their paddle.

No one did, and Ari was looking directly at her again, that familiar smirk firmly in place.

"*SOLD!*" Charice boomed, and the sound of a gavel banging echoed around the room. "St. Valentine, for twenty-five thousand dollars, to the pretty legal eagle! That brings our grand total for the night to …"

Valentine didn't hear the rest. Air canons from every corner shot out more gold confetti and people cheered and music started playing, but she didn't pay attention to any of it. She just stared straight back at Ari, having trouble breathing as her cage was lowered to the ground.

When the bottom of the cage finally made contact with the green carpet, she couldn't stand the tension anymore. Fuck waiting for the ladder, she was getting down *now*. She unclipped the safety belt from around her waist, then carefully turned herself around, gripping her seat, ready to lower herself down. As she started to, though, she felt hands on her hips. Gripping her tightly, guiding her.

Reminding her.

She lost her handle on the swing and came down hard on both feet. She would've fallen on her face if not for the hands holding her, pulling her back into a very solid chest. She held completely still, not sure what to do or say.

"*St. Valentine,*" Ari's voice filled her ear, and she was instantly blinking away tears. All this time—how did he still have this power over her? "*And* St. Patrick's Day? You just cover all the holidays, don't you?"

I'm going to kill him. I'm going to kill him, and then Del, and then everyone else who had a hand in this.

As if she'd summoned him, Del appeared in front of her. He gently grabbed her arm and pulled her away from the devil.

"Nice of you to join us, Mr. Sharapov," he said, wrapping an arm around Val's shoulders and turning her to face her bidder. "I told you it'd be an exciting evening."

"It certainly was exciting. An auction, Del? Very, very clever."

Val was still finding it hard to breathe. She was going to hyperventilate. Hyperventilate and pass out and possibly puke. Before she could do any of that, though, Del squeezed her tightly to his side.

"Valentine," he sighed. "I'd like to introduce you to your new employer for the next week. This is Aaron Sharopov, *esquire.*"

It hadn't been that long, not really. A month? Not quite? Three weeks?

But it still felt like a shock to the system, seeing Ari again. Being so close to him. She had thought she was somewhat over him. Angry at him, yes—but feelings for him, no, she didn't have those. Not anymore.

And yet her body was a complete traitor to her heart. Her fingers still itched to rake through his thick blond hair, which was as artfully unkempt as ever. Her eyes still devoured his broad shoulders, which were of course covered in an expensive suit and long trench coat. His blue eyes hadn't looked at Del once—he kept them locked on her eyes the entire time he was in front of her—and they didn't show a hint of remorse or apology or guilt. They looked … like they were laughing.

*No, not laughing. **Smirking.***

"This is fucked up, Del, even for you," she snarled. "Are you that hard up for money? I already kill myself every night bringing in hundreds—*thousands*—for you, but it wasn't enough? You had to *sell* me?"

"Calm the fuck down, kitten," Del sighed, and he started herding her across the room, away from the crowd, which was starting to celebrate the night in earnest. "I'd like to remind you that half of the money tonight is going to sick kids."

"That just makes it worse!" she snapped, yanking away from him when they got into the hallway, Ari standing close behind her. "You've made it so I can't even say no! You'll get your twenty-five fucking grand, but you can consider the week he paid for as my noti-"

"Stop it," Del ordered, his voice all business. "You've been acting like a goddamn teenager for the past couple weeks—*both of you* have been fuckin' idiots, and both of you are going to continue being fuckin' idiots until you get some closure. I, for one, am done seeing your mopey ass every day, and I'm done seeing this guy lurking around trying to catch a glimpse of you. So yeah, when I saw an opportunity to make you two deal with each other *and* make some money, I jumped on it. *Sue me*. And then grow the fuck up and stop making your problems everyone else's."

The speech had been meant to put Valentine in her place, and it worked. She felt a little embarrassed, even. Had she really been *mopey*?

Still. It had been a nasty trick. Del could've at least given her a heads up. Maybe she could've talked to a regular client, convinced him to outbid Ari. Or at the very least, she could've mentally prepared herself to see him again.

Del glared at both of them for a moment longer, then he took a deep breath.

"Look, we had a deal," he said, pointing at Ari. "And a deal is a deal. I gave you your membership back. The auction is also a done deal—Serge will be collecting payment before you leave. Beyond that, I honestly couldn't give a shit what you two do. Talk, don't talk. Work for him, don't work for him. But I've washed my hands of this situation."

And then he was stomping away, grumbling about having to run a nursery school.

Valentine folded her arms, staring after him. Hating him a little bit, but wanting him to come back. She pressed her lips into a hard line, wondering what she should do.

"You *have* to talk to me now."

Hmmm, I think I know exactly what to do.

Valentine spun around, swinging her hand as she went and slapping Ari straight across the face.

"You're a piece of shit," she told him, then she whirled around and hurried back towards the cooler and staircase down to the Club Room.

"I know this," he said, catching up with her. "And you knew this before we ever even slept together."

"That's not what I'm talking about, and you know it," she said. They were on the stairs by then, and Ari pulled her to a stop.

"No, I don't know it. I don't know anything that's going on in that crazy head of yours, because you *won't fucking speak to me*. I can't know how you're feeling, I can't apologize, if you won't let me within ten feet of you, Valentine."

She stared up at him in the dim lighting. God, he was so good looking. She'd never really realized before, but he had a slightly angelic look—wavy blond hair, soft blue eyes, tall and strong. No wonder she'd fallen so hard. But then his wicked smile ruined the entire effect. She pulled her arm free.

"I just wanted it to be over," she stated, then continued on down the stairs as people started down behind them. "Okay? I didn't want an apology—I *don't* want one. I don't want to talk to you. I don't want *anything* from you."

"That's lovely for you, but *I'm* not done yet," he said as they strode through the Music Room. "And I have some things *I'd* like to say."

"You can't make me listen to you," Valentine snapped, finally turning on him at the entrance to the club. "Just like you can't *make me* 'work' for you, Ari. I don't care what you bid in there—I'm not your *whore*, not anymore."

"I never thought you-"

Valentine held up her hand.

"Don't lie," she hissed. "I heard you. You said it. *Don't fucking lie.*"

He stared down at her for a second, and then shocked her by taking the hand she held up and gently pressing it to his chest.

"I did lie," he agreed, nodding his head. Absurdly, she felt her eyes fill with tears. "But not to you."

"God, I hate you," she groaned, yanking free of him. "You just wasted a shit ton of money, I hope you realize. I'm not sleeping with you. I'm not even leaving this club with you."

"I don't want any of those things," he assured her.

"So, what? You paid twenty-five thousand dollars just to come and apologize to me?" she snorted, not believing him at all. He shook his head.

"No. I paid twenty-five thousand dollars for my own personal 'leprechaun' to do my bidding," he informed her. She opened her mouth to inform him that would never fucking happen, but he continued on. "And I expect services rendered for money paid. For one week, you are obligated to work for me for four hours a day."

"I'm not 'obligated' to do shi-"

"You're going to be my assistant," he said, and she was finally stunned into silence for a moment. She glanced around them.

"Your *what?*"

"My personal assistant," he said again. "I've taken on a pro-bono case recently, outside of my regular work hours, so you're going to help me."

"You're literally putting me to work?" Valentine was shocked.

"That's what I paid for, isn't it?" he pointed out. "If you do a satisfactory job, I'll even kick in a bonus."

"A bonus," Valentine guffawed. "Ari, I don't want a job as your personal assistant. I don't want to be around you *at all.*"

"Then explain to Del why his charity donation will be short twelve or so thou," he countered. Ooohhh, she really hated him. "I'll even sweeten the deal—I'll pay you, myself."

"We're not doing that again—*I will not sleep with you.*"

"I'll pay you an assistant's salary," he clarified. "Twenty five dollars an hour."

Val let out a frustrated shriek and shoved him in the chest.

"I don't want your money! *Fuck* your money, Ari! Is that what you think of me? That all I want is money? *I don't want your fucking money!*"

She hadn't exactly spoken softly. As she huffed and puffed and glared up at him, she quickly realized that everyone around them had turned to stare. Gary, the bartender in the Club Room, moved to the edge of the bar, watching them closely.

"I don't think all you want is money," Ari spoke in a low voice. It was obvious he was trying to keep his own anger in check. "But I *do* realize that you *need* money, and right now, it's the best bargaining chip—the *only* bargaining chip—I've got. Whether you want to admit it or not, that extra money will come in handy. How is your grandmother, by the way?"

Valentine sucked in air sharply, and once again found herself blinking back tears. She shrunk away from him, as if his actual presence alone could harm her.

Probably because it can. He steals my oxygen and my heart and my self-worth.

"I didn't think I could hate you more than I already did," she breathed. "Yet here you are, opening your mouth and proving me wrong once again."

"Well, I suppose it's a feeling you should be used to. Love your hair, by the way."

Her hair? Valentine had practically forgotten she was at Caché, let alone all dressed up in a ridiculous costume. When Ari reached out to twist his finger in a curl, she was painfully yanked into the here and now.

"Don't touch me," she snapped, slapping his hand away. "If you want me to be your assistant, then fine, I don't really have a choice. But I am *not* your escort. You're not my client. So *don't fucking touch me*, got it?"

"I knew you'd come around to the idea."

"Work means exactly that—I'm not at your beck and call. I do whatever an assistant does, I go home, and it doesn't fuck with my classes or my job here or anything in my real life. I get paid at the end of the week. I'm Ms. O'Dell, you're Mr. Dickbag. Got it? Good, grand. Now get out," she ordered him.

"Oh, I don't think so," he chuckled, and he pulled something from his jacket pocket. A shiny gold card flashed in front of her. "My membership has been reinstated, and don't waste your time complaining to Del about it—consider it carved in stone."

"Jesus, what did you do to make that happen?" Val groaned, rubbing her fingertips against her forehead. Ari went to respond, but she held up her hand. "Don't answer that, I don't want to know how much more I cost. I never should've left New York, I swear."

He frowned down at her, but just as he opened his mouth to respond, they were interrupted. Someone stepped around him from behind, unaware of the wrath they were incurring as they did so.

"Val! You look *amazing!*"

Evans Daniels, a former colleague of Ari's, walked right up to her. He wrapped an arm around her waist and squeezed her, all while kissing her on the cheek. She stared up at Ari the whole time, watching his eyes narrow into slits.

"Sorry I got here so late—I meant to come and bid on you," Evans was chuckling as he stepped back. "But according to the bouncer out front, I would've been outclassed. You're fetching quite the price tag these days!" He was still laughing while he spoke, and his arm was still around her waist when he finally turned to face Ari. His laughter quickly died, but the smile stayed on his lips. "Ah. I see. Membership fees have gotten *expensive*, it seems."

To say the tension was thick would be an understatement. While Valentine stared at Ari, his glare dropped down to the arm around her waist. Evans grinned at everyone, a drink in his free hand.

"Noon," Ari finally spoke, but by then, his gaze was on Evans.

"Monday. In the school parking lot, after your class. Don't make me come find you, Valentine."

"You're going to regret this, *Mr. Sharapov*," she warned him. His blue eyes shifted over to her.

"Possibly," he agreed. "But not half as much as you will if you're not there when I show up."

And with that, he nodded and walked away, disappearing into the crowd in the Music Room.

"Did he really pay—" Evans started the minute they were alone.

"Yes," Valentine interrupted. "You didn't know he was gonna be here?"

"Not a clue—I haven't been near his offices in weeks. You didn't know?"

"Not at all. Del knew, and I assume Serge and Charice. But no one told me. Apparently everyone decided it was time he and I confront each other," she sighed.

"Pretty crafty," Evans nodded his head. "You're supposed to like … work with him, do shit for him, for a couple days, right?"

"Right. Del is using St. Jude's charity to guilt me, and Ari is using Gam-Gam. I can't … I can't say no," she sighed. "I thought this was all done. I thought I wouldn't …"

She let the sentence drift away. She'd thought she wouldn't ever have to see him again. People like Aaron Sharapov didn't slum it in places where people like Valentine O'Dell hung out, so it had been a reasonable expectation.

She had certainly never expected him to be quite literally thrust into her life, so abruptly, and with no escape plan in sight for her. She'd very effectively been trapped. Almost a month spent trying to get over him, and now she'd have to see him every day for the next week.

Think of Gam-Gam. Think of rent. Think of medical bills. Think of how in a year or two, you'll hopefully never need help from someone like him ever again.

"You're working in his office?" Evans asked politely, and he began to gently guide her towards a booth in the Music Room.

"He said he wants me to be his assistant. God help me, I think he has some sort of plan," Valentine groaned and dropped her head to the table in front of them.

"Well, maybe I'll find a reason to stop by more often—help you kill some time while also annoying the shit out of him," Evans chuckled.

Valentine froze when she felt his hand on the back of her head, his fingers massaging through the thick curls. She knew Evans was attracted to her, he'd never been shy about that fact. But every time they'd interacted, she'd made it very clear her services were off limits to him. Their friendship and his work relationship with Ari made it an impossibility.

"You don't have to," she said, sitting up and gently brushing his hand away. "I don't want this affecting more people than it needs to; this is my problem. I'll deal with it on my own. One week and it'll be over. That's less than last time."

She'd meant the last part of her statement as a joke, but by the time she actually spoke it, it just sounded depressing.

Two weeks was all it was supposed to be last time, and look where that got you.

4

It seemed like Ari's luck was *finally* changing. Sure, reuniting with Valentine had been somewhat of a shit-show. Every glance she'd given him had been filled with betrayal and anger, and of course there was the fact that he was now out twenty-five thousand dollars. He didn't mind blowing large amounts of money, and he would definitely be writing this off on his taxes as a charitable donation, but still. He hadn't gone into the evening thinking he'd have to spend that kind of cash just to get alone time with her.

Goddammit, Del.

Yet it had worked, and after only being back in St. Valentine's graces for twelve or so hours, he had the first bit of good luck he'd seen in weeks.

He'd told Valentine he was getting ready to do some pro-bono work. The truth was he didn't have all the info he needed for the job, not yet—he didn't have the client. He didn't know where she was, and he was having a bitch of a time finding her.

He went into work Saturday, hoping to get ahead in work so his load would be lightened for the coming week. He did the same things he did every day when he got to his office. Took off his jacket and hung it up. Made himself coffee. Checked his messages. He'd left early on Friday, in order to mentally prepare for the battle of wills that was going to happen that evening, so he'd missed a couple calls that had come in later in the day. While he sipped his coffee, he went over the messages that had been jotted down.

One from his grandmother, asking if he'd be at his grandparents' golden wedding anniversary.

One from a client, looking for some paperwork.

One from somewhere called "The Hive Agency", asking about a billing issue.

Ari stared at the last note for a while, his eyes narrowed as he racked his brain. What the fuck was The Hive Agency? What bills? Why was that name familiar?

An agency ... an agency ... when have I ever used any kind of agency ... wait a minute ...

Clarity blazed inside his head, and he remembered the name. The Hive Agency helped people find in-home nursing care. It's where Valentine had found her nurses—it was a caregiver job agency. The first nurse had been with Valentine and Gam-Gam long before Ari had shown up. The second one, though, had been hired at his request, and at his expense.

A billing issue!

Ari picked up the phone and quickly dialed the number they'd left for him, praying they'd be open on a Saturday.

"This is Aaron Sharapov," he introduced himself when someone finally picked up. "I received a message asking me to call—something about billing?"

It was explained to him that he hadn't paid for the final two weeks of Nurse Crockett's services. He was a little surprised because he'd paid any nursing bills as soon as Valentine had presented them to him. But as Ari looked over his calendar, he realized they were referring to the two weeks at the start of the current month—a new billing cycle had started at the same time as when Valentine had cut him off.

She'd used Nurse Crockett's services for two more weeks after dropping him like a bad habit, and had then stuck him with the bill.

How could he use this to his advantage?

"I'm sorry about the mix up. Can I pay over the phone? Or I can come down there on my lunch break. Also, is there a way I would be able to get in contact with Mrs. Crockett?"

After the money situation was dealt with, he was able to sweet talk the receptionist into giving him Crockett's pager number. He dialed it next, and within a couple minutes, he received a return call.

"Mr. Sharapov?" she asked, her voice light and sweet. "What can I do for you?"

"I'm trying to tie up some billing issues," he explained. "And I'm having trouble pinning down Valentine's grandmother."

"I don't think I'll be much help," she sighed. "After they moved Eugenia into that facility and I got this new job, I lost all contact."

"Gam-Gam's in a nursing home?" he asked, feigning surprise. He grabbed a pen and held it poised over a notepad.

"A skilled nursing facility," she corrected him, though he had no clue what the difference was. "That second stroke created a lot more problems, there was just no way her poor granddaughter could care for her at home so soon afterwards. The hospital had Mrs. Parker moved to the facility for recovery care and observation. But then IDHS got involved—"

Ari had gotten some of the story from Del, but he figured it could only help him to know as much as possible.

"IDHS—like social services?"

"Yes. Best I could gather, someone reported Valentine for elder neglect."

"Ridiculous, she lived her life for her grandmother."

"That's what I said when they interviewed me, and I know Nurse Grace gave a glowing testimonial for Valentine, too, as did all of Mrs. Parker's doctors. Still, it's rough going through that, poor Val."

Poor Valentine, indeed. I still can't believe she didn't call me. This is a legal issue, she knows I could've helped her.

Ari ground his teeth together for a second, then took a deep breath.

"You said Mrs. Parker was in a nursing facility—do you happen to know which one?"

"I think it was the North Branch Care Facility."

"Thank you so much for your time, and the information, Mrs. Crockett."

"Of course, dear. I hope this means you and Valentine are back together, I always thought you made such a handsome couple."

Ari grimaced, then said goodbye before ending the call. Next he immediately called his receptionist Rose at her desk.

"Yes, Mr. Sharapov?"

"I need you to make a list for me of any and all contacts we have within the Illinois Department of Health Services," he barked. "And any lawyers we know who work for health services for the city."

"On it, Mr. Sharapov."

He'd told Valentine he'd pick her up on Monday. He had a lot of work to do, and very little time to do it in—and it didn't help that a lot of the agencies he would need to get in touch with would be closed for the weekend.

Ari'd never been scared of hard work, though, so he rolled up his sleeves and took off his tie and got down to work.

Me, doing pro-bono. The lengths I'm willing to go to for this girl, it's almost embarrassing.

Despite her bravado at the club, Valentine was nervous. She'd *been* nervous ever since Friday night. The entire weekend had basically been an anxiety attack wrapped in a layer of anger and heartbreak.

And now it was Monday, and she was waiting in the open parking lot at her university, gnawing at the side of her thumb while waiting for Ari's stupid little sports car to make an appearance.

Am I really going to be an assistant? Or am I going to spend the whole time smacking his hand away from my ass?

She'd had the whole weekend to mentally prepare. After that set-up on Friday, even Del had agreed that she'd earned Saturday night off. Normally, Valentine didn't miss work for anything—Gam-Gam's new medical bills made the old ones look like pennies, she needed all the money she could get anymore.

Her stash of cash from her previous deals with Ari was all gone, and all the extra money she'd been making at work practically flew back out of her hands. It went to those medical bills, as well as a couple consultations with lawyers, trying to figure out what—if anything— she could do about IDHS's investigation against her. She couldn't afford someone like Ari, though, so all the ones she'd spoken to had taken her money and then basically told her they couldn't help.

That's what I get for going to lawyers who advertise on bus stop benches.

So missing work was usually a no-no. Ten percent of twenty-five thousand dollars, though, was a healthy chunk of change for one night's work. Del cashed her out Friday evening, so she didn't feel too bad about missing Saturday. It would give her time to think. To plan. To prepare.

To psych herself out so much, she was even more of a nervous wreck by the time Monday actually rolled around.

Jesus, what does he have planned for me!? Is he really gonna pay me? Do I want him to? I could still stop this. No, I can't, I need this. Why does he turn me into this helpless person!?

Because she'd been so close to falling for him, that's why.

She'd thought there had been something growing between them. They'd both felt it, both talked about it, both admitted it. She'd believed in them. Believed in *him*.

Mistake number one.

Yes, Ari had paid for her time. For her company. But that's what hurt the most—he'd known what a big deal it was to her that he understood she wasn't a whore. He'd assured her that he hadn't thought of her that way, and at the end, he'd said he'd *never* thought of her that way. *Would never* think of her that way.

And she'd believed him.

Mistake number two.

It had *all* been a lie.

Ari Sharapov had very little control in his own life. He'd once ex-plained to her that he was playing a long game. Do what his daddy says now, so in a couple years he'd be set for life. Sure, not a life he was en-tirely sure he wanted, but he'd convinced himself it was his best option for getting the things he *did* want.

So in order to feel like he could have some control, Ari had dumped his girlfriend, and he'd paid Valentine for her time. Just what he'd always wanted—a relationship that didn't require anything of him, he didn't owe anything to it, and he had no responsibilities within it. Just snap his fingers and she would come running. Dress up sexy for him and smile pretty for him and drop readily to her knees for him. Valentine could see the appeal of such a relationship, especially to a man like Ari.

So he'd paid her and he'd used her and he'd said anything he'd had to in order to keep that relationship going. Why would he want to give it up? It was perfect for him—a girl stupid enough to believe anything he said, and fuck him any way he wanted, just so long as he whispered sweet words to her. Shit, he could've stopped paying, and she still would've kept showing up. Kept liking him.

Kept falling for him.

Thank god she'd figured him out before it was too late.

... did I?

The sound of screeching tires broke her out of her reverie, and she glared at the large, black, Audi SUV that was stopped in front of her. When it didn't move, she rolled her eyes and went to step away from it, but then the passenger window rolled down.

"Get in, we're running late," Ari said, leaning over the center con-sole. Valentine stepped back and glanced over the vehicle again.

"This isn't your car," she stated as she reached for the handle.

"It isn't? Odd that it has my name on the registration. *Get in.*"

After she was buckled into the plush leather seat, he hit the gas, speeding out of the lot. He'd always been a somewhat reckless driver; speed limits were more like a suggestion to him.

"What happened to the ego-mobile?" Valentine asked, referring to his Porsche. He cleared his throat, concentrating as he pulled into traffic.

"I got rid of it."

"I thought you loved that car—why?"

"The firm had bought it for me."

"So?"

"So when I found out that the firm had been secretly keeping keys to the apartment they'd also bought for me, I thought maybe it would be a good idea to start getting rid of their 'gifts'. I like my apartment and changing locks is easy—but the car had to go."

"They had your keys," Valentine snorted. "Rich people are fucking weird."

"Yes, they are."

There was a long silence, and it was almost unbearable to her. Ari seemed completely at ease, leaned back in his seat, one hand on the wheel. As if this were a completely normal day.

And there she was, half ready to peel her own skin off.

"Why not another Porsche? If you can just blow twenty-five grand in a night with barely a thought, you could've afforded another sports car," she pointed out. He chuckled.

"Barely a thought, huh? Valentine, there's been very little else I've thought about in the last three weeks."

She nearly choked on that statement, and coughed into her fist to disguise it.

"You finally realized Porsches are for men with small penises, I suppose," she continued on with her car rambling. It felt neutral, safe. Ari heaved a sigh and finally glanced at her.

"I didn't get another Porsche," he started, holding her gaze when they stopped at a red light. "Because someone once told me she didn't like my car."

Noooope, not neutral. Not safe.

Valentine sucked her lips between her teeth and gently bit down on them, trying to distract herself as the car started rolling forward. She retreated into her mind, figuring no conversation was the safest bet, and she went over her plans for the rest of the day. First stop after finishing up with Ari would be to go see her grandmother.

Gam-Gam.

The break up with Ari had been horrible, and it happened at a horrible time, but even worse than all that, Valentine had realized she was a bad person. She'd not only ruined her love life, but she'd also ruined her *actual* life, too. So blinded by a stupid man. By good times and better sex.

After six months of taking care of virtually every moment of her grandmother's days, Val had loosened the reins. Just a little bit. Just enough to hire a second nurse, leaving her grandmother in trained, professional hands around the clock. Valentine had honestly thought it was for the best. After all, nurses would know better how to take care of a sickly, elderly woman, right?

Apparently, someone thought otherwise. After her grandmother's second stroke, she'd been admitted to the hospital. The social workers from IDHS had shown up not too much later, claiming they'd received reports that she'd been abusing her power as medical proxy, and had also been stealing her grandmother's money and spending it on herself. Valentine had almost laughed. *What* fucking money? All of her grandmother's retirement money was gone—there was nothing *to* steal.

None of that mattered to IDHS, though. It was all Valentine's words against her accusers, and they couldn't exactly ask Gam-Gam her opinion on the matter, because she didn't even know her own name half the time.

So an investigation was launched. She was essentially being audited—they wanted every receipt, every bill, every doctor's visit, every medical file. They wanted her grandmother's bank statements, as well as Val's own. They wanted the paperwork on the sale of the farm. They wanted to know about her tuition payments. They wanted *everything*.

They also wanted to know where her own income came from.

What a fucking nightmare. Valentine knew she'd done nothing wrong, but it was still difficult to go through it all, *and* scary. At the beginning, they'd ordered her to stay away from Gam-Gam. It was over a week before she was allowed to see her grandmother again, which had been sheer torture when the woman had been so sick—touch and go, really. Thankfully, the in-home nurses, Grace and Crockett, had spoken up for her as character witnesses, which was why she'd eventually been allowed to visit.

Just knowing something like that could happen again, or even worse, had Valentine feeling even more on edge than usual. She worked more and more hours at the bike messenger place, and she ramped up the charm when she was doing her escorting gig at Caché, hoping for those big tips. Anything to help make things easier for her, her roommate, and Gam-Gam.

Anything at all, which is how I find myself in situations like this.

"Where are we going?" Valentine asked, suddenly realizing she recognized the area.

"Oh, I forgot, I have something for you," Ari ignored her question and dug into an inside pocket on his jacket.

"I don't want any gifts from you," she replied quickly. He snorted and pulled out what looked like a plastic white business card, but without anything printed on it.

"Access card," he explained, holding it between two fingers. "To be my assistant, you'll need it. It will get you into my office at work, the main conference room, the break room—but no direct building access after hours."

"Why would I want to ever come to your work after hours?" she asked, plucking the key card out of his hand.

"I'm sure I could think of something to entice you," he suggested. She glared at him.

"I'm sure there *isn't*. Where are we going? I know this area."

"I'm not surprised. Just working on a case."

"A case?" Valentine asked. "How long are we going to be here? According to the auction rules, you only get me for four hours a day—and since you're an asshole, I'm deducting two of those hours. I don't wanna sit in a corner, taking notes while some rich guy tries to get out of paying his taxes, or whatever."

"I'm not a tax lawyer," Ari chuckled. "And I don't think we'll be here long. It's ... a new client, and a touchy situation, but an easily solvable one, I think."

"You think everything is easy."

"Because everything is for me."

"You're ridiculous," she snorted as they pulled into a parking lot. A shiver shot down her spine—she recognized the building instantly. She'd had several nightmares about it. "Are you doing work for the Department of Health Services? But you're in corporate law—what kind of meeting is this?"

"The kind that will benefit both of us, hopefully. Trust me."

"*Trust* you? Did you honestly just say those words? Are you high? I've got a half a mind to just get out of the car and walk away right now," she threatened as he parked.

"*Assistant*, Valentine," Ari reminded her while he shut off the car. "That means I'm your boss, and you have to do what I say for the next *four* hours, or those poor sick kids don't get any of my money."

Valentine's jaw dropped.

"You are *literally* the worst."

Ari smirked right back at her.

"Whatever made you think I wasn't?"

5

Ari sat stiffly at a table, working his head from side to side. He rolled it around for a moment, then jerked it quick to the side. *Snap*. Ah, he'd finally managed to crack his neck. That had been driving him crazy—he must be more nervous than he realized, he was holding all his tension in his shoulders. Then there was a noise in the hallway, drawing both his and Val's attention to the door. It was the first time she'd moved since entering the room.

When she'd first realized they were at that particular branch of the Illinois Department of Health Services, she'd asked a lot of questions. He'd been able to ignore her while he'd talked to the lady in the front office. Val had seemed shocked to hear he had an appointment all set up for the two of them, and with the social worker in charge of Gam-Gam's case. She'd clammed up then, and hadn't moved a muscle since they'd been seated at a chipped table in a small, empty office.

When the door knob started to turn, Valentine shuddered, but Ari slowly stood up. Smoothed his hand down his tie, then quickly combed his fingers through his hair, casting a glance at his reflection in a picture frame.

Valentine had always loved his hair. He didn't know why, it was unruly at the best of times, sometimes he considered shaving it all off. But of course now he never would, simply because once upon a time, she'd loved to run her fingers through it, and he had hopes that maybe she would again some day.

He cleared his throat, announcing their presence as a woman marched into the room.

"Ah, Mr. Sharapov, they told me you were waiting in here," Mrs. Abigail Flatley, Gam-Gam's case manager, said.

After a weekend of digging and a frenzy of phone calls that very morning, Ari had found out that when the report of neglect had been made, Abby Flatley had been brought in to determine the extent of the alleged abuse. If Gam-Gam was ever to be released back into Valentine's care, it would Abby Flatley's decision.

Ari had spoken with Abby several times on the phone that morning, working to reschedule a meeting she'd had with Valentine the very next day, and doing it all at the alleged request of Valentine herself. Of course that was a bald faced lie, but big gains required big risks.

"Thanks for seeing us on such short notice," Ari said, stepping forward and offering his hand. Abby gave it a strong, hearty shake, then made her way to a seat at the table.

"What's going on? What are we doing here?" Valentine finally spoke, obviously struggling to keep her voice civil.

"Mr. Sharapov called me early this morning, saying you wanted to reschedule your meeting for now. He told me he's your grandmother's legal representation," Abby said, giving them both a confused glance.

"He's—" Valentine started, but Ari didn't give her a chance to continue. She was still angry at him, and possibly enough to deny help that she very much needed.

"Offering my services *pro-bono*," he interrupted, and watched as a light dawned in her eyes. Then he dropped his briefcase onto the table before sitting down again. "Health and medical law aren't my areas of expertise, but Grandma Parker is a very special woman, so of course I had to help."

"He's in corporate law," Valentine piped up. She'd obviously gotten over her confusion and curiosity, and was now pissed that he was meddling. "And he hasn't been a part of this, he doesn't even know what's going on."

Ari looked over some sheets of paper that had been faxed to him just a couple hours ago.

"Roughly three weeks ago, IDHS received a call alleging elder neglect," he said, skimming over the details. "They named Mrs. Parker the neglected, and Ms. O'Dell the neglecter, which resulted in IDHS denying Ms. O'Dell visitation rights while her grandmother was sick and in the hospital."

"Yeah, but they started allowing me to visit at her facility now," Val said. "So I don't under-"

"A basic, cursory examination of Mrs. Parker's medical files, as well as any public records pertaining to her, will show that Ms. O'Dell has not only been an exemplary primary care giver, but has often times gone above and *beyond* what was necessary. She has worked multiple jobs to pay for her grandmother's medical care, kept meticulous accounting records of her grandmother's financial affairs, hired not one but *two* qualified nurses, as well as a live-in assistant to help monitor Mrs. Parker's well being. Those nurses both vouched for Ms. O'Dell after the case had been brought against her."

"Yes, we have all the records you mentioned," Mrs. Flatley said, going through her own stack of papers.

"I handed them over right away whenever they were asked for," Valentine added. "I brought them down here myself."

"You are aware that Ms. O'Dell is Mrs. Parker's medical proxy," Ari said, going over some other papers. The social worker nodded.

"Yes, we have that on record."

"She's Mrs. Parker's legal power-of-attorney, as well," he continued, and both women nodded.

"All paperwork we have on record, Mr. Sharapov," Abby said. "Valentine applied for medical assistance for her grandmother several months ago, that's when a file was originally started for Mrs. Parker."

"So you're saying IDHS already had proof of the excellent care

Ms. O'Dell was providing for her grandmother," Ari said, raising his eyebrows. "And proof of her guardianship of her grandmother. And yet in response to *one* phone call *alleging* possible abuse, IDHS withheld Mrs. Parker from receiving any sort of care or stewardship from her legal power-of-attorney."

Valentine's eyes got wide, while Abby Flatley's eyes suddenly looked very wary and nervous.

Good.

"We understand that it's a sensitive situation, but we must treat all calls seriously—it's protocol," she said, clasping her hands together.

"It's protocol to launch an investigation—it was unnecessary and quite possibly damaging to Mrs. Parker's health to deny her contact with her granddaughter. How was Ms. O'Dell supposed to make informed decisions regarding her grandmother's medical care when she wasn't even allowed in a room with her? Wasn't allowed to check on her to see how she was doing in the hospital?"

"In cases of abuse, we find it's best—"

"But this wasn't abuse," Ari shut his briefcase dramatically, the sound echoing in the small room, causing Valentine to jump in her seat. "This was an allegation of neglect. *Alleged neglect.* From an unknown source which provided no other details about Ms. O'Dell or her grandmother. Therefore, it is my belief that IDHS caused direct and possibly irreparable harm to Mrs. Parker, as well as emotional trauma to both Mrs. Parker and Ms. O'Dell, simply based on a phone call from a person who quite possibly doesn't even know either of them."

Valentine's jaw had dropped again, and he noticed she hadn't taken her eyes off him since he'd started speaking. He didn't look back at her, though. He kept his steely eyed gaze directly on the social worker, who was looking angrier and angrier by the second.

"Really, I feel 'irreparable' is going a bit far, it was only a couple day-" she tried to argue.

"How many days were you denied access to your grandmother?" Ari asked, finally looking at Val. She sputtered for a moment.

"Uh … a little over a week."

Ari looked down at the lone sheet of paper he'd left on the table.

"According to her medical records, in those nine days she was denied access, Mrs. Parker suffered from migraines, gastric distress, a cold, a UTI, and a kidney infection. At her age and state of health, any of those could have been life threatening, and *because* of her age and state of health, all of those things *have* contributed to a further degradation of her mental state. Before entering the hospital, Mrs. Parker needed very little prompting to recognize her granddaughter—now she has trouble remembering her own name. It is my belief, as well as her doctors, that if she had been allowed to see Ms. O'Dell and communicate with her, that would've greatly reduced her stress while in the hospital, and could have possibly prevented some—if not all—of the aforementioned health issues," Ari rattled everything off.

Of course none of that was necessarily true. Gam-Gam had been a pretty sick woman before going to the hospital, that hadn't been about to change, regardless of whether or not Valentine was by her side. But IDHS couldn't prove it *wasn't* true, that was for damn sure.

And Ari wasn't a good lawyer for nothing.

"This is ridiculous," Abby huffed and puffed at him. "We are not responsible for Mrs. Parker's current medical condition."

"I think we have a strong case that says you are," he countered. "I'm strongly encouraging my clients to sue IDHS, as well as Cook County, for damages to cover the emotional and medical struggles you've forced upon them."

Now it was Abby's turn to drop her jaw, and she looked back at Valentine.

"You're *suing* us?" she asked.

Valentine was clearly at a loss, which Ari had been counting on. He cleared his throat.

"They haven't agreed to anything yet—Ms. O'Dell is a very generous young woman, her main concern is her grandmother's well being. Against my advice, she has stated that she has no wish for monetary compensation. But I strongly believe she has an excellent case, and if IDHS prolongs this invasive investigation any further, or if they attempt to keep my clients from seeing one another again, I *will* sue this department, IDHS, Cook County, and *you*, personally."

Ari had always wanted to be a lawyer, from a very young age. Most of the men in his family were lawyers, so it ran in his blood. He'd loved watching shows set in the legal world, had loved going to work with his father. But it had never been his dream to work in corporate law—he'd wanted to be a trial lawyer.

There was just something so invigorating about matching wits with a person you knew you could eviscerate at any moment.

"You can't threaten me!" Abby babbled. "I'm a state employee!"

"You are," he agreed, nodding his head and standing up. "Which makes you partially responsible for this mess. So finish up your pointless investigation and leave my clients in peace. I'll be contacting this office at the end of the week to see how things are progressing. Ms. O'Dell?"

He didn't wait to see if Valentine was going to come with him, he simply grabbed his briefcase and strode from the room.

When he made it to the parking lot without the sound of footsteps behind him, Ari thought maybe he'd overestimated his abilities. He'd really only had that morning to prepare his little speeches, drum up some kind of legal magic act, so he'd been kind of impressed with himself in there. It had certainly worked on the social worker.

Saint Valentine's a little harder to impress, I guess.

As he was unlocking his car, though, Ari heard a small cough from behind him. Someone clearing their throat. He turned to find Valentine standing behind him.

Even after all the time they'd spent together, Ari still couldn't get over what a chameleon she was—a shapeshifter, really. At night, she looked like some sort of makeup guru, a club kid fashionista. Wearing high heels that almost brought them eye to eye, and tight clothing that left very little to the imagination. An Amazonian, a glamorous goddess.

During the day, though, all that was washed away. Wavy chestnut tresses were pulled up into messy buns. Sequins and spandex were traded out for denim and cotton, and that god awful cardigan that was constantly trying to drown her. Makeup was scrubbed away, leaving her several shades paler, and looking several years younger. Out of her "Saint Valentine costume", she seemed ... smaller. Younger. *More vulnerable.*

That was the real Val. Smart, sweet, comfortable. That was the face that was burned onto his brain, her *real* one. Those dewy lashes—all her own, the false ones thrown away the night before—blinking away tears as she begged him to let her stay.

That was the face looking up at him now.

"How did you know all that stuff?" she demanded, wrapping her oversized cardigan tightly around herself.

"Del, at first," he said. "He skimmed over the situation when I blackmailed him to let me back in the club."

"Blackmailed," she whispered, and he could've sworn there was a hint of smile on her lips.

"And then Nurse Crockett, I spoke to her this weekend. She let me know which facility your grandma was staying at—after that, all it took was a couple phone calls to the right places."

"Her medical records," Valentine continued. "How did you get those?"

"A couple more calls to the right kind of people. I have friends in medical law and family law, they know how these things go, they gave me some pointers. IDHS will drop the investigation against you soon, tomorrow or next week," Ari guessed.

"That's good. It's been ... hard."

"I can imagine."

Whoops, wrong words to say right now.

"I'm sure you can," she chuckled darkly. "Up there in your ivory tower, I'm sure you know *exactly* how this feels."

"Once upon a time, you liked it up in my tower," he reminded her. She snorted.

"Yeah, right up until I found out you weren't prince charming. You were the big bad wolf, the whole time."

"Not the whole time. Not at the end."

"*Especially* at the end," she snapped, then she pressed her hand to her forehead. "No. I'm not getting into this. I didn't ask for your help and I don't think we needed it, but thank you, anyway, *Aaron*."

Oh, he hated that name. He narrowed his eyes at her.

"Let me break this down for you, *St.* Valentine," he said, walking closer so he could loom over her. "I had to break several laws and basically sell my soul, all just to get dirt on Del so I could get into the club. Then I had to give up *twenty-five thousand dollars* just to be able to speak to you. That was all in twenty-four hour span. After two more days, I all but solved your legal issues with IDHS, and have pretty much given your grandmother back to you. I may have done some shitty things to you, and I may have fucked up in the end, but even you can't deny that I'm *trying* to make things right, and to be honest, I think I'm doing a pretty good fucking job."

Ari expected a fight, and was ready for it. Valentine was a pretty passionate person.

Or she might run away—it was another thing she tended to do a lot.

But neither happened.

Instead, her glare slowly melted away, and much to his surprise, her eyes filled with tears.

"It was awful," she breathed, and he stood upright.

"What?"

"I didn't know what was going on," she was still speaking softly, but he could hear her better. "That Abby lady was outside my grandmother's hospital room with a doctor, and he kept apologizing, but she was like a robot, like she didn't even care, and they told me I couldn't see Gam-Gam. That I wasn't *allowed* to see her. Not that day. Not the next. I began to think it would be forever. And I just … I kept thinking …"

She wasn't looking at him anymore. She was staring off into the distance next to him, her eyes watching the road. Two fat tears rolled down her cheeks, and were quickly followed by more. She raised her hand to her mouth, her sweater sleeve wrapped around her fist, but she made no move to brush away the tears.

"Kept thinking what?" Ari asked.

"I kept thinking … *if only you were there,*" she sighed gently. "You would know what to do, what to say. Who to talk to, who to yell at; you're good at stuff like that, but I'm not. And I wanted to call you *so badly*, but I couldn't, because you were … you're …"

"The worst," he finished for her. She squeezed her eyes shut tight and nodded.

"The absolute worst. Everything was shit and it felt like I was in hell and you were just the *fucking worst.*"

After the auction, Ari had told himself it would be a long road. First step would be to get the look of hatred out of her eyes. Next would be convincing her that he'd been lying to his father, not her. Maybe, eventually, somewhere down the road in the distant future, he'd get to touch her again. But it certainly wouldn't be any time soon, so he'd kept the thought of it out of his head. He'd treat her with professional courtesy until she gave him a sign that she was ready for more.

At the sound of her voice—of her heart breaking all over again—all that flew out the window. He dropped his case and closed the gap between them, wrapping his arms around her. He hadn't done that enough when they'd been together. They'd had lots of sex and spent a lot of time together, but he could probably count on one hand the amount of times he'd held her.

Not enough times.

"I'm sorry," he breathed into her hair. "I really am, Valentine. I told you I'd fuck it up, and I did. I did everything wrong. So now, *let me make it right.*"

She took a deep breath, her frame shuddering in his arms.

"You'll just get it wrong again," she replied, her voice low. He pulled back a little to look down at her, but she kept her eyes on the buttons of his coat.

"I won't," he assured her. "I'm a quick learner."

"Not quick enough, Ari. Look, I—"

No. He knew that tone of voice, he recognized that look in her eye. Worse than hating him, worse than being angry with him, worse than fighting him—she was *giving up*. The others meant there were still feelings there. She had to care about him in order to hate him. If she gave up on him, though, he probably wouldn't stand a chance. He couldn't let that happen. He couldn't let her speak the words that would end them.

So he dropped his head to hers and pressed his lips to hers and prayed a kiss could work where words had failed.

He could feel her gasp against his mouth, but he didn't move away. He moved closer, striving to *feel* her through all their winter clothing. He ran his hands down her back, pressing her as close to him as possible, relishing the moment because he knew it wouldn't last forever.

Valentine was a very sexual person, he knew—it was one of the things that had attracted him to her in the first place, was the literal basis for their entire relationship. Sure, somewhere along the way, more feelings had gotten involved, but that base attraction hadn't lessened. If anything, it had just grown stronger and stronger.

So when she kissed him back, Ari felt like he deserved a medal for not ripping off her clothes right then and there, and tossing her into the backseat of his car.

It's been waaaaaay too long.

"Come home with me," he whispered as he pulled away to take a breath.

When she looked up at him, though, he knew it was absolutely the wrong thing to say. Her mouth was set into a grim line, and he felt her hands on his chest, gently pushing him away. He didn't budge.

"You may have paid for my time," she spoke slowly. "But you didn't pay for *me*. Never again, Ari. *Never.*"

"That's not what—" he tried to argue, but she abruptly stepped back, breaking his hold on her. "I never thought of it that way."

She gave a sad laugh and rubbed her fingers across her forehead.

"I admit it, today was a good day, Ari. You did … good. Don't ruin it by lying."

He glared again, and wasn't sure who he was angrier at—himself for opening his big mouth, or her for not believing him.

"I'm not lying, and before this week is over, you're going to believe the things I tell you," he informed her.

"A week, huh," she sighed, moving around him and opening the passenger door on his car. She didn't get in, though, but pulled her backpack out. "At least our contract is shorter than last time, huh? Though you certainly got screwed on the price."

"Goddammit, Val, it's not about that, I—"

"Can we consider today's work done?" Val asked, glancing over her shoulder. "If I catch that bus that's coming, I can transfer to a line that'll take me to Gam-Gam before visiting hours are over."

"You don't have to take a bus," he said, but she was already walking backwards away from him.

"I can't work for you tomorrow," she informed him. "Or Wednesday."

"I paid for a fucking week, Valentine," he reminded her.

"I know, and you'll get it, it'll just be broken up. I started working at the school library Tuesday and Wednesday afternoons. I'll call you to find out if you need me on Thursday," she said.

He didn't like that idea, not one little bit.

"I'm not that stupid, Val—give me your new phone number," he demanded, but even as he spoke, she turned around and started jogging for the bus stop on the corner.

"What? I can't hear you! Talk to you Thursday, *byeeeeee!*"

She was practically sprinting by the time she reached the stop, and she didn't even turn back once before she got on the bus.

6

Aaron
Malachi
Sharapov

Valentine stared down at the name, her eyes wide.

Malachi. How could I not know that?

She'd never learned his middle name, that was how. They hadn't known each other very well, not really. He certainly didn't know her middle name. So it shouldn't have come as a shock, learning his for the first time.

But still …

It was so like him—Old World, yet bold and modern in its own way. Different, yet traditional. Perfect, really.

Oh no. No no no no, do not start associating the word "perfect" with Ari Sharapov. One good kiss and suddenly you're forgetting every awful thing he did.

Valentine was in the conference room at his law firm, staring down at some legal paperwork with his full name on it.

When she'd called him that morning, he'd told her to come to his office after her classes. She'd been slightly terrified—the one and only time she'd been in his work place, things hadn't worked out so well for her.

Would the senior Mr. Sharapov be there? Would he recognize

her? Would she get laughed out of the building? Have to run as people chanted "whore" at her?

She didn't want to go, but she'd made a deal, so she would stick to it.

It had *nothing* to do with the kiss.

Turned out she didn't really have anything to be afraid of—if Ari's father was in the building, he was staying out of sight. And though she'd shown up ready to battle wills with Ari again, he'd played the role of impersonal boss perfectly, not touching her at all, barely even looking at her. He just gave her a small tour of his office and the areas she'd be working in, then handed her off to some girl from the secretarial pool.

Jesus, he really did just want me to come be his assistant.

She stared down at the paper in front of her, then slid it back into the folder it had fallen out from; she was supposed to be relabeling and organizing a stack of folders. She was about halfway done, but it was boring work, and her mind was wandering.

Why did I let him kiss me? Why did I kiss him back? Stupid, Valentine. So stupid.

But he'd just done something amazing for her, and she'd been so angry at him for it. She wanted to hate him. He deserved it. He'd let her down when she'd needed him the most. Yet now here he was, *helping* her when she needed help the most. Made it kind of hard to keep hating him.

Did that make up for it? Did one good thing cancel out a really awful thing? She didn't think so.

Did she?

"I hate this," she moaned, letting her head drop to the table.

He wanted to talk to her. That's what he'd said back at Caché—he'd spent all that money, gone to all the trouble of blackmailing Del, just to have a chance to talk to her. Because it wasn't over for him; because he had things he "needed" to say. Because … what else had he said?

"I did lie—but not to you."

What had he meant by that? She'd been reminding him of the time she'd overheard him talking to his father, saying she was nothing but a whore. Ari had tried to deny it, so she'd called him a liar.

"... but not to you."

So ... what? He was lying ... to himself? To his father? What did *any of that* even mean?

And why do you even care? Only three days left to go, and then you can just ignore him at Caché. Easy peezy. Sure. Right. Fuck, how do I find myself in these situations!?

Her brain would've spun in circles like that for hours, so she was glad when the door behind her slammed open. She jumped in her seat and whirled around to find Ari standing in the entrance.

"That's all you got done?" he said, glancing at his watch with a frown. "I thought you'd be a lot farther along by now."

"I don't exactly have a background in office work, give me a break," she snapped. He rolled his eyes and gestured for her to stand.

"You can finish it tomorrow. C'mon, we're getting out of here."

She looked at her own watch while she hurried through the doorway, careful not to touch him as she moved past.

"It's four—you get to come and go whenever you want?" she asked, glancing around. The office still seemed busy, with different secretaries and assistants hurrying back and forth across the floor.

"One of the perks of being a *Daddy's boy*," he mocked himself as he shut the conference room behind them. "Which one of these people is gonna tell me I can't go?"

"Your life is so hard."

"You have no idea," he snorted. "I also got ahead on all my work so I'd have a light load during our week together."

Valentine didn't have a response for that; he'd somewhat cleared his schedule so he could pursue her. She was almost ... impressed.

"So where are we going? That social worker called me and said they were wrapping up my grandma's case. I'm going to be cleared of all the charges, so your 'pro-bono work' is done," Valentine pointed out.

As happy as she was to be cleared of any guilt, she was also a little nervous. Gam-Gam was still sick, her memory hadn't been improving at all, and without Ari's "generosity", Valentine couldn't afford round-the-clock care. The dementia was only going to get worse, so her grandmother really needed constant supervision. Valentine couldn't possibly provide that while going to work and school.

It's like I'm constantly going from one bad situation to another. Out of the frying pan, into the fire. Then into lava. Then into the lake of fire. Then into the seventh ring of hell.

She shook her head, trying to clear her thoughts. Like Scarlett O'Hara said—she wouldn't think about that stuff right now, it was tomorrow's problem.

"Where you're concerned, I don't think my work will ever be done," Ari sighed dramatically as he guided her towards the elevator. She snorted at his comment, then glanced at her watch again.

"Hey, yeah, it's four, you're supposed to be meeting with a client at five," she reminded him while they waited for the elevator to climb up from the ground floor.

"Easily taken care of."

While they stood there, he pulled out his phone and made a quick phone call, rescheduling with the client he was about to miss. He never asked for anything, either, she noticed. Didn't *request* a new time—simply *told* everyone to change their schedules. It was annoyingly rude.

And undeniably impressive. I forget that he's a powerful man in a lot of ways.

The elevator was empty when they got on it, but two floors below them, the business must have been closing for the day. Crowds rushed onto the lift when it stopped, and pretty soon the small space was wall-to-wall people. Ari immediately moved up against the back wall, and Valentine was shoved and pushed around, until eventually she found herself against him, back flush to his front.

As his hand came to rest on her hip, anchoring her to him, she felt a blush creep onto her cheeks. It was ridiculous—she'd been naked with him, he'd been inside her. In multiple orifices. But that had always been at night, always between *Saint* Valentine and Aaron Sharapov, *esquire*.

Now they were in the bright light of day, in his office building, and it was just Val and Ari. She wasn't wearing her usual eight pounds of makeup, and felt downright respectable in the black slacks and oxford button down she'd changed into for her "job". She was just a normal assistant leaving work for the day, and her boss was subtly moving his hand from off her hip to cup her ass cheek.

She cleared her throat nervously and glanced around. No one seemed to notice. Everyone was wearing heavy coats and holding umbrellas, briefcases, purses. From the waist down, everyone could be naked, and no one would know.

Talk about a mental picture.

Ari's hand squeezed and she sucked in air sharply. The elevator was stopping at about every floor, it seemed like, so there was no telling how long the whole ride down would be.

"*Stop it,*" she hissed, slowly thrusting her elbow back and into his ribs. He gave a low chuckle, then his hand dropped lower so his fingers were brushing between her thighs.

"What was that, Ms. O'Dell?" he asked in a loud voice. Several people looked their way, and Val knew her face turned an even darker shade of red.

"Nasty rain today, huh?" she managed to chuckle at the woman nearest them. The lady looked at her like she was a bug, then went back to her phone.

"It is pretty damp," Ari said, and she thought she was gonna fall through the elevator floor. "But I never did mind getting wet."

Fuck this—I'm not the same girl anymore, Mr. Sharapov.

Valentine took a deep breath, then crushed herself against him, trapping his arm between their bodies. They got a couple strange looks, but she just smiled politely back and held her ground when he tried to wiggle his hand free. His watch was digging painfully into her butt, but she managed to stay in place until they'd ridden all the way down to the garage.

As soon as the doors opened, she sprung away from him, walking brusquely across the marbled floor of the vestibule. She didn't even look back, just moved with the crowd and went straight for his car. She waited until they were both securely inside the vehicle before she launched into him.

"When I'm in this building, I'm your employee," she informed him. "And as such, you will keep your sexually harassing hands to yourself, *got it?*"

He laughed at her.

"You're sexy when you're indignant."

"Shut up and don't touch me."

"I wonder what you're more upset about," he spoke as if he were talking to himself, all while turning on his car and pulling out of the spot. "That I touched you 'inappropriately', or that you *liked it.*"

Her blush was back in full bloom, and he smirked when he saw it.

"I thought Del explained the rules to you," she growled. "I may be your 'employee' for up to four hours a day, but I also have Serge on speed dial and he has full permission to kick your ass."

"You know, once upon a time that would've been scary, but I think the giant's taken a shine to me."

"Yeah, you keep telling yourself that. Where are we going?"

"It's a surprise."

"*Oh god,*" Valentine breathed, suddenly terrified. "What kind of surprise?"

"Wouldn't be much of one if I told you about it beforehand. Just be patient, and please, *please*, have an open mind."

Ominous words, for sure, and it was then she suddenly recognized where they were—she sat upright when he turned onto a familiar street. Narrowed her gaze as he pulled into another underground parking garage.

"You've gotta be shitting me," she snapped, looking around the garage of his apartment building.

"Nope. C'mon, let's make this quick—I have an early dinner meeting after I drop you off," Ari said, then he climbed out of his car.

"I am *not* having sex with you," she announced as she hopped down to the pavement. "I told you that before."

"I don't want to have sex with you—you're a raging bitch right now," he snorted as he walked them back out of the garage and to the entrance of the building. When he held open the door for her, she hesitated.

"You deserve to deal with someone who acts like you. What the hell are we doing here?" she demanded.

Ari shook his head, but didn't respond. Simply ignored her and walked through the door. She paused for a moment longer—if she let the door shut, she'd be locked out, and it was a long walk home. But going inside with him meant going to his apartment, which meant bad things were going to happen, because good ol' Saint Valentine wasn't known for her great decision making skills. Still …

Such a long walk home.

Valentine slipped through the door just before it could shut, then she hurried down the hall. She was surprised when they walked right past the elevator, so she followed him down the entrance hall to a door that looked identical to his own. Only his was on the top floor, and this was the first floor.

She was very confused.

"I told you about this place, once before," he commented as he took out a separate set of keys from his pocket and unlocked the door. "I bought it the week after you left."

Valentine had forgotten all about the empty apartment in his building. Back when things had been good and confusing and wonderful and weird, he'd off-handedly mentioned that there was an apartment for sale below his own. He'd been considering buying it so she could stay in it.

She'd never once imagined that he'd really do it.

It was done in the same style as Ari's apartment—oak flooring, stainless steel appliances, a large kitchen island with stools, exposed brick on the side walls. But as she walked further into the space, she saw that the back wall of the living room was actually disguising a hallway, hiding three rooms. She peeked her head in one, saw that it wasn't terribly big, but had a nice sized window running the length of the room.

A stylish but modest bathroom sat between the two bedrooms, and she was impressed to see a tub. She was even more impressed when she got to the master bedroom. It was quite a bit larger than the first room, and also had en suite. What she wouldn't give for one of her own.

"I take it you like it?" he asked, twirling the keys around his fingers.

"It's gorgeous—whose is it?" she countered.

"I told you already, it's for you."

"That was something you said weeks ago—months ago—back when I was a whore and you were slightly less of an asshole. Things are a little different now, I'm not willing to be some … mistress tucked away in your lovenest, sorry."

She was a little shocked that he'd even tried this; sure, they'd kissed once, and he'd been inappropriate in the elevator, but for the most part, he hadn't put any moves on her. In fact, he'd been going to great lengths to show her he didn't think of her as being only good for sex. But now this.

Much to her surprise, though, he laughed at her statement.

"No shit you're not my mistress—mistresses have to sleep with their misters, and I haven't had sex in far too long."

"Pity for you."

His eyebrows show up.

"Are you saying *you've* been having sex?" he asked, and she laughed out loud.

"Jealous? That's what *whores* do, Ari, they sleep with lots of people."

"I never—"

"I heard you!" Valentine finally snapped. They'd danced around it, and had been dancing around each other the past couple days, but they'd yet to really talk. Apparently her brain had gone and decided now was the time, without consulting her on the matter. "We've been over this. *I heard you.* With my own ears. After everything we'd said, and you still called me that, to your own father."

"Yes," Ari snapped back. "I called you that to my own father *because* it was my father."

That threw her for a loop. She wasn't quite sure how to respond.

"You ... what? That doesn't make sense."

He strode across the room so he was standing right in front of her.

"It was a bad day, okay?" he told her. "I know you think I live some sort of golden life, but I do actually work, and sometimes things are shit. That day was a shitty fucking day, and then you stormed in, and my father saw you, and he was being an asshole, and it was the only way to get him to drop the subject. I knew if he thought you were just a prostitute, he would let it go. You and I were just barely even starting to figure shit out—how was I supposed to know what to tell him?"

"You should've known not to call me a fucking whore!" she yelled. "It was the worst thing you could've done, and you didn't even hesitate! Because you *don't care.*"

"You're so good at knowing everything, *Saint* Valentine," he snarled, looming over her. "What I'm thinking, what I'm feeling, what everything means. Since you're such a fucking genius, what does my being *here* mean, hmmm? What does me buying this apartment, buying *you* at that stupid auction, mean?"

His words stung because she knew they were true. The last couple of years had left her jaded, which she knew led to her being a little judgemental. She'd had a hard life, so she knew more than most people. Knew *better,* she figured.

But even so, that didn't just negate him being a gigantic dickhead.

"It means Ari Sharapov likes to be *in control,*" she said, refusing to be cowed. "That's what it's always been about. Poor Saint Valentine needed a break, so Ari came along and took control for her. You weren't quite ready to give it up when I left, it wasn't on your terms. And you knew I'd still need help, even without you. That's why you wormed your way back into the club, and that's why you looked into my grandma's case."

Ari rolled his eyes.

"Sometimes I forget you're practically a child," he said in a droll voice. "Such dramatics."

Her blood was boiling. Yes, she was quite a bit younger than him—eight years, to be exact. But he'd never once before made mention of it. He'd always treated her like an adult, same as him.

"You wanna see dramatic? How about me walking out on our fucking deal right now," she snapped, and went to stride past him. He grabbed her arm, spinning them around to face each other again.

"You wouldn't deny those poor kids my generous contribution," he tried to call her bluff.

"You wouldn't ever get your money back from Del," she countered. She knew Ari had paid up, so that threat wouldn't work anymore. His eyes narrowed.

"The deal was I pay for you, you have to work for me," he reminded her.

"Exactly—*work* for you. Not be sexually harassed and annoyed and practically stalked. That voids our 'contract'," she informed him.

"Jesus, you're stubborn," he cursed, raking his fingers through his hair. "Are you gonna let your pride stand in your way *now*, of all times? You needed help with your case, I put the fear of god in IDHS. Are you really gonna throw all money and help away, just because you 'don't wanna listen'? Just because you're mad at something you *think* I *might* have said?"

God, she hated him in that moment. She wanted to say "yes", to everything. Fuck him and fuck his deal. She didn't care about anyone or anything, so long as it meant teaching Ari who was *really* in control, once and for all.

Hate him because he's right.

As she glared up at him, her grandmother's face floated across her mind, and even her roommate's, Bailey. She'd hardly been home at all to spend time with the girl, so she'd become even more of a hermit. With Ari helping to solve some of her problems, Valentine would have a little more time for the people in her life. And of course most important of all, Gam-Gam—she absolutely couldn't turn down any kind of help that involved her grandmother.

I'm so angry at him, and the world, and life itself, that I'm willing to spite the nose off my face. When did I become this person?

Valentine hung her head for a moment, feeling defeated. She was suddenly tired. Exhausted. Of pushing and fighting and just trying to survive. She didn't want to be this bitter person, but she didn't want *him* to be the reason she got better.

Any port in a storm, Valentine. Suck it up and accept the help you desperately need and get over your anger.

"You're right," she breathed, finally looking back up at him. He looked stunned at her response.

"I'm sorry, what?"

"You're right," she repeated herself. "I'm … angry at you, and ashamed of myself, and because of all that, I … I'm just angry."

There was a long pause, and he had a strange look in his eyes. She couldn't quite place it. Confusion? Or possibly … hurt? Could Ari Sharapov *get* hurt? Three weeks ago, she wouldn't have thought so. He finally let out a long sigh.

"I'm sorry I made you angry," he said simply. She gave him a weak smile.

"Thanks."

"And I shouldn't have called you a whore, even if I didn't mean it," he continued. She held up her hand to stop him, but he kept going. "I know you don't understand the relationship I have with my father, but it is what it is; I'm working on changing it, but it takes time. I should've … stood up for you. And I didn't. And I will regret it for a long time."

"Thank you," she whispered. Her brain warned her not to believe him—he was literally a professional liar. But her heart was already turning over, and that scared her more than anything else that had happened. She quickly tried to think of something to turn the situation around. "Do you think this is what Del meant when he said we needed closure?"

That startled a laugh out of him, and he shook his head.

"I don't want to give Del that much credit. Are we good now?"

"I accept your apology, if that's what you mean."

"And you believe everything I said?"

"I think I do."

"Good. Can we start having sex again?"

Her jaw dropped, but then she saw the smirk at the corner of his lips, and she started laughing.

"No," she shook her head, as well. "You can't afford me now."

"We'll see about that."

"So what are we doing here, Sharapov?" she asked, holding out her arms.

"I told you, I bought this apartment so—"

"*No sex.*"

"You're so boring now," he sighed. "I bought this apartment as an investment—I have plans to eventually buy the whole building."

"God, it must be amazing to live your life. Twenty-five thousand here, a whole building there."

"It would be a lot better if the women in my life were more compliant."

"Wom*en?*" she questioned the plurality of the word.

"Jealous?" he teased, but then his smile quickly fell away. "I read your grandmother's medical records, had a doctor friend explain some things to me. Valentine … I know it's none of my business, and I didn't know her well, but have the doctors spoken to you about releasing her to your care?"

Three weeks of anger and resentment had trained her to snap at anything he had to say, so she just barely stopped herself from telling him to mind his own business.

He wants to help. In his bossy, nosy, controlling way, that's what he's doing. And you need help. Let go of control a little, and let him take it a little.

"Not in depth," she was honest. "Doctors in real life aren't exactly like they are on TV. She's got several of them, it feels like I rarely see the same people twice. They tell me what conditions she has, which new ones pop up, what treatments she's receiving, but that's about it. I know I'll need to have round-the-clock care for her while I'm working, things like that."

Ari nodded and rubbed a hand against the side of his jaw. She realized he must not have shaved that morning, he had the beginnings of a five o'clock shadow. It looked good on him.

"I also looked into the care facility she's in," he went on. "It's highly rated by the state, she's receiving excellent care there, the best a state-run facility can provide. The notes I saw from her nurses, it seems like she's also well liked there."

"Are you saying I should just ditch my grandmother in some *home?*" Valentine pieced together what he was getting at. They may have made peace somewhat, but this was going a little too far.

"No, that's not what I said at all. Obviously you'd be involved in her care and all her medical treatments, and you could still see her whenever you wanted. But Valentine … you need to consider the fact that maybe Gam-Gam *is* home now."

"No," she shook her head. "No. I won't be that person who just abandons her because she takes a little work."

"You're *not* abandoning her," Ari rolled his eyes. "She needs dialysis, Val. She needs twenty different kinds of medication. She needs to be in a memory care unit because if she walks out a door, she won't remember where it is or how to get back to it. You've taken amazing care of her, everyone knows this—*everyone*. But there's only so much you can do."

"Why are you saying all this?" she demanded, suddenly wondering what was motivating this little speech.

"Because you live in that house where all three bedrooms are up a flight of stairs, which she can no longer climb," Ari pointed out. "But if it's just you and Bailey, you only need a two bedroom."

Much like the apartment I'm standing in right now.

"So all I have to do is forget I have a sick grandmother, and I get a free apartment?" she asked, folding her arms across her chest.

"No—all you have to do is stop being a goddamn brat, and then you can have a free apartment," he growled, and she blinked in surprise.

Is that what I'm being? A brat? But ... she's my grandmother ... I love her ...

"I don't know," she finally sighed. "Even if—*if*—I were to leave Gam-Gam in that facility, I still probably wouldn't move in here."

"I wouldn't charge you rent," Ari offered.

"Yeah, for now. What happens when six months go by and I still don't sleep with you?" she pointed out. He shrugged.

"We'll work up a contract."

"Those things never work very well in my favor."

"Uh, I beg to differ."

"Baby steps, Ari," she said, pressing her hand against his chest, as if her touch had the power to stop that mouth of his. "I'm barely considering forgiving you—I don't think I'm ready to live a couple yards away from you."

"You said you accepted my apology, that means you *already* forgave me," he pointed out, placing his hand over hers. She frowned.

"That's odd, I don't remember saying that. Ask me again tomorrow, maybe I'll forgive you then."

But she was finally smiling at him again, and he smirked back down at her.

No, wait, not a smirk.

It was a genuine smile.

"Brat."

She went to quip back, but his cell phone interrupted them. He stared at her for a moment longer, then pulled the device out of his pocket. Valentine saw the screen, saw *Harper Kittering* scrolling across, and her hand fell away from his chest. Ari groaned and swiped the call to decline.

"Girlfriend problems?" Valentine asked in a syrupy sweet voice. He snorted.

"You have no idea. I've acquired a stalker since the last time you saw me."

Valentine blinked her eyes rapidly in surprise. Something about that statement ... Harper? A stalker? She'd always been a little intense, but had she really gone full on stalker?

Val shook her head, deciding not to care.

Not my boyfriend, so not my problem.

"She always was such a lovely girl."

"Tell me about it. You still doing that design project with her?"

Now it was Valentine's turn to snort.

"'With her' is being generous—she won't be in the same room with me to work on it, she barely speaks to me, I'm doing everything on my own. All she does is everything possible to make my life miserable."

"Really?" Ari's eyebrows shot up.

"Yeah. Little things, I guess, tripping me in class, being rude in the halls. Scared me in the parking lot once, when I was on my bike. She got too close with her car, made me fall," she prattled off.

"Holy shit."

Holy shit was right. Valentine realized they'd been standing there talking as if everything were normal. As if no time had passed. As if they were still two people in a strange relationship, standing on the very edge of something greater.

Or something far, far worse.

"It's five," she breathed, glancing at her watch. Then she cleared her throat. "Work is officially done for the day. This leprechaun needs to be heading out."

"Trying to escape so quickly, huh? You're a pretty shitty assistant."

"Well, you didn't exactly hire me for my filing abilities, did you?"

The joke came off more sexual than intended, and Ari clearly took it that way, chuckling darkly. When they walked out of the building together, a freezing cold breeze ripped down the sidewalk. Val immediately hunched her shoulders, and next thing she knew, Ari was pulling her in close to him. Wrapping his long, felt jacket around her and tucking her into his warmth.

And for a moment—just a moment—there was nowhere else she wanted to be.

Fool you once, shame on him. If this is a second time, there'll be no end to the shame you feel.

7

What the fuck was going on?

Valentine stared at herself in her full length mirror. She had a towel wrapped snuggly around her midsection, and held a flat iron in her hand. She did a double take at it, realizing she'd finished doing her hair a couple minutes ago, and quickly turned it off and sat it on its cooling pad.

What the fuck have I gotten myself into?

Three months ago, Ari Sharapov hadn't existed to her, and she'd just been Saint Valentine, making her ways through her days as best she could.

Then over the course of two months, he'd become everything to her. It happened so subtly, she hadn't even noticed until it was too late.

Then for three weeks, she'd hated him with a passion she was sure she'd never felt before; one she was sure would never die.

And now …

Now she had no clue what she was feeling.

Of course she was attracted him. Even raging anger couldn't take away the fact that he was so good looking, it should've been illegal. She could ignore it, but it was always there.

And now that anger had cooled so quickly. Burned white hot for three weeks, and then *poof*, almost gone, barely leaving a warm coal behind.

Stupid. Valentine had gone through too many rough patches to be tricked by fate again. Good things didn't happen to her—Ari had been the most recent incident to teach her that, and now wasn't any different.

So she clung to that knowledge. Just because he maybe wasn't the world's biggest asshole—an idiot, for sure, but maybe not an asshole—didn't mean he wouldn't fuck things up again. So she couldn't let any-*thing* happen between them again.

That was one thing she couldn't let go of control of—she'd always have to have her guard up. No matter how many sweet things he said, or flashy gifts he presented her with (seriously!? An apartment!?), he'd hurt her once already. Maybe not on purpose, but he'd done it, and he'd done it spectacularly. That meant he could, and most likely would, do it again.

"You need his help," she mumbled to her reflection. "And you need his connections. And yeah, you might need his money. But when the dust settles, just make sure you don't *need* anything else."

"Are you talking to me?"

Valentine jumped as her bedroom door opened a crack. Her roommate, Bailey, poked her head through the gap. Val laughed.

"No, just being a crazy person, babbling to myself. C'mon in."

Ever since Gam-Gam's second stroke, she and Bailey had grown a lot closer. Despite being a homebody, she kept the same crazy hours Valentine did, so they often met for pizza or coffee in the kitchen at five in the morning. She'd gotten a job online, doing some coding, so she was even bringing in a little money. It wasn't much, barely enough to pay for her own food, but every little bit helped.

What would Bailey think of living in a swanky apartment near down-town? Of exposed brick and all new bathrooms? Of no rent to worry about, because my—STOP IT. SHE WOULDN'T THINK ANYTHING ABOUT IT BECAUSE IT'S NEVER GOING TO HAPPEN.

"What are your plans for tonight?" Valentine prattled, trying to cover up her frayed nerves.

"Seriously?" Bailey laughed as she sat on the edge of the bed. "'Same thing I do every night, Pinky', sit in my room and stare at my computer until my eyes bleed."

"Honestly sounds like more fun that what I'll be doing," Val sighed as she yanked a dress out of her closet and tossed it onto the bed. Then she grabbed a bottle off her tatty dresser and started rubbing lotion all over her legs.

"Please. You get to dress up every weekend and go hang out at a fancy ass nightclub. I wish I got to do stuff like that," Bailey sighed.

Valentine glanced over at her, then paused and looked back. Bailey was nineteen, but age was only a number at Caché. How long had it been since Val had gone on a Girl's Night Out? Sure, she had to work, but Bailey deserved a night off just as much as she did—Valentine had taken last Saturday off.

Now it was Bailey's turn.

"You can," Val said, standing up straight. "Come with me tonight."

"What?" Bailey looked stunned. "But ... you always told me that place is crazy."

"It is, but it's also a good place to forget about your problems for a little while."

"But ... but ... I'm underage."

"Not a problem when you know the right people," Val winked at her.

"I ... I wouldn't even begin to know what to wear," Bailey said, glancing around as if Valentine's room somehow had a response to that.

"That's why I'm here," she replied, then she turned with a squeal and started rummaging through her closet. "You're skinnier than I am, but I think your boobs are bigger, so that should even things out. *Oh my gosh!* This is perfect for you!"

She pulled out a red tartan, pleated skirt and tossed it onto the bed. She leaned over to a different section of closet and quickly found a tight, black, button up cardigan. It joined the skirt while she went over and dug around in a tupperware bin. She let out a triumphant shout and pulled out what she'd been searching for—a pair of knee-high white stockings.

"I cannot wear this," Bailey breathed, holding up the small skirt.

"You can, and it will look awesome," Val assured her, shoving the rest of the clothing into the girl's arms. "Now go change—don't come back if you're not wearing it!"

After Bailey left, Val wiggled into her own outfit. It was a simple brown dress, with a low scoop neck and long sleeves, and a hem that went clear to her ankles. The entire thing was skin tight, hugging her body in a way that was almost obscene. She loved the juxtaposition of showing very little skin, but still looking sinfully sexy.

She was just sitting down to strap on a pair of dangerously high stilettos when there was a soft knock at her door.

"I can't wear this," Bailey whined from the hallway.

"I'll be the judge of that! Come in," Val ordered, fighting with the buckle on the second heel.

The door opened and she heard a few hesitant footsteps. Out the corner of her eye, she could see that Bailey had put on a cute pair of black boots, almost combat style. Doc Martens, possibly. They were totally her style, and she was such a tall girl, the flat shoe would probably make her feel more comfortable in her new outfit.

"I look … ridiculous," Bailey sighed. Val laughed and finally lifted her head.

"It's probably not as bad as you—*whoa.*"

"Is that a good whoa? Or a bad whoa?" Bailey asked, curling her fingers nervously around the hem of the skirt.

"That's a 'I better keep an eye on her or she'll steal all my clients' whoa," Val explained as she stood up. "You look *amazing*, Bailey! Who knew this body was underneath all those black clothes!?"

Valentine didn't have a problem with Bailey's somewhat goth dress attire—whatever made people comfortable, that's what people should wear, that was her motto. But still, there was always something neat about seeing someone step outside their comfort zone and try something a little new.

Bailey looked like a super sexy extra from the movie *The Craft*. The cardigan was just a little small on her, which only added to the effect. Her breasts were almost overflowing the low neckline, and the tight knit material hugged her slender waist, showing off the gentle slope of her hips.

The skirt was short, but of course, it had been designed to be, and it was the perfect choice for someone like Bailey. She was around five-foot-nine or ten, and the skirt made her mile long legs look more like five miles.

All in all, the outfit was sexy without being slutty, and was totally suited to Bailey's already somewhat-witchy look.

"You really think it looks good? I don't have any shoes to match," she complained.

"No, the shoes are perfect, honestly. Tones it all down, makes you look like a badass. Like are you going to fuck me? Or are you going to sacrifice me to Satan tonight? I don't know, but I wanna find out," Val joked, and Bailey burst out laughing.

"And that's a good thing?"

"Oh, for sure. Trust me. Men will line up to be your sacrifice, I guarantee it," she assured her. "Do you want any makeup?"

Normally, Bailey favored a heavy black eyeliner, a somewhat "raccoon" look, but she was fresh scrubbed that day. She had large, soulful gray eyes and generous lips. She glanced at Valentine's "vanity"—a shit ton of makeup strewn in a semi-circle around the base of her full length mirror.

"No, I'm already taken up too much of your time, you still have to do—"

Valentine laughed and grabbed the other girl's hand, yanking her down to the floor.

"We're going to have so much fun tonight! And thank god, because I *really* need it."

At nine-thirty, Valentine led Bailey into Caché and introduced her to her co-workers. Gary promised to keep an eye on her if Val got too busy with a client, and Del offered Bailey a job right on the spot. Val politely—but firmly—declined on her behalf.

Then at ten o'clock, the doors opened and people started spilling in. Some sort of big basketball deal was going on, a game or a conference or something, Valentine didn't know. But what she did know was that every basketball player within ten miles of Caché had apparently decided to turn up that night, and each one brought a small entourage with him.

The club went *nuts*. The Dance Room was pumping, wall to wall people bumping and grinding on the floor. Two rooms upstairs had been opened together, and a giant tub had been placed in the middle of them—a KY Jelly wrestling tourney was underway; clothing optional, of course.

Every go-go dancer, every escort, everyone *period*, was going full tilt. It was a night that held a lot of potential for Valentine, but as busy as it was, she knew she couldn't leave Bailey alone, not that night. So she helped around where she could, delivering bottles to VIP tables, introducing men to other escorts, helping Gary serve drinks. Bailey was always close behind her, and even helped out a couple times in a pinch.

"I'm sorry this isn't the night of fun I promised you!" Valentine yelled around midnight, leaning in close to the other girl's ear. They were on the dance floor, crushed between people and swaying to the beat.

"Are you kidding?" Bailey yelled back. "I'm having a *blast!* This is incredible! Like half these guys are famous!"

"How do you even know that? You don't watch basketball!"

"NBA 2018 for Playstation, duh!"

Valentine started laughing, but then she felt a hand on her

shoulder. She turned around, quickly shaking it off, but was pleasantly surprised when she saw Evans Daniels standing behind her.

"I thought I recognized you!" he said, grinning at her.

"From behind?" she laughed some more, teasing him.

"Valentine, I'm pretty sure I could recognize you quicker from behind than from the front," he teased right back. Then he turned the charm on Bailey. "Who's your friend?"

"This is Bailey, my roommate," Valentine said, introducing her *and* hopefully setting a boundary. "It's her first night in Caché."

"Oh, wow! You picked a hell of a night to pop your cherry," he laughed. Bailey scrunched up her nose.

"Excuse me?"

"So what do you do, Bailey?" he asked.

"She takes classes online," Valentine piped up before the other girl could. "She's *nineteen*, it's her second year in college."

At the word "nineteen", she could practically see Evans cooling his jets. Anything went at Caché, sure, but Val wasn't about to let the thirty-two year old corporate poon hound hit on her young, naive roommate.

"College!" Evans toasted his glass to Bailey. "Fun times! I loved college—I went to Columbia. You ladies want a drink?"

They followed him off the dance floor and into the Music Room. It wasn't any less crowded in there, but Evans had apparently had foresight—he'd booked a table for himself for the night, and it was all set up with a bottle ready and waiting for them when they sat down.

While Evans and Bailey made chit chat—Evans smoothly, Bailey awkwardly—Val glanced around the room. That feeling of being on edge was back and she bounced her feet under the table. Maybe it was the adrenaline still pumping from rushing around the club all night. Maybe it was nerves on Bailey's behalf.

Maybe it's a totally different problem. Maybe one that's, oh, say, about six-foot-two, with blond hair and blue eyes and all at once the life line you've been praying for and the living nightmare you've been dreading.

"Penny?"

Evans' voice interrupted her train of thought and Valentine glanced over at him. She'd almost forgotten that she wasn't alone.

"What?"

"Penny for your thoughts," he clarified, and she chuckled. Bailey was leaning back in her chair, talking to some super gothed-out chick who was wearing a bunch of leather straps covering vital body parts, and little else.

"They're not even worth that much," she joked. "Just … stuff. Life."

"Ah, life stuff. The worst," he sighed. "Anything I can help with?"

"Not really," she shrugged. "Just gotta take it one day at a time, you know? I'll be fine."

"I feel like everyone always says that," he replied, startling her.

"Excuse me?"

"Everyone always says they're fine," he repeated her statement. "Like it's a band-aid that'll cover up the fact they're not fine at all."

She chuckled again and nodded, spinning her glass between her hands.

"Ain't that the truth," she agreed. "But best to leave the band-aid in place for now, okay?"

"Okay," he nodded his head. Unlike Ari, Evans was a guy who knew when a subject was closed. "So how'd you meet Bailey? I didn't even know you had a roommate."

"I took out an ad," Valentine explained. "I'd needed help with my grandma, offered a free room to someone who'd be home during the hours I'd be gone. She was one of the people who responded."

"You're lucky you didn't end up with a serial killer."

"Yup. Instead I ended up with a quirky little gamer," Val laughed.

"Bailey's a gamer?" Evans asked, raising his eyebrows as he looked across the table. Upon hearing her name, the younger woman finally returned to the conversation.

"That's what she's in school for," Valentine explained, smiling between them. "Game design."

"One of the things, yeah. Kinda dorky, I know," Bailey said, picking at the tablecloth.

"Dorky? Are you kidding? Multi-billion dollar industry that only shows growth, as well as an industry that's at the forefront of technology—what's dorky about any of that? Plus, I kick ass at Skyrim."

And then they were off speaking another language. Valentine had never seen Bailey so engaged, she fairly lit up as they started talking about games they both knew and played. When a waitress interrupted to drop off more mixers, Val leaned close to Evans.

"Look after her for me, alright? I'm gonna do a lap," she mumbled as she stood up. "And nothing funny. If I come back and you two have disappeared, I won't hesitate to shut this entire club down to look for you."

"You're a formidable friend to have, Saint Valentine," he laughed, then he waved her away. "We won't move from this spot."

The night was still relatively young—she could easily pick up a client, and make sure to stay down there in the Club and Music Rooms, keeping an eye on Bailey the whole time. So Val made her way back onto the dance floor. It had thinned out just a little, enough so that she didn't feel claustrophobic as she danced around.

She kept an eye on the crowd, looking for potential targets. There was a rowdy table near the entrance, she didn't want any part of that, so she kept scanning. The bar was a mass of people, not worth even trying. Maybe if she moved to the other side of the—

Just as she was taking a step to turn around, a flash of blonde caught her eye and she did a double-take. Then her jaw dropped.

Harper fucking Kittering had just walked into the Club Room with a gaggle of her friends, all of them laughing and flicking their hair around. They swayed close to the rowdy table and the guys took the bait pretty quickly, talking and flirting with them.

Holy shit. **Holy shit.** *I never thought to preemptively ban her because I couldn't even imagine the possibility of her showing up at a place like this! Who told her about it, who invited her!?*

Valentine whirled around to walk off in the opposite direction, but instead, she collided with what felt like a solid wall. She ricocheted off someone's chest and started to fall backwards, but then strong hands gripped her upper arms and held her upright.

"I just love it when we bump into each other."

At this rate, her jaw was gonna fall off at the hinges, she was gaping so much.

Ari stared down at her, as if she'd conjured him out of thin air. It felt like a mirage—he'd been banned from Caché for so long, it was bizarre seeing him there again.

On top of that, he also *looked* different. He still hadn't shaved, and she was surprised to realize that Ari could probably grow a thick, healthy beard if he ever chose to; the stubble made him look rakish and sexy, complimenting his mussy hair perfectly. His clothing just added to the look—she'd rarely ever seen him wear anything but suits, but now he was in a white t-shirt and expensive looking jeans. His long, black, felt winter coat looked like it had been added as an after thought and perfectly completed his sexy, messy, roguish look he had going on.

And to round out the bizarreness, HARPER IS LESS THAN FIFTY FEET AWAY.

"What are you doing here?" Valentine gasped as he let her go.

"Membership was reinstated," he reminded her. He went to fish out his gold club card, but she stopped him, pressing both hands to his chest.

"I remember," she assured him, and she glanced over her shoulder. Harper was leaning over some basketball player, practically resting her tits on his head. "I meant what are you doing here *right now?* You didn't tell me you were coming tonight."

"I didn't know I had to ask permission. Did you know Evans is hitting on your roommate in the other room?" he asked.

"I left them together, they're talking about video games. Did you know your girlfriend is practically right behind me?"

"I don't have a girlfriend, just an annoying saint who won't—"

Valentine roughly cupped her hand around his chin and forced his head up, so he was looking over her shoulder. He glared and started to snap at her, then stopped when his gaze must have connected with Harper.

"So your timing isn't the best," Valentine growled. "On top of which, you looming over me is bad for business."

"Ah, yes," Ari said in a soft voice, and he moved his chin out of her hand so he could look down at her again. "Your *business*. I heard it's booming."

"A girl's gotta make a living, and as fun as it is being your assistant, I need something that pays a little better. I don't work for you here, so go away, Ari."

"You *could* work for me here," he offered.

"Did that really come out of your mouth? After all the ... progress, or whatever, we made today?" she asked, crossing her arms tightly across her chest.

"Too soon?" he chuckled.

"*Way* too soon. Go away, Ari."

But he didn't move. His stared down at her, his eyelids drooped low, the corner of his mouth quirked up into his signature smirk. She wanted to look away. To walk away. To slap him or shove him or turn around and ignore him forever. But she was frozen to that spot, staring up into his blue, blue eyes.

"Valentine—" he started, and she desperately wanted to hear what he was going to say. Would it be another apology? Another proposition? A declaration? A retraction?

She'd never get to know.

"*Ari!*" Harper's voice squealed, cutting through their tension like a light saber. Valentine winced and actually ducked as the blonde bombshell came barreling past her. She practically threw herself at Ari. "*O.M.G.*, did you follow me here? I knew you must still be following my posts."

Ari was staring at Valentine, grimacing as he struggled against Harper's hold. He finally managed to yank her arms away from around his neck, then he forced her a couple steps back, so she was standing right next to Val.

"I wouldn't even know where to follow your 'posts'," he replied. "And I told you—*don't fucking touch me.*"

"You don't have to be so rude, Ari," Harper huffed. "And what, you think it's just coincidence you happened to show up here on the same night I came here for the first time? I don't think so. I *knew* you …"

Harper's voice drifted off when Ari reached over and grabbed Valentine by the wrist, then gently pulled her over so she was at his side. She was too stunned to even fight the move, her eyes wide as her gaze bounced back and forth between the two exes.

"This isn't my first time in this club," Ari said simply, not pulling Valentine in tight to his side, but also not letting go of her wrist.

Harper. Looked. *Pissed.* If a person's head could actually pop off, Valentine was sure that would be happening right now. Even in the dim lighting, she could tell the other girl's face was crimson red. And not from embarrassment.

From pure rage.

"What *the fuck?*" she hissed through clenched teeth, glaring straight at Val. "*You* said you guys weren't together!"

"We're—" Valentine started, but Ari took a step forward.

"—none of your business," he finished for her. "You need to stop calling me, stop showing up at my work, stop harassing me. And you need to *leave Valentine alone.*"

"Oh, great, so you're a whore *and* a tattletale?" Harper snarled. Val stiffened at the word "whore".

"She didn't need to tell me anything—I know you, I know how you are," Ari covered smoothly. "And if you keep up with this bullshit, we'll start having some real problems."

"Oh, please, you know you can't touch me. Your father would disown you. He loves me more than he loves you," Harper taunted.

"Then I feel sorry for you. Now if you'll excuse us, Valentine and I were having a *very* important conversation and you interrupted."

"You can't just—" Harper started.

"We weren't—" Valentine tried to argue.

Ari didn't listen to either of them, though, and instead abruptly leaned down and kissed Valentine, hard. She let out a muffled squeak and started at him wide-eyed as he crushed his lips to hers hard enough she could feel his teeth.

A second later and his hand was on the back of her head, fingers tangling in her long hair as he deepened the kiss. She gasped when his tongue invaded her mouth, practically leapt out of her skin when his body pressed against hers, and felt like fainting when his teeth grazed over her bottom lip.

"You'll pay for this!" Harper screeched. "You ... you ... you *home-wrecking slut!*"

Ari let go of Valentine just in time for them to watch Harper stomp away. She didn't say anything to her friends, just walked up and stood amongst them as if nothing had happened. She tossed her head back and laughed, forcefully, and leaned close to a different guy. She kept glancing back, obviously trying to catch Ari's attention.

"She might be clinically insane," he commented, and his calm, even voice shattered the daze Valentine had been stuck in.

"*What the fuck is your problem!?*" she squealed, yanking away from and smacking at his chest.

"I'm horny and the woman who wants to fuck me, I don't want, and the woman I want to fuck, doesn't want me," he answered plainly. She hit him again.

"Well, stop making all of that *my* problem!" she demanded. "Do you have any idea what you just did? She's already a nightmare to be around, now she's just gonna be ten times worse!"

"It was kinda worth it—did you see the look on your face?"

"No! I was too busy trying to remove the tongue that had some-how found it's way into my throat!" she snapped back. He smirked at her.

"You weren't complaining much at the time."

"Probably because I was choking!"

"Admit it," Ari whispered teasingly. "It felt good, making her see red. Turning her green. Wanna try for some other colors?"

Valentine glared at him, but she couldn't maintain it. She glanced over at Harper, and she had to admit, it was pretty satisfying, seeing the blonde so discomposed. She was manically fiddling with her hair, and the guy she was attempting to flirt with looked slightly scared of her. Probably because she wasn't looking at him at all, but was still staring back across the dance floor at Ari.

"She's awful," Valentine said softly. "She's the worst. And it'll just make everything with her worse."

Ari didn't argue. He was glaring back at Harper. Valentine glanced down, suddenly realizing he was still gripping onto her wrist with one hand. He'd been holding onto it the whole time. Almost possessively. And that's what Harper was actually looking at—not at Ari, and not at Valentine, but at where they were touching. At where they were connected.

I wanna give this bitch something to really look at.

Valentine yanked Ari's head down so quickly, he actually stumbled. That was fine with her, it brought him even closer to her. She pressed every inch of her body against him, bending backwards a little as he leaned into her and kissed her with even more passion than he had moments ago.

She kept her eyes open. This was about Harper, not Ari. She wanted to watch the girl suffer. Wanted to cause Harper as much pain as she'd caused her over the past couple weeks. It was awful, sure, but watching the blonde go nuclear was almost worth it. A couple more kisses, and Harper's head might actually spin around.

But then Ari's hand was against the side of her neck, and his other arm was wrapping around her waist. And suddenly she wasn't looking at Harper over his shoulder, anymore. Her eyes were closed.

When did that happen?

She moaned against his mouth, ran her tongue along the side of his teeth, let her hands get reacquainted with his shoulders. She wasn't supposed to ever touch him again, and god, she'd wanted to *so badly.*

He was holding her so tightly, her toes were barely brushing the floor, so she barely noticed that he was moving her across the floor. Suddenly she found herself pressed up against the wall below the DJ booth and Ari wasn't holding her anymore. His hands were running all over her body, skating over the soft material of her dress.

"I love this," he breathed. "Seeing so much of you but none of you at all."

"I knew you'd love it," Valentine panted. *"I knew it."*

Ari reached out and she was stunned when he grabbed onto a door knob that was entirely painted black, practically invisible in the club's lighting. He yanked the door open and dragged her through it.

"You seem surprised," he whispered. The door shut behind them and they were in complete darkness. *"You forget,* Saint Valentine showed me all of Caché's hidden secrets."

A red light came on above their head, barely illuminating the room. Not that it need to, Valentine was very familiar with it. They were surrounded on all sides by padded walls. In the wall across from them, about six feet up, there was a large black square in the padding. Above it there was a digital clock that had started counting down from five minutes as soon as they'd entered the room. While Ari kissed a trail down the side of her neck to her cleavage, Valentine stared at the black square.

"What are we doing? This is a bad idea," she said, lifting her hands to his head. Ari's own hands were busy, as well, scrabbling and pulling at the material of her dress, lifting it up her legs.

"This is the best idea we've had in a *long* time," he countered.

"I don't want to be this girl again," she whispered.

"You were never that girl," he whispered back.

And then his fingers were between her legs and an arm was back around her waist and Valentine's eyes started rolling back in her head. Before her eyelids fully shut, she saw the clock. Twenty seconds left till zero.

"I hated you," she groaned as he started to lift her, and she wrapped her legs around his waist. "But I *missed this."*

"God, you have no idea. *No idea* how much I missed this," he moaned against her skin. She bit into her bottom lip and lifted her arm above her head, scratching her nails against the padding.

"Oh yeah? *Prove it to me.*"

Two fingers shoved inside her, and as Valentine gasped, a flash went off behind her closed eyes. She laughed and smiled just in time for the second flash. By the time the third one went off, she was biting down on his shoulder, and for the last one, she had both hands in his hair, clutching his head to her bosom.

It was a photo booth. A padded photo booth that turned on when people entered the room, and every five minutes, it would take four photos. Whenever they were done, they would just have to remember to grab the photos from the slot before they left.

Don't want to leave those behind—memories are bad enough, I don't need photographic evidence of my bad decisions.

"That sounded like a challenge, Valentine," Ari hissed, and his fingers disappeared, causing her to moan in disappointment.

"Are you up for it?" she asked in return.

"Again—you have no idea."

His fingers were at her chest, pulling at her top, and she finally opened her eyes to look down at him. Then he was pinning her against the wall with his weight, allowing him to use both of his hands. The material was stretched and pulled and dragged over her shoulders, down her arms, under her breasts. At the same time, Valentine was shoving and pushing at his heavy coat, letting out a small cheer when he finally dropped it to the ground.

"Perfect. Did I ever tell you that you have *perfect* breasts?" he sighed before wrapping his lips around one nipple. She hissed when she felt his teeth, and raked her nails down his back in response.

"You were never very giving with compliments," she replied, sliding her fingers along his belt to the front of his pants before yanking everything apart.

"Well, they're perfection."

STYLO FANTÔME

"You obviously didn't look very closely at Bailey's outfit tonight."

"If you want to do a side-by-side comparison, I'd be happy to judge," Ari offered, but then it was his turn to gasp. Valentine had forced her hand inside his pants, delighted to find he wasn't wearing any underwear, and she quickly wrapped her hands around the base of his cock.

"Hmmm, I'm a little busy at the moment. Maybe another time."

"A verbal contract is binding in—"

He choked on his words when she squeezed her hand, then groaned when she started pumping that same hand up and down. His forehead dropped to her chest for a moment, both of them breathing hard, then he was upright again. His hand joined hers, stroking along with her for a moment while he kissed her quickly, and then he was shoving her away before pushing his pants over his hips.

"I can't believe you made me wait this long," he growled in her ear, and she shuddered as she felt his hot, hard length between their bodies. "I should make you *beg* for this."

"Try it—you'll find yourself waiting even longer."

"*Bitch.*"

Valentine almost thought he was going to do it, but then he was slamming into her so quickly, so abruptly, she figured he must've decided punishing her would be better than making her beg.

Too bad this is my favorite kind of punishment.

"*Oh my god!*" she shrieked, and at the same moment she threw her head back, the flashes started going off again.

"My name," Ari was panting as he slammed his hips against her over and over again. "I want you to say my name."

Had his dick always been this big? Had he always been this aggressive? Had it always felt this way? Valentine felt like her whole body was expanding and contracting, just one gigantic pending orgasm. And with each heaving breath, her nipples were brushing against his rough t-shirt, acting like a match trying to light a fuse.

"Fuck, Ari, was it always like this?" she asked, shoving her fingers into his hair and holding his head so she could look into his eyes.

"No," he managed. "Sometimes it was even *more* amazing."

"*Fuck.*"

Valentine abandoned herself then, stretching her arms out to the sides just in time for the last flash. Ari's arms were hard at work, one wrapped under her hips, his hand clutching her ass, fingers scratching. His other hand was on her left breasts, squeezing almost painfully tight. While he lavished her other breast with his tongue, the hand moved up her body, pausing to gently squeeze her throat before moving into the hair at the base of her skull.

"Goddamn, Valentine, you're not holding out on me anymore," he growled, then bit down on the top of her breast. She let out a shriek and her thighs started to tremble.

"Ari, I'm … I'm …"

I'm gasping for air and there's no oxygen and I always forget how he steals it all.

"So fucking close, I can feel it," he whispered, moving his mouth to her ear, catching her earlobe with his canine tooth.

"Yes," she whimpered, coiling her arms around his shoulders, tightening her legs around his waist. "So close."

"I've been dreaming about this. *Praying* for this," he sighed, slowing his thrusts, but not losing any depth or power. Every time his hips met hers, she swore she could feel his dick interfering with her breathing. She shrieked in time to those thrusts.

"Fuck, that's it, I can't—"

She shrieked in earnest when the entire world tilted. At first she thought he was dropping her, but then she realized he was laying them down on the floor, her head at the base of the padded wall. She groaned when her shoulders came into contact with the cold floor, but was soon shouting again when he began pumping his hips again.

"You can," Ari assured her, and she felt his fingers between their bodies, slip sliding around where he was pounding into her. Pinching and rubbing and caressing.

Her entire body started to shake.

"I will," she assured him, her voice a high pitched whine. She clawed at the padding above her head, trying to get away from the sensory over load. And from the wall across from them, the flashes started going off once again.

"Jesus, I'd forgotten how fucking beautiful you are like this," Ari breathed, and he moved away from her, standing up on his knees so he could look down at her body.

"Fuck, I'm coming, Ari. I'm going to come."

At that statement, he leaned down close, his lips once again at her ear.

"How beautiful you are *always*."

Valentine screamed when she came, her eyes squeezed shut so tightly, she couldn't even tell when the last two flashes went off. Hell, a bomb could've been dropped on top of them, and she probably wouldn't have noticed. She was just raw nerve endings and waves of incredible pleasure and feelings of satisfaction that she hadn't even re-alized she'd been missing.

This whole time, I didn't feel wanted. A different guy to dance with, talk with, flirt with, every single night, and none of them made me feel wanted. Fifteen minutes with his guy, and I've never felt so wanted in my life.

Valentine sobbed as the orgasm crested and fell away, then dou-bled back into a tidal wave and crashed over her body once again. Ari's hands were on her hips, his grip bruising, holding her tightly as he physically pulled her into his thrusts. She covered her face with her hands, screaming into her palms while he came with such force, she could feel it inside her.

Ari let out a shout, hitching his hips in tight to hers, his cock puls-ing and throbbing. Then he was collapsing on top of her, his breath hot against her dewy wet chest. They both fought for air, trying to remember how to breathe. Or figure out if they were even able to anymore.

Valentine wasn't sure how long they laid like that; enough that she started to shiver as her skin cooled down. When Ari finally pulled away, she adjusted her dress, pulling it back to rights and covering her chest up.

By the time she stood up and was scooting the skirt of her dress back down her legs, Ari was standing with her, putting his belt back together. Sticking out the top of one of his pockets were three photo strips. Valentine reached for them, but he pushed her hand away.

"We'll look at them together," he informed her, then he scooped his heavy jacket off the floor. He placed it around her shoulders, ran his fingers through his hair one last time, then opened the door so she could walk through it.

The loud techno music and hyper crowd brought Valentine a little bit back to her senses. She'd just had sex. Nasty, hot, raunchy, quickie sex, with nothing more than a door separating her from the rest of the club.

An *unlocked* door.

I swore I'd never do something like that again, and here I am, doing the same fucking thing, with the same fucking guy.

As if he could tell the direction her thoughts were headed in, Ari grabbed her arm and practically yanked her across the floor. They hurried through the Music Room, both Bailey and Evans giving them an interesting look as they passed. When they finally got to the stairs, though, Ari slowed to a stop. Flourescent lights rimmed the walls there, and he stood close to one, leaning in to use the light to look at the pictures. Valentine squeezed in close, biting her lip and wondering just how embarrassed she was about to be. As he held each strip up, though, Valentine was surprised. She didn't feel embarrassed at all.

The camera was up high enough that all the pictures were from about butt height and up. Ari's back had been to the camera the whole time, his loose jeans and t-shirt covering him up. Valentine's legs were visible around his waist, as were her head and shoulders and arms, but his torso always covered her own, so there was no nudity.

There was just Valentine, her head tilted to the side, smiling while biting her bottom lip, an arm stretched above her head. There was just

Ari, his head almost reverentially bowed to her chest while her fingers were speared into his hair.

It didn't look nasty, or hot, or raunchy.

It looked … like he was worshipping her. Like she'd been gone for far too long, and he was welcoming her home in the only way he knew how.

"I'm keeping these."

His low voice broke the spell the pictures had been weaving, and she glanced up at him. He was still staring at the photos, almost glaring, his gaze intense. Before she could argue or comment or say anything, he was pulling her around to face him. She thought he was going to kiss her again, but he didn't actually touch her. He pulled his wallet out from the inside pocket of his jacket and opened it, then delicately dropped the strips alongside the cash in the long pocket. She was glad he used a flat wallet instead of a bill fold, so the pictures wouldn't get damaged.

"I want copies," she informed him, and his eyes finally met hers.

"I'm surprised. The Saint Valentine I remember could be shockingly modest," he teased, pulling his jacket tight around her.

The familiarity was a little too much, too soon. Valentine wasn't sure what had just happened, but she knew it wasn't what he was thinking. They were not back together. She couldn't allow that, not now, and probably not ever.

If he could hurt you once, he could hurt you again.

"That saint has left the building," she forced out a laugh as she shrugged out of his jacket. "And *this* saint needs to get back to work."

"Are you serious right now?" Ari asked, taking his coat when she handed it to him. She nodded and smoothed her hands over her dress, trying to get rid of any wrinkles or creases.

"Don't worry, we'll call that one a freebie," she tried to joke.

He didn't laugh.

"No shit—I don't have to pay for your time anymore," he informed her, as if it were a given.

"No," she agreed. "You don't. Because I'm not for sale to you. When should I be at work tomorrow?"

Ari looked *mad*. It sent a shiver down her spine and she wished she hadn't given back his jacket.

"You know, fraternization between staff members is strictly prohibited at Sharapov, Heimer, and Schimmer law firm," he informed her. Valentine barked out a laugh.

"Oh yeah? Then someone should tell my asshole boss to stop sexually harassing me."

"Maybe he'd stop if he weren't so sure you liked it."

She stopped laughing. Cleared her throat once. Licked her lips. Then cleared it again.

"Goodbye, Ari," she spoke softly. He glared at her for a second longer, then that infuriating smirk spread across his lips.

"See you tomorrow after your classes, Valentine."

And then he was gone, taking the stairs two at a time.

What the fuck have I gotten myself into now?

By the time Valentine made her way back to the Music Room, she felt slightly more in control of herself. She'd stopped in a bathroom and fixed her hair, touched up her makeup. Put her armor back on. When she slid into their booth, though, she realized she could've come back looking like she'd just gotten done with a gang bang, and no one would've noticed.

Bailey and Evans were deep in conversation as if they'd been best friends for years. Several napkins were spread across the table, incomprehensible notes scribbled across them, and then Valentine noticed something else. A phone was propped up against the candle in the center of the table. They were facetiming somebody.

"Oh hey, Val! You're back!" Evans exclaimed, just noticing her for the first time when she reached for the vodka bottle.

"Yup, Saint Valentine is back," she replied, all while pouring herself a healthy slug of the liquor.

"Was that Ari you were with?" Bailey finally noticed her, too.

"Yup. Who are we talking to?" she asked, then she tossed the shot back and immediately poured herself another.

"His younger brother, Devlin," Bailey sounded excited as she grabbed the phone and turned it around. A younger, scruffier version of Evans waved at her and said hi, then Bailey put the phone back. "He works for Muse Games in New York!"

"Wow, that's ... super cool."

Valentine had no idea was "Muse Games" was, but she toasted her shot to them before drinking it down, as well. She quickly when about pouring a third.

"You okay?" Evans asked, his eyes bouncing between her and the vodka bottle.

"Better than ever. Your brother's name is Devlin Daniels? Evans and Devlin Daniels? What is wrong with your parents?"

"They're sadistic bastards," Evan laughed, and she could hear Devlin laughing over the phone. "So I take it you and Ari have ... made some sort of peace?"

"You could say that," Val replied before taking her third shot, gasping as the vodka burned a fiery path down her throat. "So let's have one last drink to me, Saint Valentine."

She poured everyone a shot, even Bailey, and they eventually all held up their glasses.

"Saint Valentine—patron saint of beekeeping," Evans chuckled.

"Patron saint of love?" Bailey guessed, glancing between them. Valentine thought for a moment, then nodded her head.

"Patron saint of whatever the fuck I want," she added, then quickly took the shot before anyone else could add some pearls of wisdom.

8

Ari really didn't know women as well as he liked to think he did—he hadn't had many girlfriends, and the few he'd had, he hadn't paid much attention to them. They'd just been … *there*. A decoration, something for effect. Harper Kittering had been pretty to look at, impressive on paper, great pedigree. A fucking show dog.

Valentine had been a thoroughbred race horse, a completely different animal, and one he didn't have any experience with—he'd thought he could just whip her into shape and then just rein her in. Stupid man. Instead, *she'd* tamed *him*, then bolted, and it was like he was the different animal, now. One that found itself begging for attention and acting irrationally.

The sex the night before had been incredible. Mind blowing. Three weeks really wasn't all that long to go without sex, but still. It was like they'd been starving, and in that photo booth room, they'd been presented with an all-you-can-eat buffet. His only was regret was not getting seconds when he'd had the chance. He pulled the photos out of his wallet and looked over them again, something he'd found himself doing several times through the day, then he looked at the clock.

He still remembered Valentine's schedule well from when they'd been spending almost every day together, and he knew her last class on Friday got out around two—it was already half past that time. He narrowed his eyes. She was supposed to come to work right after class.

If she was riding her bike, she should've been there ten minutes ago. If she was taking the bus, she should've been there even earlier.

She better not bail on me now.

This was all proving even harder than he'd thought. PayING that obscene amount of money to get her attention had been staggering, at first, but then he'd realized it was a good idea. Maybe taking her out of the club and bringing her into his world would show her how serious he was about wanting to be with her. Maybe forcing her and his father into somewhat close quarters would force Ari to stand up to his own personal monsters.

He twisted around to stare out his office window. It was funny, Valentine had once called him a "Daddy's Boy", and he'd brushed it off. He'd always been very aware of the hits he had to take in order to get to where he wanted in life. So sure, he'd figured he could be a daddy's boy for a while, if it meant he'd eventually get his name on the side of a building.

It was no different from what a lot of people did in their life. George W. Bush had been the president of the United States for eight years—and he'd gotten there based on the strength of his father's accomplishments. An American dynasty, and Ari had always thought of himself as being part of that kind of dynasty, which meant he occasionally had to kiss the ring.

But Valentine had changed his perspective about a lot of things. It wasn't a dynasty—it was a business, that's all. A business he did want, something he'd been working his whole life towards. His father had met presidents, regularly dined with the mayor of their city and the governor of their state. Ari wanted those things for himself, and he didn't think there was anything wrong with that; walking a path in his father's shadow was just the simplest way to get those things.

Walking in his father's shadow, though, was coming with a higher price than he actually wanted to pay, he was beginning to realize. Valentine had forgiven him for the harsh words he'd spoken, and sure, they'd slept together. But she was still closed off from him. She didn't trust him. And for the first time, Ari was having to deal with the fact that she may never. She hadn't jumped as his offer for a free apartment, and she hadn't rolled over and confessed her love for him after they'd literally made love.

She didn't need him, and quite possibly didn't want him, and all because he was so attached to a future that he wasn't even sure he really wanted. As long as he was stuck in this job, living under his father's rule, she would probably never trust him.

My name on the side of a building, or a saint in my bed ... too many choices.

He flicked his gaze back to the wall clock and immediately glared. Ten more minutes had gone by while he'd been lost in thought. She was now almost half an hour late. Valentine was stubborn, but she wasn't rude, and she was usually pretty punctual. He picked up his phone and shot her a text, then thought better of it and actually called her. After several rings, he heard her voicemail pick up.

"I'm shocked—is Saint Valentine too embarrassed to come into work? I've seen you in much more compromising positions than the ones we were in last night," he said. "We have a deal—you owe me four hours today. I'll come find you if I have to."

He hung up and tapped the edge of his cell phone against his chin. She wouldn't like that message. He smiled as he imagined her bristling with indignation. If she was avoiding him, he'd pretty much guaranteed that she wouldn't come within a ten mile radius of his building. She'd probably lock herself inside her house and curse his name.

Perfect, then I know exactly where she is.

Ari laughed to himself and collected his jacket and car keys, then headed out the door, locking it behind him. The receptionist Rose popped out of her cubicle.

"Mr. Sharapov," she spoke in a low voice. He raised his eyebrows. "Is something wrong?"

"Your father," she said, glancing around. "He's been asking some of the girls to monitor your phone calls. I thought you should know."

Ah. So his father had noticed that Ari had cleared out a lot of his schedule. The old man was still pushing for him and Harper to get back together. He must have figured Ari was either talking to her again, or to another woman. Either way, it was ridiculous. Ari was a grown man, his thirty-first birthday was only a couple months away. His father shouldn't be meddling in his love life, let alone listening in on his personal work calls.

"You're a peach, Rose," Ari sighed, then he shoved his keys into his pocket and strode the hall, calling out as he went, "if I ever escape this hell hole, I'm taking you with me."

"I certainly hope so, sir."

Valentine's class had actually been cancelled, so she'd spent the morning with her grandmother, then she'd gone to the bike messenger place and picked up a couple jobs. She was trying to burn off some restless energy. She rode hard all around the city for three hours, working up a healthy sweat but doing nothing to quiet the storm raging inside her.

What was I thinking!? How could I do that last night? And jesus, now I have to go see him today, work for him. I hated him a couple days ago—how could I sleep with him? One apology doesn't fix everything, doesn't even really change anything. He's still trying to buy me, he's still answering to Daddy, he's still got a psycho-ex. Stupid, Valentine, so fucking stupid.

And the worst part of it all was she knew—*she knew*—if given half the chance, she'd do it again. From the first moment she'd met Ari, there'd been something about him. His eyes watching her from behind that mask. A spark, a connection. They were linked, and it horrified her. She didn't want to be connected with him. He was all wrong for her. The *worst* for her. She couldn't live life in his world, and he would never condescend to live in hers. It could never work, so what was the point in trying?

As she thought that, she could practically hear his voice inside her mind.

"Coward."

Valentine gritted her teeth as she biked home around one in the afternoon. She was *not* a coward. Despite being slightly ashamed of her behavior the night before, she would go to work and she would act professional. She would use the job to build a wall between them, and after the three days were up, the wall would be finished.

Easy frickin' peezy. Sure.

As she came down her street, her eyes zeroed on her house. There was a bright yellow piece of paper attached to her door, and her heart instantly sank. It was a notice of some kind—she'd gotten enough over the past couple months to know what they looked like. But what could it be for? She racked her brain as she slowed down. She'd paid the water bill, and she'd worked out a payment plan with the utility offices. The rent had been paid in full on the first, that was the first bill she always paid. So what could it possibly be?

Valentine licked her lips nervously as she climbed off her bike and pushed it through the gate. She put down the kickstand and left it at the bottom of the stairs, then slowly marched up the porch steps, as if she could delay whatever the paper had to say.

Just get it over with.

Valentine snatched the notice off the door and skimmed over. Blinked her eyes in confusion, then read over it again. Her breath caught in her throat, and she wondered if Bailey had already seen this notice. She struggled to yank out her keys and quickly unlocked the front door.

"Bails!" she shouted up the stairs. "Bailey, have you seen this!?"

"Is that you, Val?" Bailey shouted back, and a moment later, she poked her head around the banister. A huge set of noise cancelling headphone were resting around her neck. She must've been gaming or working.

"Something happened," Valentine said, and she realized she was practically panting. Bailey stared at her for a second, then finally made her way down the stairs. Both girls moved into the kitchen and sat at the chipped formica table.

"What? What's going on?"

Valentine stared down at the sheet of paper, gripping it so hard that she was starting to crinkle the edges.

"We're being asked to vacate the premises."

Bailey gasped.

"We're being *evicted!?*"

"No, no," Valentine said, shaking her head. Then she let out a dark chuckle. "It's worse than that—we could fight an eviction. The realty company who owns this house, this block, I guess they're working on massive gentrification. They're going to gut it, or tear it down, or something. Either way, we have thirty days to vacate."

There was a long pause, a sense of defeat hanging heavy in the room.

"What are we going to do?" Bailey finally asked in a small voice. "I can't ... I don't want to go home, Valentine."

"I don't want that, either," Val breathed. "Where am I going to go? And IDHS is dropping their case—where am I going to bring Gam-Gam? My credit score is shit, where am I going to find a place big enough for all of us so quickly?"

"We'll think of something," Bailey rallied. "You have tons of friends, and you've got Ari back. He'll think of something."

Valentine laughed.

"I don't have him back, Bailey."

"Really? Didn't look like that last night."

A little surprised at that comment, Valentine cut her eyes to her roommate.

"Excuse me?"

"Can I be honest with you?" Bailey asked. She looked nervous, the long sleeves of her sweater wrapped around her fists. Valentine sighed, then gestured for her to continue.

"Sure, why not. Today's already shitty," she laughed.

"When you told me why you and Ari broke up, or whatever you want to call it, I was kinda surprised," Bailey confessed. Valentine had told her the whole story a couple weeks ago, finally confessing to the real nature of her job and everything that had happened between them.

"Surprised? What do you mean, how?"

"I mean, yeah, what he said was totally shitty," Bailey said, not making eye contact as she continued with her confession. "Talk to his dad about you like that, I mean, what a dick. And also yeah, him being so up his dad's butt, that's shitty, too."

"All things I already know, Bails."

"But I mean ... those are just shitty things. And hardly things at all," Bailey said, holding up her arms in a shrug. "He liked you. A lot. He did things for you—he's still doing things for you. And you liked him, too. A lot. So I was surprised that you just let the whole thing end over ... over some words. Some words you just over heard."

"Are you serious?" Valentine was shocked. "He called me the worst possible name he could, and he said it to his *father*. How are we supposed to have a relationship if he's too ashamed of me to tell his own dad about me?"

"How are you supposed to have a relationship if the first moment he messes up, you run away and refuse to talk to him?"

Valentine felt like she'd been slapped. For the past three weeks, she'd been so sure of righteous indignation. Ari deserved all of her anger and vengeance, surely.

Didn't he?

Is that what I did? Run away at the first sign of trouble? Ari had known he was going to fuck up at some time, and what did I do the minute it happened?

"I ... I ..." Valentine babbled articulately. "Gam-Gam was in the hospital! I just needed ... help! I just wanted his help, and he threw me out!"

"Yeah, but he didn't know about Gam-Gam, you said," Bailey pointed out. "Again—I'm not denying that it was shitty, and he deserved to have his balls kicked up into his throat. But I don't know ... if I liked someone as much you said you liked him, I think I'd at least give them a chance to explain themselves."

No, no, no, no—Valentine was the patron saint of thinking of others. Her entire life revolved around taking care of her grandmother, and from the first moment she'd read that notice to vacate, she primarily been thinking of how to keep her, Gam-Gam, and Bailey together—and Bailey wasn't even related to her. There was no way she'd been selfish about this Ari situation, no way at all.

We said we wanted to be together, that we wanted to try to figure shit out. If I had screwed up, and Ari had stopped talking to me, how would I have felt?

"I have to go to work," Valentine breathed, staring off into the distance over Bailey's shoulder. "Don't ... don't worry about this for now, okay? I'll ... we'll figure something out."

"I'm sorry, Val, I shouldn't have said anything. He deserved everything he got from you, and possibly worse!" Bailey called as Val stood up and started walking away.

"It's okay, Bailey. It's okay. I have to go to work."

Valentine was in such a daze, she sat down on her bed and didn't move for almost forty-five minutes. Just stared at the wall and thought about everything Bailey had just unloaded on her. Ari had definitely deserved her wrath, but had he deserved to be frozen out? Abandoned?

I was falling for him. Had fallen for him. Is that how you treat a person you think you're in love with? I don't know, I've never been in love. We're both two idiots stumbling around blindly in this piss poor excuse for a relationship. One thing is for sure—he's trying to make up for it. He tried to get in touch with me for three weeks, he paid that ridiculous amount at the auction, hell, he even offered me a free place to live, what else could—

Valentine gasped and dropped the vacate notice.

He offered me a free place to live.

What were the chances!? Ari offers her a place to live, and twenty-four hours later, she gets some random ass vacate notice. She hadn't heard *anything* about the area's gentrification plans—isn't that something a management company would talk to their renters about? Notify them of?

Ari had enough pull to get dirt on Del. Enough clout to get the details on Gam-Gam's IDHS case. Enough resources to drop twenty-five thousand dollars without batting an eyelash. So surely, bribing her rental company to evict her wouldn't be out of the scope of his abilities.

"That mother fucker," Valentine growled, leaping to her feet.

She didn't bother with taking a shower or changing her clothing—she wouldn't be working today. She scooped the notice up off the floor, then strode out of her bedroom and stomped down the stairs. Bailey was back in the kitchen, brewing up a pot of coffee.

"Hey," she said. "I really am sorry. Your relationship with—"

"I don't have a relationship," Valentine snarled, then she yanked open the front door and practically ran out it, slamming it shut behind her.

Even pedaling hard, Ari's office building was a far ride for her. Valentine was even more sweaty when she finally dropped her bike right in front of the building's doors. She glared at everyone she came across, and when she got to his office's floor, she made a beeline for his door.

"He's not here!"

Just as she was about to grab his door knob, a voice stopped her. Valentine glanced around, then found the secretary who'd shown her around—Rose? Her shiny redhead was barely visible over her cubicle wall.

"Where is he?" Valentine demanded.

"I don't know, he left maybe ... ten minutes ago?" Rose said, looking at a wall clock. Valentine followed her gaze. She was forty minutes late for work, he'd probably gone out looking for her.

She nodded at the secretary, then hurried out the building. When she climbed back onto her bike and rode away, she finally took out her phone. Yup, sure enough, there were several missed calls from him. She didn't bother listening to his voicemails, just immediately called him back. He answered on the second ring.

"Where are you?" he said immediately.

"Where the fuck are you?" she countered.

"Feisty today."

"Shut up. Where are you?"

"I was at work," he replied. "But my assistant was too embarrassed to come to work, so I'm on my way to her house to pick her up."

"Your 'assistant' isn't embarrassed about anything," Valentine snarled. "And I just left your work."

There was a long pause.

"You're mad, aren't you?" he finally sighed.

"Goddamn right I am."

"Well, I don't really feel like driving to the sound of your shouting. Are you still near my office?"

"Yes."

"Meet me at my apartment."

"I'm not going anywhere near—"

"Meet me at my place, or you'll have to wait to yell at me about whatever it is you think I've done now."

Valentine let out a strangled shriek and hung up the call. She was tempted to throw her phone, but she couldn't afford a new one, so she squeezed her hand tightly around it before shoving it back into her pocket.

Ari must not have been very close to her house when she'd called him. She'd just barely finished up locking her bike when his fancy new car coasted into the garage. She glared at it, then went about finger combing the tangles from her hair. She hoped she looked slightly less insane when he finally emerged on the sidewalk.

"Has anyone ever told you that you're really sexy when you're mad?" he asked.

She punched him in the arm.

"I'm not flirting with you!" she snapped, following him inside after he got the security door open. "I came here for answers."

"I'm sure I have some for you. What's the problem now?" he asked as they got into his elevator.

Valentine pulled the crumpled up vacate notice out of her pocket and shoved it against his chest. Ari barely caught it before it fell, then unfurled it and read it over. Seemed to pause for a moment, then read it again.

"This doesn't look too good for you," he spoke in a low voice. She opened her mouth to snap again, but the doors behind her dinged open. Ari pushed past her and moved to the center of the hall, unlocking his front door when he got to it. Now it was Valentine's turn to push past him, storming into his apartment like she had a right to.

Her bravado almost left her when she glanced around the space. He hadn't changed a thing. Of course, why would he, it had only been three weeks, but still. It was like a punch to her gut, seeing the apartment she'd grown to love so much.

Then she was shaking her head, clearing her thoughts before tossing her bike helmet and jacket onto his couch.

"It's not good for me," she finally replied, turning to face him. "Or Bailey, or Gam-Gam. Did you do this?"

Ari's expressions shifted from guarded to confused and surprised.

"Do what?" he asked, holding up the paper. "I think if I managed your rental house, you would've noticed, Valentine."

"No, but Aaron Sharapov, esquire, has an awful lot of connections," she pointed out. His eyes narrowed.

"Don't call me that," he said quickly. "And while yes, I do have a lot of connections, how would it benefit me to get you evicted from your house? I'm trying to make your life easier, Valentine."

"Don't you think it's awfully coincidental that yesterday you were practically begging me to move into your apartment downstairs, and then today I get a notice to vacate my home?" she pointed out. He nodded his head.

"Yes, yes I do. Good thing I got that place—good rentals are a bitch to find, anymore."

"Get fucked, Sharapov," she snapped. "I'm not moving into your apartment, I don't care if you have me evicted."

"*I didn't do this*," he snapped back. "Your faith in me is astounding, *O'Dell*. All I've done for the past goddamn month is try to get back in your good graces—why would I lie about this now? You're pretty great at jumping to conclusions, you know. Pity they're always the wrong ones."

Valentine opened her mouth to make a retort, then froze. Jumping to conclusions. Just like she'd done last time. Her conversation with Bailey flitted across her mind, and it had a dampening effect. Valentine looked at Ari, *really* looked at him.

He was angry, that was for sure. He was breathing hard and glaring at her, still holding the notice aloft. And he looked offended, and possibly even a little hurt.

But he didn't look like he was lying.

"What are the chances of this happening?" Valentine asked, finally lowering her voice. "What are the chances of you coming back into my life at the same time as I get evicted?"

"Small," he agreed, taking cues from her changed demeanor and calming down, as well. "But stranger things have happened. The rental company who owns your house has probably been planning this for a while—a simple call to them would've absolved me, Val."

She refused to show her embarrassment on her face. Instead, she let out a groan and dropped her head, staring at the floor.

"Maybe, but there hasn't been a whisper about any rebuilding or gentrification in that area. This came out of nowhere. God, it's just one bad thing after another," she complained. "I finally wrap up all the bullshit with IDHS, and then this. When is going to end!?"

When he didn't respond, Valentine lifted her head. Ari wasn't looking at her, didn't even appear to be listening. He was reading over the fine print at the bottom of her notice. He squinted at the small lettering, then pulled out his phone and started typing something into it.

"Holy shit," he breathed as he worked.

"What? What's going on?" Valentine asked, moving around so she was standing next to him, trying to looking at his phone.

"Your rental company—Cook Property and Rental Management."

"Yeah, what about it?"

"It's owned by a much larger real estate corporation."

"Okay, so?"

"And so," he sighed, then tilted his phone screen so she could read it. "Look who's on the board of directors."

Valentine let out a shout and grabbed his phone.

Roy Stevens Kittering.

Kittering.

"Harper!" she spat out the name like it was a swear. "Could she really do something like this!? She couldn't. Could she!? *How?*"

"Her dad has already paid her way into several different schools—this really isn't a leap. When did IDHS get that phone call about your grandmother?" Ari asked, taking his phone back and turning to fully face her.

"I don't know, a couple days after you and I broke up, after Gam-Gam had her—*holy shit, you don't think Harper did that, too!?*"

Ari's eyes drifted shut, and he let out a long, suffering sigh.

"I am so, so sorry, Valentine."

Valentine couldn't believe it. Sure, Harper didn't like her. She did everything she could at school to make her life miserable. But there was a big leap between tripping her in class to getting her evicted and trying to get her charged with elder neglect.

She did try to hit you with her car. The bitch is clearly unhinged.

"Oh my god," Val breathed. "Caché. She was there. Does she

know I work there!? She could get Del in trouble, get everyone in trouble!"

Ari opened his eyes again.

"She doesn't know," he shook his head. "She thought we were there together. I never told her what you did for a living, and neither did you. But you should probably warn him, just in case."

They both retreated to opposite ends of the living room, typing away at their phones. She gave Del the heads up, then sent Bailey a series of texts, filling her in on the situation. When she was finished, it was to find that Ari was already done with his message. He'd taken off his jacket and he was kneeling on the floor, turning on his gas fireplace. She frowned, then moved across the room to stand next to him.

"She's fucking crazy," she said, and he nodded as he stood up.

"She really fucking is," he agreed. "I should've done something about her a long time ago. But she ... her dad ..."

Valentine connected the dots.

"Is good friends with your dad," she guessed. He winced.

"I'm sorry."

"It's ..." Valentine almost said *it's not your fault*, but really, it was just a little bit. He should've gotten a restraining order, or confronted her father, long before any of this could happen.

"You can still have the apartment," he assured her. "For long term, or just until you can find something that can hold all three of you. Whatever you want. I won't bother you."

That last sentence almost broke Valentine's heart. For three weeks, she hadn't wanted Ari to ever bother her again. Now, just after a couple days, the idea of him not bothering her actually made her sad.

"I'm sorry, too," she surprised herself by blurting out.

"What? Why?"

"I should've talked to you," she said, shrugging her shoulders. "I acted ... immaturely. I was having the worst day, I heard something awful, and I just got angry and I ran. That probably hurt a lot. I should've at least let you explain yourself. I'm not used to that, having to answer to anyone or listen to anyone. I'm usually the one in charge, the one explaining things. Apparently I've been doing it for so long, I started thinking I didn't need to hear anyone else's side. And that's shitty. I'm sorry."

Ari looked absolutely stunned for a moment, then he shocked her by bursting out laughing.

"For weeks and weeks," he chortled. "I worked on all these apology speeches. Memorizing and tweaking and changing. Then I finally get you alone in my apartment, and you beat me to it. You are a constant surprise, Saint Valentine."

"I try."

"Does this mean I can kiss you now?"

"Sure."

He bent down and practically devoured her mouth. When he pulled away, she actually felt dizzy.

"Does this mean I can fuck you now?"

"Baby steps," she breathed, putting a hand on his chest. "Your ex-girlfriend is psycho and your dad is still … your dad. We're still a bad match, Ari. Good sex doesn't solve problems."

"No," he agreed, and he ignored her hand and stepped up close to her. "But it makes them a lot easier to bear."

He certainly has a point.

Last night had been a whirlwind. A fantasy—she was so good at those, after all. Now, it felt different. His lips were back against hers and his hands were under her shirt, smoothing up her back, and it felt … like home. Like reality. Like *them*.

Just when she was about to rethink her whole never-sleep-with-him-again policy, someone banged on the front door.

"I knew it," Ari breathed, his teeth clamped down on her bottom lip.

"What?" Val asked, deftly pulling his tie apart.

"We're going to settle this, once and for all."

He abruptly pulled away from her, so quickly she didn't even have time to let go of his tie, the material sliding loose from his collar as he moved. He strode across the apartment and opened the door, and Valentine felt bile rise in her throat when Harper Kittering stepped through the door.

Out of the frying pan, and into the dumpster fire. Story of my fucking life.

9

Harper was babbling about something, but Valentine couldn't hear what she was saying. There was a faint ringing in her ears. Probably caused by the bomb that had just gone off in her head.

What is she doing here? Did he plan it this way? Is this the part where they point and laugh at me, before dragging me out and stoning me in front of a crowd?

"What is she doing here?" Harper all but screeched when she finally turned and saw Valentine.

"She came looking for legal advice," Ari replied smoothly. Valentine and Harper shared a confused glance, then they both looked back at him.

"*Valentine* needed legal advice? You're in corporate law—she's a stupid ho," Harper pointed out.

"A 'stupid ho' who just received a notice to vacate her rental unit. Know anything about that, Harp?" Ari asked casually.

*Oh, I see now, he **did** have a plan, and I **am** stupid, because it wasn't a plan with her. It was a plan **with me**.*

"Why would I know anything about her getting evicted from whatever shithole she lives in?" Harper replied with a sniff, all while flinging a long strand of hair over her shoulder.

"Well, because you've spent the last month making her life a living hell," Ari told her. Harper went still as he spoke. "And while close calls with your car are cute, and all, filing a false report with IDHS I'm sure is a punishable offense. But convincing your father to have his company sell off a bunch of low-income housing? I'm almost impressed."

There was a lengthy pause. Valentine slowly moved forward so she could stand near Ari, present a more united front. If he was going to argue on her behalf, she could at least support him. Harper was batting her expensive false eyelashes rapidly, and it was so obvious she was trying to think up a lie, it was embarrassing to watch.

"You give me too much credit, Ari," Harper sighed in a bored voice.

"I didn't give you enough," he countered. "You're much more industrious than I ever imagined. What was the plan, Harper? Get her kicked out and make her move, I'd forget she exists? Scare her in a parking lot, she'd quit school? Take her grandma away, she'd crumble? None of those things happened."

"You don't understand," Harper whined, finally dropping her cool-as-ice act. "Some of my friends found out you dumped me for her, and I *cannot* have that! Daddy is also disappointed in both of us. You know if you don't take me back, you can kiss a career in Illinois politics goodbye."

"He doesn't want a career in 'Illinois politics'," Valentine blurted out, surprising everyone, including herself. But she licked her lips and pressed on. "You're fucking obsessed with him, bragging to everyone you're around that he's gonna marry you some day, and you don't know the simplest things about him. Why? Why do you wanna make something happen with a person you clearly don't even like?"

"I was with him forever before your skanky ass showed up, so I probably know him better than you," Harper challenged. Valentine actually laughed out loud, but Ari took back control of the conversation.

"Apologize to her, right now," he stated. Both women went quiet and stared at each other for a moment.

"You must be joking," Harper started.

"Apologize to her, or I put *Daddy* on speaker phone right now and we have this conversation with him."

It was a slightly surreal moment. Ari standing up for her, defending her to Harper, treating her like she was his proper girlfriend; even though she wasn't.

Yeah, and it's also surreal because these are two adults—he's thirty and she's twenty-six? Twenty-seven?—and they're using threats to tattletale to 'Daddy' against each other. They both need so much therapy.

"I think we both know you won't do that," Harper said, fiddling with the ends of her hair.

"I think I can also make a couple phone calls to the Tribune and tell them all about how the deputy mayor's daughter got into the University of Illinois and then got kicked out, and then miraculously got into a prestigious design school without any background in design whatsoever."

A pink stain started to spread across Harper's cheeks.

"You wouldn't," she breathed, and Ari nodded.

"I'm not like you, Harper, I don't want to ruin someone's life just because I'm mad at them—but I'll do it if you don't leave Valentine alone. *This* isn't going anywhere," Ari said, gesturing between him and Valentine briefly before moving to gesture between himself and Harper. "And *this* is never happening again. Accept it, and move on."

Ooohhh, Harper looked mad. Valentine wondered if she'd ever been truly threatened before? She looked so angry, like she was thinking of hitting Ari, so when she snapped out her arm, Valentine wasn't too surprised.

What did surprise her, though, was when Harper slapped *her*, and not Ari.

There was a collective gasp between Ari and Valentine, both stunned by the blonde's action. Harper glared down the length of her nose at Valentine.

"Doesn't matter anymore. Without that project grade, you're done at that school, anyway."

Valentine was not a violent person, typically. She'd been in many a situation at Caché that would've made a less zen person flip out, but she'd always kept her cool. Always kept her hands to herself. She wasn't a fighter. She was Saint Valentine. She was a lover.

Not today.

With a shriek, Valentine swung wildly and punched Harper, her fist glancing off the other girl's nose. Harper let out a startled scream, and then it was fists and hands windmilling, and so much blonde hair everywhere, Valentine felt like she was in a blizzard.

So she grabbed onto two handfuls of the platinum tresses, and she yanked as hard as she could. Harper bent sideways, shouting again, and Val was suddenly thankful that she'd yanked her hair into a ponytail before coming into Ari's apartment. She used her advantage and jerked on Harper's hair again, spinning the girl in a circle before slamming her to the ground.

As fights went, it wasn't much of one—obviously neither Valentine nor Harper had much experience with brawling. Sharp nails scratched down Valentine's neck, so she balled up her own hand into a fist again and rained blows down on Harper's chest, both of them shouting and screaming the whole time.

And then it was over, almost as quickly as it had begun. Arms were wrapped around Valentine's waist and she was plucked off of Harper before being practically tossed onto the couch. She bounced roughly on the cushions, sitting upright just in time to watch Ari yank Harper to her feet. The blonde was crying almost hysterically, her nose *and* upper lip bleeding, and Valentine felt a swell of pride.

"Are you fucking kidding me!?" Ari shouted, his grip on the other girl's arm so hard, she was wincing. "You *hit* her? What the fuck is wrong with you, Harper?"

He was marching her across the apartment while he spoke, and then he shoved her into the hallway.

"*She's* awful! *She's* trash! How could you choose her over me?" Harper was sobbing.

"That's what you're not getting!" Ari yelled, leaning down to point his finger in her face. "It was never about that—never you versus her! I didn't 'choose her' over you, she didn't even exist when I decided to break up with you. I just didn't choose you, *period*. I never would have; was never going to. *Do not* attempt to contact either of us ever again."

Before Harper could respond, he had stepped back through the doorway and slammed the door shut in her face.

"Holy shit," Valentine said when they were alone. Ari stared at the door for a moment longer, breathing hard, then he turned to her.

"Holy shit," he panted, nodding his head in agreement. "Are you okay?"

"I'm fine," Valentine nodded towards the door. "But did you see her?"

"I did."

"I kicked her ass! I've never done anything like that before! I mean, I *really* kicked her ass!"

Ari started laughing, which set Valentine off, and pretty soon they were in hysterics. Crashing down off the adrenaline. When it finally settled into just chuckling here and there, he joined her on the couch and gently put his hands on either side of her head, forcing her to look up.

"She got in a few good licks," he murmured, and she felt his thumb tracing over the scratches in her skin. She winced at the sharp pain.

"Not as good as mine. Is it bad?"

"You'll heal, Slugger."

"Did her father really buy her way into her schools?"

"Did you think Harper was really getting those good grades on her own?" he asked, letting her go. Valentine frowned.

"I never thought about it. She's fashionable, she's in school for fashion, I didn't question it. Explains why she was so shitty at our project," Valentine said. She paused for a long moment before continuing on. "Is that like … a standard rich person thing?"

"What, paying off college administrators and teachers?" he asked.

"Yeah. Did your dad do that?"

"I graduated from Northwestern—on a full scholarship, and then I went to Yale Law, where I graduated in the top percentile of my class. *No*, my father did not pay to get me into school," Ari said in a serious voice. Valentine held up her hands.

"Hey, just checking."

"How'd *you* get into one of the most elite design schools?" Ari countered, his pride obviously wounded.

"Oh, the old fashioned way—slept with the admissions officer."

That startled another laugh out of Ari. He stared at her while he smiled, and it occurred to Valentine that as much as she loved his signature smirk, he really looked best in a genuine grin. He already didn't look his age, with his youthful good looks, but his smiles knocked another ten years off his face.

"You look good when you smile, Ari," she commented. He nodded his head.

"So do you, Val."

There was another pause, and then they were crashing into each. As clothing was torn apart and hit the floor, Valentine knew it was a bad idea. Knew she should be walking away, not digging herself deeper into this hole with him.

But his hands knew her body so well, and his voice was like her favorite song ever, so when he pulled her on top of him on the couch, and when he bent her over the coffee table, and when he laid her down in front of the fire, she couldn't say no.

She didn't even know the word anymore.

10

A ri Sharapov was the kind of person who liked to know where
things stood.

But with Valentine, it was kind of like he was balancing on
a pedestal—one on wheels—a mile in the air, and the whole thing was
wobbling.

Who knew where he was.

The sex had been explosive, once again. It was like they were picking up right where they'd left off, and also making up for lost time. It
was incredible, amazing.

But was it smart?

He worried it was too much, too fast. Valentine had always been
an emotional, passionate person. Her feelings were wrapped up in
everything she did, yet here she was, jumping into sex with him so
quickly.

Don't get him wrong, he loved it. The more naked time the better.
But the logical part of his brain warned him that if he didn't pump the
brakes for them, it was going to become too much for her. She would
convince herself that the only thing they had in common was sex, and
that just wasn't true.

They were both strong willed, and independent. They were both
blunt. They both liked to have a good time. They liked to butt heads
and argue and laugh. He liked to be in control, she liked to let go of

control. She was completely wrong—they weren't a bad match. They were the *perfect* match. He just had to make her see it.

*Now that IDHS is taken care of, and hopefully Harper's off her back, we can focus on each other. Really **actually** pick up where we left off and work on **us**.*

"You're here."

Ari swiveled around in his office chair to find his father standing in his doorway.

"Had a few things to catch up on," he replied, sitting up straight.

"Ah, but too busy to catch up with your old man?"

Normally, Ari didn't work on the weekends, but he was still trying to stay ahead of everything so he could have a looser schedule during the weekdays. So he could have more time to deal with Valentine. Which of course meant he hadn't had much time for his father.

Of course, ever since he found out his father had kept keys to his apartment, their relationship had been somewhat strained. The family Sunday dinners had stopped, Ari hadn't been to the house, and even missed his father's birthday—mostly because Harper's father had thrown the party for it, but also because he just couldn't maintain the same relationship with his dad. It wasn't working anymore.

For the first time ever, he wondered if it ever really had.

"I've got a couple minutes before a phone call," Ari sighed, glancing at his watch. "What did you need?"

"Do I have to need something to want to spend time with my son?" Don Sharapov asked as he strolled into the office.

Yes. That's how you've always been. I'm only your son when you can get something out of me. A grunt to do your work, a protege to brag about, a scapegoat to blame. It never bothered me before, but now, even a name on a building doesn't seem worth dealing with you.

"No," Ari said. "But I know you're not big on social calls at work."

"Always observant," his father chuckled. "I heard Harper came home pretty upset last night."

"Did you?" Ari rubbed his hands down his face. "Did you also hear that she had a fat lip?"

"There was a mention of some bruising. She wouldn't tell her father anything, but sounds like you know the story."

"I do."

There was a long pause.

"Care to share?"

This was the moment. The moment to stand his ground. To either stake a claim in this law firm, or stake a claim on Valentine. She might not have been there right that moment, but he could still fight for her.

"No, I don't. But I'll tell you this—I will *never* get back together with Harper," Ari said, leaning forward to rest his arms on his desk and stare his father right in the eye. "I only ever dated her to make you happy, but it just made me miserable. She's been unbearable ever since. She calls my cell phone twenty times a day, sends me even more text messages, shows up randomly at my apartment."

His father scowled.

"Surely it can't be as bad as all—"

Ari took out his phone and scrolled back to his missed call log from Thursday, then turned it around to show him.

"All of those are her."

His father leaned close to the phone, his scowl deepening.

"Kittering should've taught her better," he grumbled. "But son, maybe if you gave her a second chance, you could teach her—"

"I'm with someone else," Ari blurted out.

Well, it's done now. No going back.

"Excuse me?"

"I'm in a relationship with someone else," Ari clarified. "And pretty much have been since things ended with Harper. Someone I … who means a lot to me."

His father's eyebrows shot up.

"Someone you're serious about?"

"*Very* serious about."

He was ready to go to battle. To wage war with his father. Even if Valentine did decide she didn't want anything to do with Ari, he still wouldn't go back to Harper. And he still shouldn't have to hide a relationship from his own father.

It's a tiny dragon, but I'm slaying it for you, Saint Valentine.

"Well, I suppose as long as you're happy, I'm happy."

Ari almost fell out of his chair, he was so stunned.

"Is that a joke?" he asked. "You've been haranguing me for weeks—*months*—about getting back together with Harper!"

"Because I thought she was a good fit for you," his father shrugged. "And yes, I wanted the connection with the Kitterings. But if you've got a new girlfriend, there's not a whole lot I can do about it."

"I … am shocked," Ari was honest.

"I'm not a complete ogre, Ari. Besides, Harper sounds like a train-wreck waiting to happen, and we wouldn't want to be in any sort of scandal."

"You have no idea how right you are."

"So tell me about this new girl," his father said. "Who are her folks? And if it's so serious, why haven't you introduced us yet?"

"She's from New York," Ari spoke slowly. He wanted to slay all the dragons in the world for Valentine, but he could only do so many at a time. It would be best to approach this particular beast *after* he'd had a chance to speak with her. "Her parents died several years ago. She goes to design school here."

"Harper's school, I assume," his dad sighed, and Ari nodded. "That would explain why she's been so testy. You couldn't have looked elsewhere, had to kick up a fuss."

"In my defense, I didn't plan on being in another relationship, and I didn't have any idea Harper was going to become deranged," Ari said.

"Fair point. I want to meet this girl, Ari. Make sure she's up to snuff—not just anyone can be a Sharapov, you know," his father stated.

Ari wasn't even sure how to respond at first, and then was saved from having to—his cell phone started ringing. He dug it out from his back pocket, and was surprised to see Valentine's contact info on the screen. She rarely called him.

"This is important," Ari said, waggling the phone. "We can continue this conversation another time."

"Alright," his dad said, and he exited the office. Before he turned the corner, though, he looked back at his son. "But we *will* continue it, and I *will* meet her."

Ari nodded and stood up, hurrying around his desk and moving to the door.

"We will, and you will. Very soon."

"I hope so."

And with that, Ari shut the door, then locked it for good measure.

Talk about timing, Valentine. I hope you're in a good mood, because we need to have a long, long conversation.

"Do you know my daughter, Patricia?"

Valentine smiled and settled back into the chair next to her grandmother's hospital bed.

"I do, as a matter of fact," she replied. "She was an awesome person."

Her grandmother beamed.

"She was lovely. She had two lovely daughters, too."

"She did," Valentine nodded. "But maybe one was a bit lovelier than the other."

She laughed, and her grandmother even chuckled a little.

"I always did enjoy Valentine so."

Late Friday night, Valentine had been woken up by her phone

buzzing. She'd been disoriented at first, not remembering that she was in Ari's bed, and that they'd crashed there right after their sexfest in the living room. She'd had to crawl around naked in order to find the phone under the couch, and then her heart had gone still when she'd seen that it had been her grandmother's care facility calling.

Her grandmother had been battling a respiratory infection ever since her second stroke. It seemed to come and go in flares. The facility had told Valentine that her grandmother was fine, but because of her high fever and other medical conditions, they had decided it was best to send Mrs. Parker to the hospital. It was standard procedure for them to alert Valentine, and they assured her she had nothing to worry about.

Still.

When Ari had hopped in the shower around six o'clock, Valentine had crept out of his apartment and biked back to her own home. She wasn't sneaking away, really. Just getting some space. Things had been … intense, the day before.

Oh, hell, they'd been intense ever since he'd shown up at that stupid auction.

She didn't know what she wanted anymore. Her brain and her heart were at war. Logically, she knew that she and Ari were a bad idea, for almost too many reasons to name. But emotionally, it was like she became twitterpated any time she was near him. He took over her senses and her rationality and whoopsie, next thing she knew, she was almost always naked and begging him to do things to her.

That was not the right state of mind to be in when making big decisions, and anything involving her and Ari would be big. Huge. They'd barely been anything at all before, and their break up had shattered her. This time around? It would be so much worse. She was barely even put back together; she would just turn to dust this time around.

She took a shower while at home, and checked in with Bailey. The younger girl had been up all night, playing some sort of online game with Evans' younger brother. Love was most certainly in the air, and

Valentine wondered how long it would be before Bailey transferred to a school in New York, and Val lost her roommate.

Calm down, this isn't a romance movie. They're just talking over a video game.

At eight o'clock, when visiting hours started at her grandmother's hospital, Valentine hopped back on her bike and rode straight over. She spent the next hour chatting with her grandmother, reminding her of old stories and relatives. Her memory still wasn't good, but overall mentally, she seemed a little better that day.

"Valentine is very enjoyable," Val agreed. "Can I ask you a question, Gam-Gam?"

"Of course," her grandmother said, stifling a yawn.

"Did you have any boyfriends before your husband?" Valentine asked. Her grandmother chuckled.

"Oh my, yes. I was very popular. Very pretty."

"I know, I've seen pictures," Valentine laughed. "Did you ever … I like this guy, Gam-Gam. Or at least I think I like him. A lot. Maybe. But he's different from me. Very, very different. He wants to be together, but I … I think it's maybe a bad idea. What do you think?"

Her grandmother seemed to think on it for a long time.

"Well … have you two been *intimate* together?"

"Grandma!"

Valentine was shocked and felt a blush immediately creep across her face.

"I think if he likes you, and you like him, and you enjoy being intimate, then there's no harm in trying. What have you got to lose?"

Everything. My heart. My soul. My self-respect. He offered me help, and money, and a place to live—but all I ever wanted was him. He still doesn't get that, which means he still doesn't get me.

"That's excellent advice, Gam-Gam," Valentine breathed. Her grandmother nodded.

"I'm very good with advice," she agreed, and then yawned again. Valentine smiled and slowly got out of her chair.

"You seem tired. I'll go so you can take a nap," she offered. She leaned over the bed to kiss her grandmother on the cheek, but the old woman didn't move. Just stared up at her for a long time.

"Why, Valentine," she gasped softly. "It's so nice to see you, I love it when you visit me."

Val was once again shocked. It had been so long since Gam-Gam had recognized her, she'd begun to think it would never happen again. She smiled down at the other woman, tears filling her eyes.

"I love visiting you, too," she whispered, then had to clear her throat. "I'll visit you every day, Grandma."

"Oh, I would like that. Do tell your boyfriend I said hello, he's such a nice man."

Gam-Gam had only ever met Ari once, but he seemed to have left an impression on her. Valentine nodded, and one tear slipped free, falling onto the thin hospital blanket. She quickly wiped at her face.

"Of course. Have a nice nap, Gam-Gam," she whispered, finally kissing her cheek before standing upright.

"I will, dear."

"I love you very much, thank you for letting me come to Chicago," Valentine added. Her grandmother beamed for a moment.

"I love you, too, dear, and I'm so glad you came. You can stay as long as you like. Stay forever."

"I will," Valentine agreed.

She patted her grandma on the hand, then slowly backed out of the room. By the time she was at the door, her grandmother was already out, wheezing lightly in her sleep.

Valentine left the room feeling great. She slowly made her way across the wing and towards the exit, taking a detour through the cafeteria to check the specials, checking her messages as she went. She'd been neglecting all of her regular clients at Caché for the last week, all of her time and energy focused on Ari and her multitude of problems.

As she finally emerged outside, she skimmed through all the

texts. Offers for dinners and trips and gifts. Money. Such easy money. But she didn't respond to any of them. Didn't want to. No, the only person she wanted to talk to was—

Her phone rang in her hand, startling her. She was even more surprised by the phone number scrolling across the screen. She glanced up at the building behind her, then answered the call.

"This is Valentine O'Dell," she said automatically.

"Ms. O'Dell, this Dr. Yamamoto at Mercy Medical University Hospital," a doctor spoke in a clipped voice. Valentine looked up again at the big sign above her head, the one that said MMU Hospital.

"Hi, yes, I'm here at MMU right now," Valentine said.

"Yes, we were hoping so, the nurse told us that you'd just left. You need to come back in, I'm afraid we have some news about your grandmother."

Valentine stiffened.

"What about her? I was just with her, maybe ten minutes ago."

"Please come back inside, Ms. O'Dell, and we can discuss everything."

A slow, meandering walk through the different areas of the hospital had taken her ten minutes—jogging through the direct route took her less than five. She was slightly out of breath when she came down the hall towards her grandmother's room. A CNA she'd met earlier was outside the door, talking to a doctor in a lab coat. There seemed to be some sort of commotion going on in the room, but she wasn't close enough to see anything, and before she could get close enough, the CNA noticed her.

"Ms. O'Dell," the woman called sharply, and both she and the doctor headed down the hall to meet her halfway.

"Yes, I was just here. Let me go in and put my stuff down," Valentine panted as she shrugged out of her backpack.

"I'm sorry, Ms. O'Dell, to have to tell you this—your grandmother is gone," the doctor said. She blinked her eyes in surprise.

"What do you mean? They told me she didn't have any appointments scheduled today. Did they bump her dialysis up?" she asked, holding her backpack at her side.

"No, miss, she's gone," the doctor repeated himself. She was so confused.

"Like you lost her? Her room is right there, where could she—"

It was like a curtain dropped in her mind. One second, she was confused, and in the next second, she understood perfectly. Her backpack fell to the ground with a loud thud.

"I'm so sorry, Valentine," the CNA said softly, reaching out and rubbing Val's arm.

"Wait. Wait, wait, wait. I was *literally* just here!" Val said, shoving the woman's hand away. "Minutes ago, and she was fine. *Fine!*"

"Your grandmother was a very sick woman," the doctor told her. "She had a fever of one hundred and three, and a nasty lung infection. There were attempts to revive her, but we have a DNR on record for Mrs. Parker. There was nothing else we could do. I'm very sorry. She was asleep, it was most likely painless."

Was that supposed to make her feel better? What about this situation was painless? Valentine felt like every single one of her internal organs had turned to glass, and were now shattering. She pressed her hand to her forehead.

"But … but … I was just talking to her, I don't understand," she said, and realized she'd started crying. "Minutes ago! How can she be gone? She was doing so much better! *Minutes!*"

"At her age, and in her condition, some times that's all it takes. I'm sorry for your loss," the doctor said again.

"*Stop saying you're sorry!*" Valentine shouted. "That makes it sound like it was your fault! Like there was something you could do! Why didn't you do anything!?"

"C'mon, Valentine," the CNA cooed, wrapping an arm around Val's shoulder and guiding her towards the nurses's station. "Let's go into a quiet room, give you some time to process."

Val didn't hear a word the girl said, she was crying so hard. She simply stumbled along next to her. They went down a different hallway, and after a few moments, she was placed into a small room that muffled all the outside noise. There was soft lighting, several comfy chairs, and tissue boxes on every end table.

This is where they bring people to tell them their family members are dead. She's dead. She was everything, and now she's gone. What am I going to do?

"Is there someone I can call for you?" the CNA spoke softly as she knelt at Valentine's side. She suddenly felt guilty for not knowing the woman's name.

"No. No," she hiccuped. "God, I yelled at him. I'm so sorry. I didn't mean to, I just …"

"Don't be sorry—he understands, we all do. Are you sure I can't call anyone?"

"No. I'll … I'll be okay. I'll call … someone."

"Alright. I'll check on you in a little while. There'll be some paperwork," the CNA warned her as she climbed to her feet. "Take your time, stay in here for as long as you need."

When she was alone, Valentine started sobbing again. Grief washed over her in waves. She'd almost forgotten this feeling from when her parents had died. It was *awful*.

After giving into the depths of despair for five minutes, she struggled to pull herself together. She needed … something. Someone. Help. She fumbled with her phone, going through her contacts. Del would rush over and do anything he could for her, she knew. But she didn't think she could handle his crass demeanor right now. Charice would also come, but probably in her corset and pasties.

Bailey was at home, Valentine knew, but not only did the younger girl not have any kind of means of transportation, the news would probably hit her hard, too. That pretty much left only one person that Valentine felt she could call.

The only person I want to call, and the only person I'm afraid to call.

Last time I called him for something like this, he didn't answer. Last time I called him for something like this, he just made it so much worse.

But she was upset and she was scared and she was alone, and she wanted Ari *so badly* it was like a physical ache in the center of her chest. So she pressed the button and raised the phone to her ear. It took him a while, but eventually he answered, and she let out a sigh of relief.

"You'll be happy to know I've been slaying dragons for you," he said.

"What?" she asked, her voice scratchy and watery.

"I may be a 'Daddy's boy', but I just informed him that under no condition will I ever have anything to do with Harper ever again, and that I also happen to be seriously involved with someone else. You better not make a liar of me, Saint Valentine."

He'd told his dad about her. Valentine had been worried he wouldn't answer, and there he'd been, making her an official part of his life.

I can only handle so many things, god, maybe take it easy on me now, okay?

"I ... I ..." she stammered.

"I love it when I can make you speechless," he chuckled. "And don't think I didn't notice how you snuck out this morning. Where are you? I'm coming to get you, let's do brunch."

"I'm ... at the hospital," she finally managed. There was a long pause at the other end.

"The hospital?"

"Ari ..." she whispered his name, her voice cracking. On the other end of the line, she could hear his office chair being abruptly pushed back.

"What happened? What hospital? I'm coming right now," he was speaking fast, his voice full of authority.

"She's gone, Ari," Valentine sobbed. "She's gone and I'm all alone."

"You're not alone," he informed her. "You have me. What hospital?"

"I was just talking to her. Just talking to her, and she remembered me, and remembered you, and now she's *gone.*"

"*Valentine!*" he snapped, forcing her to shut up. "What hospital?"

"I'm at MMU," she sniffled. "In the left wing, near room 319—they … they put me in some sort of cry room."

"I'll be there in fifteen minutes."

She chewed on her bottom lip for a moment.

"Please," she finally whispered. "Please hurry."

I hate to be alone.

It was almost comical.

For months, Valentine had done everything for her grandmother.

Literally everything—fed her, bathed her, changed her. Made doctors appointments and kept records and organized meetings. By the end, Valentine had felt almost superhuman. She could do anything for her grandmother.

Yet when the end really did come, she wasn't able to do a thing.

So Ari did it all for her.

Fifteen minutes after they hung up, Ari was striding through the cry room door. She all but collapsed against his chest, sobbing into his tie while he attempted to answer questions from a nurse. When his arms finally came around her, Valentine calmed down. She wrapped her own arms around his waist, anchoring herself to him.

She wasn't sure how long they were in the hospital for, at least another hour. Maybe longer. She spent all of it attached to him, surprising even herself by how scared she was of letting go.

Because when you let go, that's when bad things happen. You let go, and ten minutes later, the person is gone.

The doctor walked her through the events as best as they could figure them out. Valentine had left the room at roughly nine thirty. At nine thirty-five, her grandmother had experienced respiratory failure. Different medical procedures had been attempted to start the flow of oxygen again, but due to her Do Not Resuscitate order, those procedures had been limited. At nine forty-three, Mrs. Parker had been pronounced dead.

"I know this may not make you feel better right now," Dr. Yamamoto spoke in a calm, reassuring voice. "But your grandmother was a very sick woman. Even if we had been able to revive her, she would have been on a ventilator, at best. Her heart would've been weakened further, and her mental state would have declined even quicker. She went peacefully, in her sleep, after spending a nice morning with her granddaughter."

"Thank you, we understand," Ari said, his voice low and serious. Valentine had come to think of it as his "lawyer voice", when he was all business. When he was Aaron Sharapov, esquire. "Thank you for taking such good care of her."

"If you have any questions," the doctor sighed and handed over his card. "This is for my office here. Again, I'm sorry for your loss, Ms. O'Dell."

Ari and the doctor shook hands. Valentine stood still and just watched as the doctor disappeared down the hallway.

"Are you ready to go home?" Ari asked.

Valentine glanced around. All the necessary paperwork had been filled out and signed. The hospital had alerted her grandmother's care facility, they would be packing up her meager belongings. She hadn't had anything at the hospital, itself.

There's nothing left for me here. Not in this hospital, not at my house. Not in this town.

"I'm ready to go."

They went to her home, and it was Ari who broke the news to Bailey. It was a surreal moment, seeing him standing in her sparse living room. Valentine couldn't even remember, had Ari ever actually been inside the house before?

Briefly, one time, when he helped Gam-Gam up to her room after a walk. She'd been half in love with him by the end of it. So had I.

Bailey cried, and the two girls hugged while Ari stood by the front door, giving them their privacy. They sat and talked for a bit, reminiscing about Gam-gam, sharing fun memories. Forgetting the sad ones. When Bailey disappeared upstairs to call her own grandmother, Ari came back into the living room.

"C'mon," he said, grabbing Valentine's hand and pulling her up.

She didn't have the energy to argue. Didn't even want to, didn't even ask. Just followed him out the front door and back into his car and eventually all the way back to his apartment. Just stood there as he stripped her naked and laid her down in his bed.

Just like this morning. Maybe this has all be a nightmare and I'm just now waking up?

"Is this real?" Valentine whispered while he turned out the lights.

"Yes," he whispered back, joining her under the covers. He was still wearing his suit, the fabric cool against her skin as he pressed himself to her side.

"How did this happen?" she asked, staring at the ceiling.

"She was very old, Valentine," he sighed, his arm wrapping around her waist. "And she was very sick. I'm sorry."

"Me, too," she sniffled. "Me, too."

They were silent for a long time after that, her trying to stop crying. When she felt like she could speak again without breaking in half, she heaved a deep sigh and opened her mouth.

"Thank you for answering the phone."

It was simply said, but it had a lot of weight. He paused for a moment, and she knew he understood. He squeezed her tightly.

"Thank you for calling me."

11

The next few days were a whirlwind, and a lesson in what a great support network Valentine actually had—she'd always thought of herself as somewhat on her own, but that had really never been true. She'd thought it before, but now she knew it for a fact.

Charice practically moved into Val's house, cooking for her and Bailey, making lots of casseroles and easy to store dishes. Val pointed out that her grandmother hadn't been the one cooking their meals, but Charice had just told her sit down and she'd served her another piece of apple pie.

Del paid for all the funeral arrangements, the cremation and the service. It was a small affair; any of Gam-Gam's remaining friends were either too old or too far away to attend. Valentine's sister Janette also couldn't make it in from New York, though she did thoughtfully ask if she'd be receiving any kind of inheritance.

Bitch.

Del came to the memorial, though, as did Charice, Serge, Gary, and even surprisingly Angel. Valentine had actually never seen the other girl out of her angel get-up and almost hadn't recognized her. Evans also made a surprise appearance, sitting next to Bailey, his arm around her shoulders comfortingly.

It's a weird little family, but it's also a pretty amazing one.

Ari stayed by her side through everything, not going back to work for the rest of the week, telling his client's that someone close to him had just passed away, so he would be unavailable. It meant a lot, it really did, knowing he was willing to do that for her.

He was also willing to do other things. He offered to hire movers to bring her stuff over to the empty apartment. He offered for her to move in with him, letting Bailey live in the apartment by herself. He drove her everywhere, took care of her, slept next to her at night. It was almost overwhelming, and undeniably comforting.

And confusing as fuck. We went from sleeping together, to me hating him, to practically living together, with hardly any conversation.

And a conversation needed to happen.

Valentine did very little speaking throughout that week, which gave her plenty of time to think, something she was realizing she hadn't done enough of in her life.

She'd been solely focused on taking care of Gam-Gam. Working at Caché so she could take care of Gam-Gam. Running herself ragged to take care of Gam-Gam. Getting through school, so she could get a good job, so she could take care of Gam-Gam later on.

Ridiculous, really, that she'd never really in-depth thought of what she would do when Gam-Gam died. Her grandmother had, after all, been a sickly elderly woman. Death had been sure to happen sooner rather later.

When taking care of a person is pretty much your sole purpose in life, what do you do when that person is gone? So much of her life revolved around a person that wasn't there anymore.

Did she *need* to work at Caché still? She liked the club, and she loved the people, and she had a lot of fond memories there—but if she never had to flirt with or makeout with someone for money ever again, it would be too soon. The club had been a means to an end. That end was gone.

I could get a real job. An easier job. A job that I'm not ashamed to tell people about.

And what about Bailey? The girl had been brought in as a

roommate solely as a sort of babysitter for Gam-Gam. Gam-Gam no longer needed a babysitter, and they were losing their house in less than three weeks. Valentine loved Bailey, felt like she was family, but ultimately, the girl wasn't her responsibility.

She could keep coming out of her shell. Go to school in New York. Meet Devlin Daniels.

Which all led her to Ari.

They'd been brought together out of her need for money, and kept together by that same need, and brought back together by it this last time. Now there were no more medical bills to pay. No more ambulance rides, no more care facility, no more hospitals. She didn't need Ari's money. She didn't need his legal help. She didn't need to his protection.

When it boiled down to it, she didn't need him.

God, she wanted him, though. He'd blossomed into a whole new man right before her eyes. He still had his rough edge, his authoritarian manner that she found so sexy. He still took control in that way she loved so much.

But now there was another edge to him, another side. A softer one. He listened to her now when she spoke. He was thoughtful. He showed how he cared for her in lots of different ways. He let her into his home, and she thought maybe even into his heart just a little.

But still …

His father called multiple times throughout the week, ranting loud enough over the phone that Valentine could overhear it if she was in the same room. The elder Mr. Sharapov didn't give a shit what had happened to Ari's new girlfriend, he needed to get his ass back to work. Needed to figure out his priorities! Needed to get his shit together!

The words bounced and rolled off Ari, he was obviously used to them, but they made Valentine uncomfortable. It was admirable that he could handle all that venom without returning it, but he should also stand up for himself once in a while. Tell his father not to speak to him like that; tell him he'd go back to work when he was goddamn good and ready.

It was just another way of rolling over and taking whatever his father dished out, and Valentine just didn't think she could handle that. She was about to start a whole new chapter in her life, and though she was pretty positive she was completely in love with Ari Sharapov, she didn't want to start that new chapter with all of his excess emotional baggage.

He couldn't stand up to his father before, and he can't stand up to him now—he'll never be able to. Mr. Sharapov will always be between us, until he dies, and by then, he'll have poisoned Ari, and he'll just be a carbon copy of his father. I love him too much to watch that happen, and he doesn't love me enough to stop it from happening. It's just like I always said, we're a bad match.

So almost two weeks after her grandmother died, Valentine pulled herself together and made some hard decisions. Ari had gone into the office for the day—at his father's request—and she was at his apartment. He'd brought over her makeup bag a couple days before, so she spread all her stuff out on the kitchen table, set up a mirror, then sat down to transform herself. While she got started, she called Ari and put him on speaker phone.

"I'll just be here another hour," he answered, and she smiled to herself. He almost never said "hello", at least not to her. It had gotten on her nerves for a while, but now she found it kind of cute. Like he'd already been thinking about talking to her before she'd even called him.

"Maybe don't come home," she suggested.

"What?"

"Let's go out," she said, dabbing concealer under her eyes. She hadn't worn makeup since that night at Caché, when they'd had sex in the photo booth room.

"You want to go out?" he asked, sounding surprised.

"Yes. I mean, not to the club or anything like that, but it's been long enough. Gam-Gam was a go-getter, she'd hate me sitting at home moping. And she loved you, so she'd want us to be having fun. Let's go on a *date*."

She put emphasis on the word, and he didn't miss it.

"A date, huh. We've never been on one of those."

"Not unless you count that time we had dinner with Evans and his boss," she said. He snorted.

"I brought you to show you off, and he eye-fucked you the entire time, and I couldn't say anything because I was trying to land his business as a client. *No*, that time doesn't count. Where do you want to go?"

"Dinner somewhere," she said. "Somewhere nice. You can show me off this time, too."

"Hmmm, and if the date goes well, then what happens?" he asked. Valentine held still, a blending brush forgotten in her hand.

"Then you get dessert, Mr. Sharapov."

"Sounds *delicious*. Give me an extra hour so I can find us a table somewhere, then I'll swing by and pick you up."

"I can't wait."

And she wasn't lying.

Ari liked expensive, and Ari liked sexy. He liked a healthy dash of taboo, and maybe just a pinch of trashy. Valentine had brought a dress from her home that fit that description perfectly.

It was a thin black material, the neckline wide at the shoulders and coming to a V between her breasts. It hugged her waist and hips before flowing into a long, loose skirt that went almost to her toes. Long sleeves covered her arms to her wrists, and she accessorized with a silver cuff and silver hoops. Simple, elegant, rich.

The taboo and trashy part came in at the skirt. Hidden in the drapey fabric were two long slits, going all the way from the hem clear up to her hips bones. When she stood still, it looked like a regular skirt. When she strode forward, flashes of her legs, her inner thighs, tantalized people, and sometimes when she turned, a person would catch a glimpse of the sides of her skimpy black panties.

She curled the ends of her hair, then pinned the left side of her hair back, but left the right side to fall in gentle waves over her shoulder. She was still in the bathroom when Ari got home, putting the finishing touches on her makeup. A classic cat-eye, paired with a deep burgundy, matte lipstick.

"Still here?" his voice suddenly echoed through the apartment. She smiled sadly at her reflection. He said it every time he came home and she wasn't somewhere he could see.

I left last time without giving him a chance. He's nervous I'm going to do it again. Good, Ari. You needed a little fear in your life.

"Still here," she called back. She puckered her lips, checking her liner, then adjusted her breasts in her top.

"I'm always so curious to see what you'll look like each night." Valentine turned to find Ari standing in the bathroom doorway. "It's like coming home and getting a different present each day."

Had he just called her a gift? It was too much. She brushed off the compliment and waved him away.

"Well, this present isn't fully wrapped—I usually don't let people see me till I'm completely ready, so they can get the full effect," she told him. His gaze skated up and down her form.

"You look ready to me."

Valentine smiled widely, suddenly glad he'd first seen her when she'd been standing still. It just looked like a plain dress with a plunging neckline.

"Still need shoes," she informed him. "So out, out, out. We can go in a couple minutes."

After Ari disappeared, Valentine lost her smile and almost collapsed on the toilet. She had to transform every evening into 'Saint Valentine', but Ari *always* looked amazing. Like a Greek god brought to life, like an angel fallen to earth. A fallen angel, ha, what an accurate description. With his expensive suits and gorgeous hair and old money vibes just rolling off him, he was the ultimate present.

But not for me. Not the kind of present I want. I've spent half a year fighting just to survive. I don't wanna spend the next year fighting his father for his soul. Not my battle. Not my boyfriend.

Valentine pulled herself together. She'd promised herself she'd give him this last night—to thank him for everything he'd done for her since coming back into her life. So she grabbed her heels from off the floor, a simple pair with just a strap across the toes, and a strap around the ankle. Delicate and feminine, rounding out her whole look.

Saint Valentine, one last time.

"Alright, let's do this!" Valentine called, striding purposefully out of the bathroom and across the apartment. Ari turned around and took a step forward, then held still. He watched her until she came to a stop directly in front of him.

"See?" he spoke in a soft voice as he reached out, tracing his finger up and down the inside of one of the slits. "A constant surprise."

When his finger hooked around the strap of her thong, she pulled away.

"Uh uh, you can't unwrap this present until after dinner," she warned him, shaking her finger playfully in his face before heading over to grab her backpack off the table. It had her purse in it, so she'd leave it in the back of Ari's car while they ate.

"Dessert is better at the beginning of the meal."

"I guess we'll never know. Now take me somewhere expensive, I feel like lobster."

They drove through the city, not speaking, just sitting in a comfortable silence. It was nice. And then when they pulled up to the restaurant, it took Valentine a second to recognize it. She gasped softly, then started laughing.

"I wondered if you'd remember," he murmured from behind her. She snickered and glanced back at him.

"Ari, this is the restaurant where you almost fucked me in the women's bathroom, all while your psycho ex and my date were just a couple yards away. I will never forget this place."

"*Good.*"

A valet attendant helped her out of the vehicle, and a moment later, Ari was at her side. His hand came to rest on her lower back, and then he was guiding her into the restaurant.

"It's Friday night—you were able to get a table at such short notice?" she asked as they made their way slowly up the steps to the maître d's stand. He snorted at her comment.

"I'm insulted. I'm Ari Sharapov, Valentine—of course I got a fucking table."

He wasn't lying—the maître d' didn't even ask who they were, he just called Ari by name, then gestured for them to follow him. They were led to an excellent table, in a far corner of the room. Her back was against the wall behind her, and then an entire wall of glass was next to them, overlooking a garden full of glowing lanterns.

"This is gorgeous," she sighed after Ari had given the wine order. "Last time I was here, I was at a shitty table in the center of the room."

"That's because the last time you were here, you were with someone else."

She looked back at him.

"Wanna know a secret?" she asked, leaning low over the table. His gaze dipped to her chest.

"Sure."

"I think you had a crush on me back then. I think that's why you were so angry about me being on a date," she teased him. Ari rolled his eyes.

"I was angry because we had a literal contract that said you couldn't go out with other men. I don't get crushes. I get what I paid for," he informed her as their wine was delivered.

It stung a little, that he hadn't gone along with her, but Valentine was actually glad for it. It helped remind her of how incompatible they really were; it didn't matter if they looked good together or not. Looks would fade. So would good sex and passion, and then what would be left? Wandering eyes and broken hearts. No, no thank you.

"You certainly did," Valentine chuckled, and she toasted him with her newly filled glass. He lifted his glass, as well, and then they drank. They ordered their meals and were finally alone again.

"You're in an awfully good mood this evening," Ari commented. Valentine shrugged.

"It's been a weird, rough couple weeks. Felt like it was the right time to ... start a new chapter," she answered sideways. He nodded.

"Good, I'm glad."

"And what about you?" she asked. "That day, when Gam-Gam passed, you said you'd slayed a dragon for me. I don't remember why, or what kind."

"A *small* dragon," Ari corrected. "When you called me that day, I was actually talking with my father in my office."

Yes, Ari talked to his father often. She'd overheard several phone calls between him and the senior Sharapov. Excuses made about why he wasn't working or why he'd missed meetings.

"Oh?"

"I told him I was seeing someone else, and that it was serious—or that I hoped it was," he said, giving her a Look. "And that I didn't want anything else to do with Harper Kittering."

Valentine had spoken with her teachers about her grandmother's passing and hadn't been back to classes since it had happened. She'd have work to make up, but they all seemed very understanding. The only thing she was really dreading was going back to dealing with Harper.

"Ah. And how did father dearest handle that news?"

"Much better than I thought," Ari said, and Valentine was surprised. "But was still an asshole. He wants to meet you to see if you're 'up to snuff'."

"And what if I'm not?" she asked quickly. Ari shrugged.

"We'll just make sure you are, don't worry about it."

Sting number two. Valentine already was up to snuff—by her standards and by her friends' standards. She should be for Ari's, too.

He said it off the cuff, obviously not giving much thought to what came out of his mouth, but that just made it worse. This was her life he was talking about; his life, too. He should care about it more.

Should care about me more.

"Couldn't have a sub-par girlfriend, now, could we?" she laughed darkly, then crossed her legs, one of her slits falling open to reveal her leg clear up to her hip. She was sitting at an angle, her chair and person open to the restaurant. Ari glanced down at her exposed skin.

"Sometimes sub-par is sexy. I wonder if the women's room still has that accommodating bathroom attendant."

Their food was brought soon after, and they tucked into their meals. There hadn't been any lobster on the menu, so Val had settled for a filet mignon. Ari had salmon. They made idle chit chat, Valentine waiting for dessert before addressing anything serious.

"I wanted to tell you something," she said after a choclate torte had been sat in front of her. "Or some things, I guess."

"Oh, god. And here I thought we were having a nice evening," Ari joked, grabbing a fork and reaching over to steal a bite. She moved the plate to the center of the table so they could share.

"All good things, I think," she assured him.

"I'm intrigued."

"Three weeks ago, I thought I'd hate you forever," she told him. He watched her warily. "You were a jerk the entire time we were together, and then you did something awful. But I have to admit—you've more than made up for it. You've done so much for me, and you've ... still been kind of a jerk, but also wonderful. Thank you."

Ari leaned back in his seat and nodded his head.

"You're welcome. Where is this going?"

"I just ..." Valentine had practiced what she was going to say to him, but her nerves were getting in the way. "You have the potential for so much greatness, Ari. You're a great lawyer, and a great son, I'm sure. But you could be a great *person*, and you can be that with or without your dad's support. Who cares if he cuts you off? Will you die? If *I* can survive something like that, being alone in the world, then I know *you* could—you're the strongest person I've ever known."

Ari was silent for so long, she began to get nervous that she'd said something wrong, or offensive.

"You're wrong," he finally spoke, clearing his throat.

"Excuse me?"

"I think *you're* probably the strongest person you've ever known."

She blushed, and for once it wasn't because she was angry, or embarrassed, or ashamed. It was because he made her feel special. Because he was being sweet, which was a rarity.

Because I'm so in love with him, and he'll never know it.

"Yeah, but we're talking about you," she teased. "You want all these amazing things, and maybe I don't know you as well as your father, but I know you well enough to know that no matter what life throws at you, you're going to get whatever you want. With or without his support. So if you want to become a trial lawyer, I say fuck him—go tear it up in a courtroom. Don't … keep doing all these things just because he wants you to do them. Don't do them just so that stupid sign on the side of your office will be for your name instead of his. Get your own fucking building and know that the only name on it *always* belonged to you."

Again, she seemed to have given him a lot to think about—Ari stayed sitting far back in his chair. The dim lighting made it hard to read his face, his reactions. He cleared his throat, and then his gaze shifted to look out the window. A couple was wandering through the garden below them, a woman in a long white dress, the skirt rippling in the breeze. The man took off his jacket and draped it over her shoulders.

"Your belief in me is somewhat surprising," Ari finally spoke. "And very flattering. I appreciate it. I can see I still have several dragons to slay for you."

Valentine's heart dropped, and not even for herself.

It dropped for him.

Because as awful as her life had been for the past five years, she'd never known the kind of pressures Ari did—she'd never been as re-stricted as him.

She felt sorry for him.

"Ari," she sighed. "You don't *have* to do anything for me—you should *want* to do them for yourself."

"What if I don't know what I want?"

"Then your life is even sadder than I thought it was," she answered immediately. Thankfully, he didn't get angry. He barked out a laugh.

He thought she was joking.

"Oh, yes, my life is tragic. I had lunch with the mayor today, and now I'm having dinner with the sexiest woman in Chicago—people should weep for me."

They really, really should, Ari. Because you have every chance for happiness, and you choose cynicism instead.

The bill was brought and Valentine didn't see it at all. She didn't think Ari even saw it—he just handed over his credit card, then signed the slip when it was brought back to him. When they were standing outside, waiting for valet to bring the car around, Valentine took several deep breaths, trying to think how best to initiate the next part of her plan. Thankfully, Ari gave her the perfect opportunity.

"What's next?" he asked, turning and wrapping his arms around her waist. "Home? Or are you ready to go back to the club yet? I spoke with Del the other day, they're organizing a water balloon fight."

Valentine laughed. It did sound like fun. God, she was going to miss that place. She lifted her hands to his chest, smoothing them over the expensive material of his blazer, sliding her fingers up and down his lapels.

"No," she finally answered just as his SUV was pulled up to the curb. "No, let's go to my house."

His eyebrows shot up.

"Your house?"

"Yeah, there's something I need to do there."

They got into the car. Valentine's nerves were through the roof, but Ari didn't seem to notice. He drove with one hand on her thigh, silent some of the time, telling her about his day other times. She leaned her head back and closed her eyes, soaking in his voice.

It was so good when it was really good, but when it was bad, it was the worst. I'll miss these hands and that voice, but I already miss myself even more. How long has it been since I've been … just me? Just Valentine?

"Did you fall asleep?"

His fingers squeezed her thigh, then ran up to where it met her pelvic bone, and she opened her eyes. Her rickety old rental house was outside her window. Strange to think that in two weeks, she wouldn't be living there anymore. She'd hated it for most of the time she'd lived in it, but now she was almost sad to leave it.

Sad because I'm leaving it? Or sad because I don't know where I'm gonna go yet?

"Just thinking," she breathed.

When his fingers started toying with the strap of her underwear, Valentine opened her door and lurched out of her seat. She moved fast, opening the back door and pulling out her backpack before he was even out of his seat. She dropped it to the ground, near the back tire, then turned to face him when he came around the bumper.

"How long is this going to take? It's freezing tonight," he grumbled, tucking a thick scarf into his jacket. She put her hands on her hips and smirked up at him.

"You're such a baby. I'm not even wearing a jacket, and I'm not cold at all. New Yorkers are so much more hard core than Chicagans."

"Chicagans? *Chicagoans*," Ari corrected her, putting his hands over hers on her hips and pulling her close. "You may be more 'hard core', but at least we're smarter. Have I mentioned how much I love your dress?"

"I had a feeling you would," she chuckled, then shivered when his hands smoothed their way up her body, pausing briefly on either side of her breasts before continuing on to cup her neck.

"I'll love it even more when it's in a ball in the corner of my bedroom."

"Okay, first of all, that is basically the sleaziest pick-up line ever invented, and second of all, technically you don't have a bedroom, you have a—"

He kissed her so aggressively, she squeaked in shock as they fell back against the car. His tongue was in her mouth, overwhelming it, and his hands were skating back down her body. Squeezing her hips, fingers digging into flesh. Moving around to grope her ass.

Since her grandmother had died, they hadn't slept together once. He hadn't even acted like he'd wanted to—he'd given her space, respected her mourning period. She'd been impressed.

But now she could literally feel how ... *frustrated* he was, as his entire body pressed against her. It felt good. Sex with Ari had always been better than anything ever had been, and they'd only gotten to have it twice since coming back into each others lives. So many missed opportunities to roll around with each other and play with each other and push each others buttons.

"I love this," Valentine breathed, unwilling to say the words that were actually in her head. "I missed this."

"Remember that," he growled, then he nipped her neck sharply with his teeth. "Next time you think of running away."

I will remember. I'll remember everything. And I'll miss all of it.

Valentine initiated the next kiss, clawing her fingers through his hair. Balling her hands into fists, gently pulling at the strands. He hadn't cut it in a while, so there was a lot to grab onto; she would miss it the most.

No, she would miss his lips. Overpowering her own and bringing her to her knees and turning her inside out. Or no, maybe his tongue—that's what she would miss, his tongue against her bottom lip. Dropping down her chest to trace along her cleavage.

Silly girl, no way, it was his hands. Squeezing and bruising and pushing and pulling. Or maybe his shoulders, so broad under her own hands. Or his back. His chest. His whole body.

His everything.

"Ari."

She was whispering, and yet she felt like the sound of her voice echoed all around her, saying so much more than just his name. He froze in her arms, then lifted his head to look down at her.

"*Don't*," he spoke softly, and her eyes teared up.

He knows. Somewhere deep down, he had to know this was coming. I'm so sorry, Ari.

"I have to go home now," she breathed, her teeth starting to chatter. He shook his head.

"This isn't your home."

"This has been my home for over six months."

"It's *not* your home," he insisted. "Your grandmother is gone, she was the only thing keeping you here."

"Exactly—she was the only thing keeping me in this lifestyle," she added to his statement. He shook his head.

"Don't do this, Valentine. It's not right."

"I …" she shook her head, hoping it would help settle her thoughts. "I've been thinking a lot."

He pulled away from her so quickly, she gasped as the cold air invaded the space between them.

"Which means bad news for me. This shit you have in that brain of yours," he growled. "What have you convinced yourself of now? I'm a liar? I'm an asshole? Always convicting me without letting me defend myself."

Valentine quickly shook her head and stepped towards him.

"No, that's not what's happening. You're … jesus, I never thought I'd say something like this, but you're a great guy, Ari, I—"

"If I'm so 'great', then what's the fucking problem?" he snapped. "I saved you. I took care of you. I do *everything* for you, and it's still not enough."

She took a deep breath.

"It's not," she agreed softly. "And you *are* a great guy. Just not great for me."

"Jesus christ. Next thing you're going to say is 'we can still be friends', right? I don't want to be your fucking friend, Valentine."

"Then what *do* you want, Ari?" she asked, throwing up her hands. "A fuck buddy? A puppet? A *whore?*"

"You *know* that's not what I want."

"No, you just want someone who's 'up to snuff'," she used his words against him. The anger in his eyes went from a simmer to a full boil.

"*Do not* use his words against me," he snapped. "I am not my father. I told you I was working on it, I told you I was going to introduce you two. You want everything to happen *now*, but what about what I want?"

"What do you want?" she cried again. "Do you even know? Is it even me? Or is it just the idea of me?"

"That is such a fucking girl thing to say," he snarled. She blinked away tears and bent over, unzipping her backpack and yanking stuff out of it.

"*This* isn't me," she told him, standing upright and tugging at her sleeves. He looked at her like she was insane as she pulled her arms free of the sleeves, the dress barely clinging to the tips of her breasts. Then she pulled a ratty hoodie over her head and jerked it into place. The dress fell loose while she moved, and soon enough it was puddled at her feet.

"Have you gone insa-"

"And these aren't me," she continued, taking off her earrings and dropping them to the ground. "And not these." Her shoes were yanked off next, with some difficulty. While she was still bent over, she pulled a pair of harem sweatpants out of her bag and put them on, quickly followed by a well worn pair of Vans slip-ons. "None of this." She threw her hair pins across the sidewalk, then yanked her hair up into a mess bun. "And least of all this." For her final act, she took out a bag of wipes and deftly pulled one free of the pack, roughly rubbing it across her face. She knew she probably looked like the Joker when she was done, but it was good enough. "*This* is not me, Ari." She tossed the balled up wipe at his chest, watched as the blotchy tissue fell to the ground.

"What exactly are you trying to say?" he asked, looking at the mess around their feet.

"I'm saying that *this* is me," she said, gesturing to her homeless-chic outfit first, and then her house. "*That* is me. Everything else is pretend, and this is the real Val. A woman your dad will *never* approve of, which means ultimately, *you'll* never approve of."

Ari's face looked pained.

"I've *always* approved of you," he insisted. "I'm just asking for a little time."

"Time is up, Ari," she sighed. "I fought a losing battle with my grandmother. I'm ... I'm not willing to fight another one for you."

Harsh words, but they needed to be said. He wasn't saying the words she needed to hear from him, so she would have to say the words she needed to hear from herself.

He glared down the length of his nose at her, then stood up straight, pulling himself to his full height. An intimidation tactic he used often; she wondered if he knew it had the opposite effect on her. She loved his height and his stature and his presence, and god, this was even harder than she thought it would be.

"Are you calling me a lost cause, Valentine?" he asked. She took a deep breath.

*I'm calling you weak. I'm calling you lost. I'm **begging** you to fight for me. To stand up for me. **To stand up for yourself.***

"Yes," she whispered. "Yes, I am. Thank you for everything you've done for me, Ari. I can't even tell you how much I appreciate it. And I ... I really hope you get what you want out of life. I really, really do."

"You mean, you hope I get what *you* think I want," he said in a low, angry voice. She shrugged her shoulders.

"Whatever makes this situation easier for you."

Ari swallowed thickly and glared down the street. Valentine

refused to look anywhere but his face. At his angry blue eyes. Such blue eyes. Ocean eyes. His eyebrows were thunderous above them, the same shade of perfect blonde as the perfect hair on his perfect head. As the perfect stubble starting to show on his perfect jawline.

"I want you to know," he spoke slowly, still refusing to look at her. "I think this is a bad idea."

"Duly noted," she nodded. "And I would like to point out that if you put together all the time we've known each other, most of it was spent having sex, making deals, or not speaking to each other. I'm not the girl for you, Ari. I was just a good time. I was just ... Saint Valentine."

*I **hate** Saint Valentine.*

"You're so stupid," he breathed. "You were so much more than that."

She wiped away more tears and went to respond, but before she could, Ari was moving. Bending over and picking her pack up off the ground. He shoved it into her arms, then stood back from her.

"Are we done here?" he asked. She was a little stunned.

"I ... I guess so," she stammered. "Ari, I—"

"If there's nothing I can do to convince of how absolutely fucking wrong you are," he talked over her. "Then we really are done. I have an early meeting tomorrow."

"With your father," she guessed. It was a low blow, but his attitude stung. She hadn't said or done anything to be intentionally cruel, so she didn't feel like his anger at her was justified.

"With my father," he nodded. "Goodbye, Valentine."

"Goodbye, Ari."

He nodded once, then twice. Paused, then nodded a third time. He still hadn't looked her in the eyes, and it killed her. So before he could step off the curb, she grabbed his collar and yanked him down to her. He stumbled, but she still didn't miss when she pulled his lips into hers.

They didn't touch anywhere else, just her hand on his jacket.

Their lips against each other. She tried to infuse him with all of her feelings for him, all the things he didn't believe she felt for him. Her admiration, and her desire, and her ... her ...

And my love.

"I believe in you, Aaron Sharapov," she whispered when they broke apart. She looked up at him, and when she saw his blue eyes looking down, she felt like she was falling into them. "You just have to believe in yourself."

He took a deep breath and closed his eyes, shuttering his soul from her once again. Then his forehead came to rest against hers.

"Just believe in myself," he sighed. "Just change my life and my goals and my dreams and slay every dragon in the land, all for Saint Valentine."

"All for *you*," she corrected him. "You're nothing to anybody if you aren't worth something to yourself."

"Sage words from a living saint," he said. Then he pulled away gently, stepping off the curb and moving away from her. "Goodbye, Valentine. Thanks for a good time."

She smiled at him, then wiped at her tears.

"Bye, Ari. Thanks for the *best* time."

His smile was tight and his eyes were flat, but at least she got to see them one last time before he turned around and got into his car. He turned on the engine and sat for a moment, staring out at the street. Her heart leapt in her chest, hoping for she didn't know what. The magic words, the perfect moment.

And then he peeled out of his parking spot and took off down the street. Before he turned the corner at the end of the block, his tail lights were a complete blur to her as the tears started pouring down her face.

12

The next morning, Valentine felt like absolute shit. Like she had a hangover, but none of the fun memories of a wild night.

I could've gone to Caché and had an awesome water balloon fight. I could've gone home with Ari and tested how flexible I still am. I could be waking up right now in a luxury apartment complex in downtown Chicago, surrounded by silk sheets and fine décor. But nooooooo, I have to have self-respect. So stupid.

After Ari had left the night before, she'd picked up her belongings from the street and had dragged herself inside. Left everything in a pile by the door. When she'd gotten to her room, seeing all the empty boxes—packing preparations—had just depressed her more. Knowing she wouldn't be going to Ari's place. So she'd collapsed face down on her bed and she hadn't moved for almost ten hours straight.

When she finally emerged downstairs, she couldn't find the filters for the coffee pot. Bailey had started packing up the kitchen, and had apparently gotten a little overzealous. So she grumbled and cursed to herself while she dug around the different boxes.

"Is there a problem?" her roommate asked, appearing in the doorway, looking as tired as Valentine felt.

"Yeah, can't find the filters," she replied. Bailey gave her a strange look, then walked across the room and opened a cupboard. A roll of paper towels had fallen over, hiding the filters from view.

"There where they always are," she replied, handing them over. Valentine snatched them out of her hand, then went about making a thick, strong brew of coffee.

"I didn't sleep very well," Valentine explained her attitude as she sat down and slumped across the kitchen table. Bailey hesitated for a moment, then sat down across from her.

"I saw you and Ari pull up last night," she commented casually. "Did he not stay the night?"

"No. No, he did not."

They settled into an awkward silence, both watching the coffee pot. When it was finally done, Val jumped out of her seat and poured cups for them both. Hazelnut creamer went into Bailey's, but she left hers black and bitter.

Just like my soul.

"You two ... doing okay?" Bailey asked when she'd sat back down.

"Doing okay," Valentine grunted, then she made a face when she took her first sip. She hadn't just made it strong, it was nuclear. She felt like she was swallowing a cruise missile.

"You don't sound okay," her roommate pointed out. Valentine groaned and let her head fall to the table with a thunk.

"I totally fucked us."

"I'm sorry ... what?"

"I don't know where we're gonna go," Valentine said, not lifting her head. "We have to be out of here in two weeks, and the couple places I've looked at in my budget, they're awful."

Her new budget, she should've said. She would be putting in her two weeks notice at Caché whenever she went back to work, and then she'd be getting a regular job. Between those two events, they'd be living off Valentine's ten percent from the auction, and whatever miniscule income Bailey earned.

"But Ari told me about that apartment he had for us, why not just go there?" Bailey asked.

"Because 'Ari and I' are not 'Ari and I' anymore."

There was a thunk as Bailey almost dropped her mug, and Valentine finally looked up at her. She managed to put it down carefully, then slid it towards the center of the table.

"Okay, let's back up. Last I saw, you two were making out against his fancy car last night. What happened?"

"We weren't making out," Valentine informed her. "We were kissing goodbye."

"Why were you kissing goodbye?"

"Because I ended it," Valentine said. "Whatever we were, I told him it was over."

"Okay … can I ask why?" Bailey pressed in a slow voice. Valentine shrugged.

"He's amazing. Even when he's awful. But after everything that happened, and *a lot* of thinking, I just know we're not right for each other."

"You *know* that?"

"Yes."

There was a long pause, then Bailey sighed.

"Bummer. I liked him," she said, pulling her coffee cup closer. Val's eyes got wide.

"You did?"

It had always seemed like Bailey was slightly afraid of Ari. He was an intimidating man, and Bailey was extremely easy to intimidate.

"I mean, he seemed kinda like an asshole," Bailey shrugged. "But also like he was really into you. You know, like in high school, one of those boys who's too cool to admit they like you, when really they've got like a secret shrine built to you. That's him—secret shrine, all the way. And then when Gam-gam got sick that first time and you stopped talking to him, he'd come around. Even after I told him I wouldn't help him talk to you, I'd see his car outside sometimes. And like normally, that would totally set off my creeper radar. But it wasn't like that, I think he just wanted to see you. Make sure you were okay, or something, even if you weren't speaking to him. I like that. I like him."

Valentine was blown away. She hadn't realized Bailey paid such close attention to her goings-on. She also hadn't quite realized just how badly Ari had wanted to speak to her after she'd cut him off.

"That's nice," she finally responded. "And he was ... I like him, too. A lot. But we ... we were weird, okay? Our relationship wasn't normal."

"Fuck normal," Bailey snorted.

That got a laugh out of Val.

"I totally agree," she chuckled. "But this was different. It was more of an arrangement than a relationship, that's how he said he wanted it, until the end, when we decided to be something more. But even then, it's still not enough for him. He has this whole idea of what he thinks he wants in life, and he doesn't really. I don't think he even likes his life now all that much. And even if he really did, *I* don't. You can't be with someone like that, you know? Trying to change yourself, or trying to change him the whole time. That's awful."

Bailey shrugged again.

"Or maybe both of you could change just a little and meet in the middle."

Valentine grabbed a crumpled up napkin off the table and threw it at the other girl.

"Stop being wise beyond your years," she laughed. "Just trust me, okay? Even when it was happening, when I was telling him I couldn't be with him, I ... I kinda hoped he'd say something to stop me. To prove to me that this, that *I'm*, what he wants, beyond a shadow of a doubt. And he didn't. He didn't even quite get what I was trying to explain to him. He gets a thought in his head, and he's so smart, so he thinks he's right, and then he won't listen to anyone else. Even when they're practically screaming the right answer at him, he can't hear it. It's ... exhausting."

"Maybe he just needs time," Bailey suggested. "I'm not trying to be awful, but you know, you guys *just* started working things out. You went from not speaking to him at all, to staying at his house every night, all in the space of a couple days. Some people can't up-shift that fast, you know?"

"If you like him so much, *you* date him," Valentine suggested snidely. "I made my decision. He's stuck in first, and I've been in that gear for too long. I'm hitting the throttle and going full speed to fifth. I'll miss him, and I'll miss us, but that's life. We're done, for good."

"You know how ridiculous you sound, right?" the other girl snorted and chortled. "I wonder how many rom-coms have that exact same line in it—then cut to two hours later, when the couple that swore they'd 'never', be wind up saying 'I do'."

Valentine rolled her eyes and laughed as well, but she grabbed her coffee mug and stood up.

"Not this movie," she sighed. "The credits have rolled, and this heroine is beyond tired. I just want … a normal life, now. I want to get a small apartment somewhere, and go to a normal job, and do my school work, and just be *me*."

She started walking out of the kitchen, but Bailey's laugh stopped her before she could head up the stairs.

"I'm sorry, but 'normal' and 'Saint Valentine' don't co-exist. Normal is boring."

Valentine paused, one foot on the bottom step.

"I wasn't always Saint Valentine," she said softly, but Bailey still managed to hear her.

"Maybe not, but it's a part of you now, and not such a bad one. You should stop thinking so badly of yourself, Val. You're an awesome person, no matter what kind of clothes you've got on."

She blinked her eyes rapidly, then hurried up the stairs, not bothering to respond. She just went straight into her room and sat on her bed.

Did she want 'Saint Valentine' to be a part of her? Could she even get rid of that side of herself if she wanted to? She wasn't sure.

But she was positive that she didn't want to be anyone's savior, and most certainly not Ari's. She'd tried, and it hadn't worked out, like so many other things in her life. Now she had to move on. She wished him well. She wished him so many good things.

Wish he would've told me, just once, that he loved me. Would've told me, just once, that I meant as much to him as his job. Just once, that among all those lofty dreams of his, I had a place. Just once.

13

Valentine went back to Caché that Thursday, a couple days later. She'd called Del so he'd know she was coming in, but she was still shocked when there was a small welcome back party waiting for her. Everyone was very sweet, giving their condolences, giving her hugs, welcoming her back. Gary gave her an expensive bottle of vodka, and Del gave her a two-night-stay voucher for The Peninsula Chicago, one of the nicest hotels in the entire city. She had no doubt that the vouchers were a regift, something he'd gotten from someone else, but she didn't care.

Charice gave her a vibrator.

I swear, it's like she's psychic.

"I need to talk to you," Valentine said when the small crowd of coworkers started to disperse and head downstairs. Del nodded and led her towards his office, eating a piece of cake with his bare hands while he went. When they sat down, he licked the frosting off his fingers, then glanced at her.

"You're quiting."

She was stunned into silence for a moment.

"I … yes. How did you know?"

"Because I know you, kiddo," he sighed. "I knew this day was coming from the moment I hired you, and when you told me your grandmother had passed, I could count the hours. You were perfect for this job, Vally, but you weren't meant for it. I'mma miss you."

STYLO FANTÔME

She sniffled, then laughed at him.

"Miss all the money I make for you," she teased. "Miss staring at my ass all the time. Miss me giving you a hard time."

"Miss all of that, and more. Tonight your last night?" he asked, leaning back to glance at a schedule next to his desk.

"No, I figured I'd end on a good note, give two weeks. Give you time to hire someone new, have me train someone, and I can also let my regular clients know, try to pawn them off on the other girls."

"You're a good kid, Valentine. Nutty as a squirrel, but a good kid," he told her. "And you're welcome here *any* time, you got that? I don't care if it's noon on a Tuesday, you feel like saying hi, you come say hi. All access membership for life."

"Thanks for that."

"And anyone ever gives you any kind of shit, you call me. Serge would kill me if I ever let anything happen to you."

"For a mean old man, you're pretty sweet sometimes, Del," she laughed at him. He glared and started shooing her away from his desk.

"Don't say it so loud! You'll give me a bad rep! Get the fuck out of here before you ruin everything," he hissed, but he winked at her before she walked through the door.

Everything felt different. She was wearing her neon two piece outfit, and her makeup was on point, but it wasn't the same. Knowing this wasn't who she was anymore, this wasn't something she had to do. She just couldn't bring forth the energy. She danced and she smiled, but flirting just wasn't happening. It felt pointless. She'd neglected her regular clients for so long, they weren't particularly interested anymore, and she certainly didn't need any new ones.

There was no drive.

No fun.

Being in the Club Room was almost depressing, so she decided on seeing if Angel wanted to switch places—the younger woman worked the door most nights, checking membership passes and IDs, easy work. While Valentine was going up the stairs, though, she ran into a familiar face.

"We keep bumping into each other," Val laughed as Evans Daniels stopped a couple steps below her.

"Maybe you're stalking me," he teased. She rolled her eyes.

"Don't flatter yourself."

He laughed and closed the distance between them, standing just one step under her.

"I wouldn't dare," he assured her. "Done for the night?"

"No, I'm bored. Just heading up to find something else to do."

"Hmmm, could that something else possibly involve me? And possibly involve getting out of here?"

She folded her arms across her chest.

"Are you asking me on a date?" she became all business.

"No, just as friends. Unless payment is absolutely required," Evans said quickly, holding up his hands. She narrowed her eyes.

"I wouldn't take payment from you—you would *never* be a client of mine," she stressed. Then she remembered that she only had a matter of days left where she would have to refer to the men in her life as "clients", so she decided to loosen up. "But you are a friend, and I think if we time it right, no one will know I've left."

They snuck out the front door. Too many employees hung out around the back door, taking smoke breaks and telling stories. There was actually a new girl at the front—Angel was nowhere in sight. The poor girl was still green at her job, struggling with a large group of Chinese businessmen, and she barely paid attention as Valentine and Evans passed her. They dashed down the street to his car.

"Would you really get in trouble for leaving early?" he asked, driving them further into downtown. Val waved her hand.

"Oh, no, not at all. Sneaking around is just fun."

Evans laughed, then pulled the car into the stream of traffic.

He took her to a tiny, dimly lit hole-in-the-wall restaurant. Or bar. A bit of both, from what she could see as he led her towards an empty booth at the back of the room. There was heavy gold and black brocade wallpaper, and tiny black chandeliers above each table. A full bar

ran the length of the far wall, and at the end of it, a man played a pi-
ano, crooning softly in French. She slid onto the plush leather seat of
the booth.

"How on earth did you find this place?" she asked, carefully pulling her hair up into a ponytail.

"I spend a lot of time alone," Evans shrugged. "And I'm a night
owl. A colleague told me about it. Chicago only has so many late night
bars-slash-eateries, and this has better ambiance than Denny's, so I've
become somewhat of a regular."

She laughed.

"I can see why. I like it."

"I figured you would. Its funky vibe suits you," he nodded, looking
over her form. She dropped her eyes to her menu, hoping she wouldn't
have to have a "talk" with him before the night was over.

She ordered a beer, surprising Evans, and some truffle fries. He
ordered a Manhattan, then surprised her by ordering two burgers.

"Hungry?" she asked when the waitress walked away.

"Starving. Been pulling long hours. I've never been good at taking
care of myself, there's no food in my place. I think I'm in desperate
need of a woman to take care of me," he chuckled, running his fingers
through his hair. He had well trimmed, soft brown hair. Neatly styled.
Nothing mussy or messy or sinfully sexy about it at all.

Stop it.

"Pity the woman who raised you didn't teach you to take care of
yourself," Valentine replied, but she kept her tone teasing. He laughed
louder and nodded again.

"I was always too busy reading and taking advanced classes to
bother with cooking. I make a mean batch of brownies, though," he
assured her.

"Well, I mean, what else does a man need?"

"I can think of a few things."

Evans had always been hard to figure out, since the first time she'd
met him. She could never quite tell when he was joking, or when he

was being serious. When he was flirting, or when he was just being playful. She waited for the waitress to drop off their food and drinks, then Val leaned across the table a little.

"You and Ari work together," she stated.

"Our companies do, yes."

"Ari and I 'worked' together," she added.

"So I heard."

"So even though Ari and I aren't anything anymore, *you* and I will never be anything *at all*," she informed him. He cocked up an eyebrow.

"Is he *that* good? Or am I *that* repulsive?" he tried to tease. She shook her head.

"Neither. But I … I have a tendency to make bad decisions, and fuck things up. I won't fuck things up for you. Or for him, for that matter. I'm done with bad decisions," she explained.

"And if I were to, uh, offer to pay? Same thing?" he checked. She nodded.

"I'd turn you down, same as I did before. I like you, Evans. Please don't make me not like you."

It was a tense moment, but he finally laughed. He had a great smile, very broad, and for the first time, Valentine wondered why Evans was single. Why he spent his weekends paying for escorts at Caché. Even if he was new to Chicago, a man like him shouldn't have any problem picking up girls on his own.

"I would hate it if you didn't like me," he said, and he reached across the table and covered her hand with his own. She smiled back at him and squeezed his hand. "Now. What are we gonna do about my baby bro, and your funky little roommate?"

Valentine wanted to answer. She had all sorts of ideas. She was slightly obsessed with the pair—if she couldn't get her happily ever after, then she would help Bailey get hers, goddammit. She was sure that between Evans' impressive brain and her own talents at getting men, they would have the goofy little pair together in no time.

Before she could say any of that, though, she was frozen in place.

A throat was cleared from close by, and out of her peripheral, she could see that a man was coming to a stop right in front of their table. He was wearing a suit, tailored to fit. His hands were in his pockets. If she lifted her gaze, she knew she would find a smirk on his lips. But she couldn't lift her eyes. She was too busy praying for a hole to open in the floor and swallow her whole.

"This looks very cozy," Ari Sharapov said in a bored voice. "When you said you were becoming a regular at Caché, Evans, I didn't realize exactly how much you meant it."

Ari could be very patient when he need to be—his job required it. But when it came to Valentine, that flew right out the window.

She broke up with me. We weren't even dating, and she broke up with me. What the fuck. Typical fucking Valentine.

She'd said a lot of things. Things that had really messed with his mind. Ari had an enormous amount of self-confidence, but he was pretty sure no one had ever believed in him as much as Valentine did; it was a somewhat shocking revelation. It made him feel …

Unworthy.

No. *Angry.* He was so goddamn angry at her. For judging him. For not giving him a chance. For believing in him just enough to make him feel like shit, but not enough to stay with him. Fuck that woman. He'd done everything he could for her, and it wasn't enough. What else could she possibly want? What kind of person basically demanded their significant other give up all their hopes and dreams for them?

*Well, really, they're not **your** hopes and dreams. They're your fathers. You've just gotten so used to them, you think of them as yours.*

His birthday was in June. He'd be thirty-one. His father was sixty. Just five more years, and he'd retire. Ari was so close to his goal. *So close.* That's what he wanted, he didn't need Valentine confusing him. Making him lose sight of that, demanding he choose one or the other.

Her or his dreams. She could've offered to be a part of them. Selfish. She was so *selfish*.

Yeah, so selfish, she only wanted the best for you and thought better of you than anyone you've ever known. That's all.

He didn't need her. He'd survived for a long time without her. *Fuck* her. He was done with her. She lived on the opposite side of town, hung out with a totally different crowd, lived a completely different kind of life. They'd never run into each other. Easy peezy. Ari Sharapov was officially *done* with Valentine O'Dell.

All of which he repeated to himself when he headed down to Caché on Thursday night.

I'm a member. A member for life, at one of the hottest places in the city. There's a lot of rooms in Caché, I probably won't even run into her.

He hadn't been down to the Club Room in a long time. Just walking into it filled him with a sense of deja vu. He scanned the floor quickly, and though it was packed, he could already tell Valentine wasn't in it. The girl ... *shined* when she danced. Like there was always a spotlight trained on her. It's how he'd found her so easily that first night, that first time.

She wasn't in the Moon Room, thank god, because there seemed to be an orgy going on in there. She wasn't in the Music Room, either. She wasn't in the rooms upstairs—one of which was hosting some sort of fight club. He stopped looking when he realized that he was actually actively looking for her. That's not why he was there, not at all. Before he could leave, though, the gorgeous, large and in charge, "Lady of the House" stepped into the hallway and rubbed a long feather across Ari's chest.

"Long time, no see, handsome," Charice purred low in her throat, then she tickled the feather under his chin. He batted it away.

"Always a pleasure," he grumbled. "Seen our little saint anywhere?"

"Maybe," she sighed, stepping close and pressing herself against him. "What's that kind of information worth to you?"

"Sorry, sugar," he chuckled. "After what I bid a couple weeks ago, I'm fresh out of payments for people."

Charice stepped back and plunked her hands on her hips. It was funny; she was a tiny woman. Even in her kitten heels, she was maybe five-foot-three, at the most, almost a foot shorter than him. Yet her presence was so large, he almost—*almost*—felt intimidated by her.

"She left maybe half an hour ago. Saw her sneaking out with a date," she explained. Ari resisted the urge to scowl.

"So she's gone for the night."

"Yeah, I doubt she's coming back."

"Of course," he grunted. He felt like he wanted to vomit. Or kill someone. Instead of doing either, he straightened out his jacket and tie. "I guess I should've shown up a little earlier if I wanted to see someone who's in such high demand."

He went to turn away, but the ostrich feather brushed against his cheek, so he looked back.

"Or you could go find her right now."

Well, well. Charice was full of surprises.

"You know where she is?"

"No. But I think I know who she's with …"

Evans Daniels was somewhat nondescript when a person attempted to describe him—brown hair, brown eyes, average height. Yet Ari still knew *exactly* who Charice was describing. His blood turned into straight up magma, setting his entire body on fire with rage.

It was late, and if Evans had bought a date, that meant they had to go somewhere there was food. At least, that's how Ari had interpreted Val's weird rules about her dates—she only went to restaurants and/or Caché.

There were only so many places open after midnight that served decent food, even in a large city like Chicago, so that narrowed down the choices. As Ari pulled away from Caché, he ran through a list of places he knew off the top of his head. When he landed on the name *Dots*, he paused for so long at a red light, the car behind him honked.

Dots—a dark, funky little after-hours pub. He'd recommended it

WHAT WE DO IN THE LIGHT

to Evans when the man had complained about having trouble finding good late night spots. It was also the kind of place Valentine would love, with its vintage décor and eclectic style.

Why didn't I ever bring her here?

It didn't matter. Why was he even thinking about? Valentine was no longer his concern—she'd made it *painfully* clear that they were over. That she wanted nothing to do with him. She was free to date whoever she wanted, do whatever she wanted. It didn't concern him. Didn't bother him.

Nope, doesn't bother me at all.

That was the thought running through Ari's head as Valentine quickly pulled her hand free from Evans'.

"This isn't what it looks like," she spoke quickly, and he was surprised. Why defend herself to someone who didn't mean anything to her?

"Looks like two friends enjoying some late night food," he replied. That took some of the wind out of her sails, and her mouth opened and closed a few times as she sought for a reply.

"Looks like it's about to be three," Evans chimed in, and he scooted further into the circular booth. "Take a seat."

"I think I will."

But he didn't take the empty space next to Evans. He simply started to move in next to Valentine, leaving the pair of them with no choice but to quickly slide out of the way. When they were finally all situated, his knee was brushing against hers.

What am I doing? Why am I here? When did I become so pathetic? I just stalked her down. Sweet jesus, I'm Harper. Valentine was right—all us rich people are fucking weird.

"What brings you downtown tonight?" Evans asked good naturedly, smiling broadly at both of them. Valentine was staring at Ari like she couldn't decide if he was a mirage or not.

"Just looking for something to … *nibble* on," he replied, smirking at her. "I had to work late, so I decided to go out and look for trouble."

"You found it. I haven't seen you in a while, Ari. What's new?" Evans asked, swirling his drink in his glass before taking a sip.

"Not a whole lot," Ari replied casually. "Hired a new assistant a while back."

"The man who hates to work with others has an assistant?" Evans laughed. "I'm almost impressed. Must be someone really special."

"You could say that," Ari said, still staring at Valentine. "Pity she quit without giving notice. We have unfinished business to work through."

Valentine abruptly stood up, causing the table to rock and tip forward. Evans managed to grab ahold of it before it went over, and Ari saved their drinks from sloshing everywhere. Then he was quickly moving as Val tried to shove her way out of the booth.

"Thanks for the drinks and food," she spoke quickly as she reached into the side of her cleavage and pulled out a small coin purse. Evans held up his hands.

"No, no, on me. I dragged you away from work, so my treat. You can get it next time we go out."

His stupid grin was back, despite Ari glaring at him.

"Whatever," she grumbled, then she gave both of them a half hearted wave. "Bye, guys."

She all but ran out of the pub, the door slamming shut behind her. It belatedly occurred to Ari that Evans must have driven them there. Would she run all the way back to Caché?

"I take it that went exactly how you hoped it would?" Evans asked in a casual voice. Ari glared at him, then stood up, his movements slow as he tucked his tie back inside his jacket.

"I take it this all went exactly how *you* planned it," he countered. "I warned you about her."

"Ah, but she's a free agent now—you don't own her time anymore," Evans pointed out. "You fucked that all up."

"She told you that?"

"Her co-workers like to gossip with big tippers."

WHAT WE DO IN THE LIGHT

"Fuckers," he growled. "And it doesn't matter—she's still off limits. Don't push me on this."

"I won't," Evans sighed. "She already gave me the same speech."

"She did?"

"Yes. She won't have anything to do with me because of you."

"She said that?" Ari checked, and his heart dropped a little when Evans shrugged.

"Not exactly, but pretty close. What's going on with you two, anyway?" he asked. "First you had a whole 'Pretty Woman' thing going on, and then she hated you, and just now she looked like she wanted to swallow her own head when you walked up."

"What's going on is none of your business," Ari replied, then he grabbed Evans' drink and knocked back the contents in one gulp.

"Ooohhh, I see," Evans spoke in a soft voice. "Fucked it up again, didn't you, Sharapov. Two cracks at an amazing woman like Val, and you still couldn't hang onto her."

Ari glared down at him, but he wasn't really mad at Evans.

He was mad at himself.

"What can I say? I'm just exceptionally talented that way."

Evans sighed, then slid out of the booth, as well.

"We're not friends, are we, Sharapov?" he asked. Ari thought for a second.

"Not particularly, no."

"Which is a shame, because we're alike in a lot of ways. Both a couple of cocky bastards."

"If you say so."

"But the difference between us is you get your cockiness from everything you *have*," Evans explained. "I get mine from everything I *am*."

"Do you sell tickets to your self-help seminars?" Ari asked, glancing at his watch. "I'll buy some next time you're having a show—I'm a little busy right now."

"So no matter what happens to me, I'm good," Evans continued.

"I've always got me. But what'll happen to you if something happens to all those things you have? Your lofty job, your nice apartment, your fancy car? Your rich daddy? Your connections?"

"Are you saying I shouldn't own nice shit because it makes me shallow?" Ari checked. "Because last I saw, you were driving a Range Rover."

"That's not what I'm saying at all, and I think you know that. Christ, why am I even bothering? She deserves way better than you," Evans groaned before storming out of the bar. Ari sighed and watched as the front door slammed shut for a second time that night.

Finally, Evans, we agree on something.

14

Between Evans and Valentine, Ari had a lot to think about.

The next day, Ari stood in front of his desk, his gaze bouncing around his office.

His degrees hung in frames on the wall. A teak desk dominated the room, with matching bookshelves behind it. Several awards were displayed on their shelves. An original Basquiat hung on the wall—a gift from his father when he'd landed his first account for the firm.

For the *firm*.

He couldn't even remember what company it had been. He hadn't even cared, he'd just wanted to impress his father. Impress the partners.

He hadn't even cared.

He didn't want to work in corporate law. He'd never wanted to; he found it boring and soul sucking.

He wanted to be a trial lawyer.

He didn't want to wait five years to inherit his father's share of this firm.

He wanted to have his own practice, his own firm.

These were all thoughts he'd had before, but he'd always quieted them. Had always taken the path of least resistance. Valentine had practically been screaming them at him the other night, begging him to listen to her, to listen to *himself*, and he'd refused. He was a robot, built from the ground up by his father, to do the things his father had taught him, to follow in his footsteps.

I want to walk my own path. How come I automatically believed that attempting to do so would only end in failure? How come it never once occurred to me that was an option? Not once. Not in high school. Not in college. Not in law school. I'm a Sharapov—this is just what Sharapovs do.

Valentine didn't want him, but he didn't want to let go of her.

He wanted to be with her.

Which would I prefer, to have my father like me, or to like myself?

Such a simple question, yet so deep. It was embarrassing that he even had to ask it. His father should like him no matter what, and a good father would want his son to like himself.

*I don't ever want to see Valentine with Evans Daniels again. I don't ever want to see her walking away from me again. I don't ever want to let her down again. Jesus, when did I become such a quitter? Spent three weeks trying to get her back, and then when I had her in my hands, I let go at the first push. She's right—she believed in me more than I ever did. I'm such an idiot. She said it, and I didn't even understand it. Didn't even believe it. Didn't even hear it, and then I was too angry to even think about it. **Such a fucking idiot.***

"Rose!" Ari shouted. By the time he turned around, the secretary was standing in his doorway.

"Is everything okay?" she asked, glancing around.

"Better than okay," he said, loosening his tie. "Is my father in?"

"Yes, he's—"

"Tell him I need to speak with him, now."

"Alright," she said, but then she hesitated. "Are you sure you're okay?"

He opened his mouth to repeat his answer from before, then hesitated.

Baby steps. Slay a tiny dragon now. Slay the bigger ones as they come.

"No," he responded. "I've been fucking miserable for so goddamn long, I got used to it, and then forgot about it. Didn't even realize it."

Rose's eyes blinked rapidly behind her tortoiseshell glasses, then she slowly smiled at him.

"I know how you feel, sir. I'll go get Mr. Sharapov."

After she disappeared, Ari yanked his tie completely loose, pulling it over his head and shoving it into his jacket pocket. He dropped his briefcase on his desk and opened it, then walked over to the wall and started pulling down his diplomas one by one. He placed them all carefully in his case. It may not be the life he wanted, but it hadn't been all bad. He'd accomplished some amazing things, all while doing something he didn't even like. How must better would he be when he was doing something he enjoyed?

"Rearranging?" his father's voice asked from behind him. Ari glanced at the older man, then he moved over to his shelf, picking up the few awards and putting them in the case, as well, before shutting it.

Someone else could pack up the rest for him.

"Something like that," he replied. His dad waved his hand.

"Leave that to one of the girls. Give them something to do, they're all so lazy," he grumbled.

This. This was Ari's future if he stayed. A bitter, angry old man. A hateful old man who drove everyone away from him, all in the pursuit of stature. A bigot. A misogynist. Ari wanted power, and money, and accolades, but not if it meant becoming like his father. How had he not thought about that before?

This whole time, I thought I was killing time until he was gone so I could do something different, when all along, I was becoming more and more like him.

"I hate corporate law," Ari blurted out. His dad gave him a strange look.

"Really? You've been practicing it for a long time for someone who hates it."

"I practice it because that's what *you* wanted," Ari said. "All my life, you told me I had to go into the family business. You told me you wouldn't pay for school unless I studied law, and then you told me you wouldn't pay for law school unless I specialized in corporate law. You never gave me any options, and I'm a fucking pussy, because I never even thought to ask for any."

His father looked shocked for a moment—they'd had their share of fights and rows, but Ari was pretty sure he'd never spoken to his dad that way before. Then shock gave way to anger and the elder Sharapov's face started turning red. Ari wondered if his face did the same thing.

"You're goddamn right I told you what to study," his dad sputtered. "You were an asshole who didn't know any better, you needed a firm hand to guide you! And it was *my* money! You think I'm going to invest in something without having a stake in it?"

"Your stake was *me*," Ari said, pressing a hand to his chest. "I'm your *son*. Who gives a shit if I practiced in your law firm or not? I could've been an amazing lawyer working for anybody, but I could only work for you, that was all you'd accept."

"You're goddamn right. I *made* you—you owed me."

Ari suddenly had an acute idea of how Valentine felt when she tried to argue with him. It was like talking to a wall. A very annoying, egotistical wall.

"I shouldn't have to *owe* my father anything," Ari argued.

"Sentimental babble bullshit," his father spit out. "What's gotten into you? Where is this all coming from? That new girlfriend? If this is the kind of bullshit she's putting in your head, you have to get rid of her."

"She's not going anywhere. That's twice now you've almost ruined us," Ari said, snapping his briefcase shut. "I won't let you do it again."

"What are you even talking about? I haven't even met her!" his dad shouted.

"And until you can learn how to act like a human being, you won't ever meet her. You're not worthy of meeting her."

"This has to be a joke," Don Sharapov grumbled. "All these years, all the time I've invested in you. I've given you *everything*, and what, you're just going to walk away?"

"Yes. Yes, I am."

Ari could literally feel a weight lift from his shoulders, one he hadn't even realized he'd been bearing his whole life.

"The hell you are!" his dad roared. "You walk away from me, boy, and I'll *destroy* you. I'll take every contact you've got. Every client! And after a couple phone calls, you think any other firm in town will hire you?"

Before, Ari would've said no. But Evans' words rattled around in his brain.

"No matter what happens, I'm good, because I've always got me."

Ari finally got it. For such a smart person, sometimes he was so incredibly dumb.

"Yes," he said firmly. "I think someone will. And even if they won't, there's other cities. Other states. Other countries. Other jobs. Someone, somewhere, will believe in me. Pity my own father doesn't."

As he snatched his briefcase off the desk and headed for the door, his father started raging behind him.

"I believed in you more than anyone else in your whole life!" he shouted, following his son out of his office and onto the main floor, seemingly not caring that he was airing the family laundry in front of all the other lawyers and secretaries. "I raised you, I built you up, I *made you*! I can tear you down! Don't you walk away from me!"

Literally every single one of Ari's worst fears was coming true, and shockingly, he felt like laughing. Opening his mouth as wide as he could, and just *guffawing*. Why did he go so long without doing this? To get the love and acceptance from a father who could treat him like this?

Oh, Saint Valentine, we're gonna have a lot of shit to work through after I get you back.

"Rose!" he snapped, looking around for her cubicle. Everyone on the floor, including his father, turned to look at the redhead in shock. She stared back at Ari, her eyes as big as saucers.

"Uh … yes, Mr. Sharapov?" she asked.

"Remember my offer?" he asked back, holding out his arms. "Now's the time. I'm getting the fuck out of here, and according to my father, no one will hire me. Wanna come be a paralegal for an out of work lawyer?"

A pin drop could've been heard in that moment. His father's eyes looked like they were going to roll out of his head. Rose glanced around at everyone, then bent down behind her cubicle wall. There was the sound of things being hastily shuffled around, then she appeared on the floor, hurrying towards him.

"Sounds fun, sir," she said. She was breathing hard and looked nervous, but she beamed up at him.

From beside him, his father's rage reached Defcon 4.

"If you walk out with him," he hissed, spittle flying from between his teeth. "I will personally make sure you never work in law *ever* again. *Anywhere* in this country."

"With all do respect, sir," she took a deep breath. "Screw you. You're mean, you give the worst Christmas bonuses I've ever seen, and your breath stinks."

Ari barked out a laugh. Who knew the tiny girl had it in her?

He gestured towards the exit with his case, so she hastily turned around and hurried towards it. He followed, with his father close at his heels. When they emerged into the lobby, his dad pulled him to a stop.

"*Aaron*," he growled. "Do not walk away from this! This is your life! Are you really going to ruin your life for some girl? For some piece of ass?"

Ari thought for a long moment.

"No," he answered, shaking his head. "I'm going to *save my life* for that piece of ass. Goodbye, Dad. Call me if you ever decide you'd rather be a father than a boss."

And with that, he stepped onto the elevator, pulling Rose along when she just stood there gaping at him. His father kept ranting and cursing, but Ari didn't hear him at all. Just smiled back as the doors slid shut.

An awkward silence settled over the elevator for a couple floors, then Rose couldn't hold it in any longer.

"What was *that?*" she burst out. "What just happened? What is going on?"

"We just quit one of the most prestigious law firms in the country," he clarified for her. Her face went pale.

"Are you okay, sir?"

"Never better, why?"

"You're breathing hard," she pointed out. Ari glanced down at his chest. He hadn't even realized it, but he was breathing like he'd just run a race.

I did—I just barely managed to outrun a terrifying future.

"I'm okay, I promise. Are *you* okay?" he asked. She shook her head and shrugged.

"I have no idea."

"You better figure it out—you might be able to get your job back if you head back right now," he offered. She pursed her lips.

"Did you mean what you said?"

"About quitting? Every word."

"No, about me working for you."

"I don't have a job right now," he was honest. "I didn't even plan on doing this today. But I have a healthy savings account, as well as a trust fund. I can pay you out of my pocket until I figure shit out."

She nodded her head.

"Then I'm with you, sir, on one condition."

"What's that?"

"I want my job to cover my education expenses," she said. "I'm not a certified paralegal yet."

"We can make that happen."

"And one more thing."

"Jesus christ, I'm already regretting this. What is it?"

"If you ever do start your own firm, I want a chance to invest in it."

Ari's eyebrows shot up.

"You have a lot of faith in me, Rose," he said, and she nodded her head.

"After what I just witnessed, I do. Just don't fuck up, okay?"

He grinned at her.

"I'll try my best not to."

The elevator dumped them out in the garage. Security was actually waiting at the doors to escort them from the building. They knew Ari well, though, and the elder Sharapov was not well liked. They hung back, apologizing for even being there. Ari offered to give Rose a ride home, but she had her own car, so they just exchanged contact information. They agreed upon a two week break—during which she would still get paid—before meeting up again to make some solid plans.

"Starting from zero is gonna be hard," she sighed as she slid into her car. "No references, no clients."

Ari paused at the word client, then smiled.

"I wouldn't say zero. My name still carries some weight—I won one of the biggest settlements in Cook County's history," he reminded her. "That'll mean something to somebody, regardless of what my father says. Besides which, I'm pretty sure I already have a client."

"You do? Someone outside of here?" Rose asked, glancing around them.

"Yeah. Someone who'll give us a lot of business, too. I'll talk to you in two weeks, Rose."

"Talk to you in two weeks, *boss*."

He shut her door for her, then headed to his own car. He sat behind the wheel for a while, almost shaking from all the adrenaline rushing through his veins. He felt high. He felt invincible. He felt … nervous. What if this was all for nothing?

No. He wouldn't think that way. If he could finally stand up to his dad, and he could finally take control of his future, then surely he could get Valentine back, and he could make it work between them. Though to be fair, Valentine was a lot scarier than his father.

One dragon at a time, Valentine. You may not be a damsel in distress, and I'm beginning to think you never were, but I'm still slaying them for you.

15

"So. Got another hot date tonight?" Valentine teased.

"What? No, it's not like that," Bailey mumbled, her pale cheeks turning bright red as she practically dove head first into a large box. "We've got a mission around five, that's it."

"Jesus, do you ever sleep?"

"Who needs sleep when there's orcs to kill?"

"Ah, young love. So romantic."

"Shut up."

Valentine laughed, then looked around the sea of boxes around them. They had the house pretty much packed up and ready to go. On Sunday, Serge was going to come with huge pickup truck and haul it all to a storage unit for them. Then Bailey and Valentine would share a room at Charice's house, just until they could find a suitable place of their own.

Just because there's a gorgeous, empty, perfect apartment open in Ari's building doesn't make it suitable.

She wasn't allowed to think Ari's name, it was one of her rules. It had been a week since she'd ended things, and she hadn't heard from him at all. It was just like she'd thought, he wasn't willing to fight for her when it came down to it. Didn't make it hurt any less.

You're still thinking about him. Stop it.

"So do you think you two will ever meet?"

She distracted herself by focusing on Bailey's budding romance with Evans Daniels little brother, Devlin. *Devlin Daniels,* she wanted to laugh every time she heard it. Bailey loved it, though; her online crush had a superhero name.

"I don't know," Bailey sighed. "Maybe. Some day. In the far off future."

"Evans is going there next week, I bet you could hop a ride with him," Valentine pointed out.

"Oh, sure, okay—let me just whip air fare out of my ass," Bailey laughed, and Valentine chuckled, as well.

"Fair point. But still. You like him. He likes you. You should go for it. Grab life by the balls."

"Says the woman who dumped the man she's in love with, and now spends all day moping around her room."

Moping. There's that word again. Del had called me "mopey" the first time Ari and I broke up. I hate that word.

"I do not 'mope'," she argued. "I ... think very hard while laying in a horizontal position."

"And also while occasionally shuffling to the kitchen to eat another pint of ice cream."

"Gee, will you look at that!" Valentine gasped, holding up her wrist and pretending to look at a watch that wasn't there. "Time for my last day at work."

"Sounds riveting. I'm gonna head to work," Valentine sighed, and she sat down to pull on a pair of houndstooth print, knee-high boots. They had a high stilleto heel, and were a perfect pop of funk for the white tube dress she was wearing.

"Where do you find all your clothes?" Bailey asked, gawking at the outfit.

"Thrift shops, mostly. Then I alter them myself. You good?" Valentine asked, raising her hands to gently feel at the elaborate braids all around her head. They were artfully messy and carefully pinned in place, and it didn't feel like she'd messed any of them up while helping Bailey pack.

"All good. Have fun tonight—I can't imagine the kind of send off they're going to give to their Saint Valentine."

"I told you that you could come," Valentine remind her as she shrugged into a flared black trench coat.

"Nah. Flirting with Devlin online is more fun than any party," Bailey replied.

"*Ha!*" Valentine clapped. "I knew you were flirting! Killing orcs, my ass."

"I didn't mean it—"

"Just remember to name your first born after me. See you on Sunday!" Valentine laughed as she hurried out the door. A sleek Lincoln town car was waiting for her at the curb—a going away present from Del. No last bike ride into the city. No sketchy Uber drivers. Saint Valentine really would be going out in style.

Of course Del had made a production out of her leaving. She hadn't been allowed to see the club all week, so she was stunned when she walked inside. The hardwood floors had been covered with red shag carpets, and red chandeliers hung down the center of the main hall. All the rooms had been opened, and different love-themed events were happening on either side.

There was "Pin the Heart on the Cupid"—a sexy guy was painted in gold from head to toe, and was wearing the tiniest pair of gold man-panties. His *very* generous bulge was *very* distracting. Blindfolded men and women were taking turns attempting to slap a heart sticker over his actual heart. The people who managed to accomplish it got a naughty lap dance, sans gold panties.

His bulge was also *very* real.

The other side of the room held something very different—at one end, a professional matchmaker sat behind a desk, giving free consultations. At the other end, an alleged psychic specializing in relationships had set up shop. Del had been showing Valentine everything, and he led her straight to the psychic's table.

"This chick right here, she needs help, Madam Zolo," he said.

"*Zolo?*" Valentine laughed. "No offense, ma'am, but I don't believe in this stuff."

"Then what I have to say won't matter. Sit," the psychic—Zolo—offered.

"I'm good, I don't—"

Del all but pushed her into the chair. She sat down with a jolt, then glared up at him.

"Your hand, please," Madam Zolo requested. Del didn't even give her a chance to resist, he just grabbed her hand and slapped it into the psychic's.

"I wanna go downstairs, Del," she whispered out the side of her mouth. "This is sweet and all, but isn't this supposed to be *my* night?"

"Shut your yap," he whispered back.

"Ah, so many problems," Zolo clucked her tongue. "But that is to be expected. Do you know the story of Saint Valentine?"

"Yeah, yeah," Val said, trying to pull her hand back. The old lady had a surprisingly strong grip. "Patron saint of beekeeping, epilepsy, the plague, love, all sorts of shit."

The psychic shook her head.

"He was a bishop," she said. "When Emperor Claudius banned marriages, Valentine continued marrying people in secret. For the crime of defending love, of loving love, and of loving those around him, Valentine was imprisoned, tortured, and then beheaded. He was quite literally a martyr for love."

Val swallowed thickly. Of course she'd generally known the story of Saint Valentine, but the woman spoke with such gravity, the story took on a new meaning. One Val didn't care to delve into too much.

"I suppose if you have to be a martyr for something, that's a pretty good one. Are we all done?" she asked, jerking on her arm. The woman held fast.

"Your road has not been easy. You have been imprisoned in a life that was not always your own choosing, and you have been plagued—*tortured*—by cruel twists of fate."

Valentine went very still. The woman was pretty spot on. She swallowed thickly and glanced around. Del was listening intently, chewing on his thumb nail.

"What are you saying? I'm about to be beheaded?" she tried to make a joke.

"I'm saying it has already happened. The mind and heart have been separated. *Severed,*" the psychic explained, slashing her free hand across her neck dramatically. Valentine winced. "You are at once love's executioner, *and* its martyr."

"I feel like we're taking this analogy a little too far," Val replied.

"A," the psychic blurted out.

"A ... what?"

"A ... a ... two a's?" Madam Zolo seemed to be talking to herself more than anything.

"Two a's for what?" Valentine asked. Zolo closed her eyes and seemed to concentrate.

"No wait, there's more," she murmured. "A ... a ... ron. A A Ron?" Valentine almost burst out laughing at the psychic's unintentional joke, but when she said the next word, Val completely froze in place. "No, *Aaron.*"

"How do you know that name?" Valentine demanded. Zolo opened her eyes.

"Aaron—do you know what this word means?" she asked.

"It's his name," Val whispered.

"Is rooted in Hebrew," Zolo continued, staring very directly at Valentine. "And means *'bearer of martyrs'.*"

Valentine yanked her hand away so violently, she started to fall backwards in her chair. Luckily Del was able to grab her before she completely tipped over, and when she was stable again, she scrambled out of her seat.

"This is sick," she snapped, her glare bouncing between the two of them. "Play your games with your clients, Del, but not with me."

"Whoa now," her *ex*-boss held up his hands. "I had nothing to do with this, doll. Madam Zolo is the real deal!"

"And I'm the real saint," Val snarled, and then she whirled around, stomping out of the room.

While she hurried through the building, ignoring all the cheers and catcalls being shouted at her, she pulled out her phone. She Googled the meaning of the name "Aaron", and sure enough, Madam Zolo had been telling the truth. The name had several potential meanings, one of which was "bearer or martyrs".

What are the chances? I'm named after a martyr, and he's a bearer of martyrs. **What are the chances!?**

All it really meant was Madam Zolo and Del had done their homework. It was a sick trick to pull, especially on her last night. She'd barely spoken about Ari at all to anyone at work, had just casually mentioned to Charice that they weren't together anymore, so he probably wouldn't be coming to the club much more.

Gossip spread around Caché like wild fire, though, so she wasn't shocked that it had reached Del. She was more surprised that he'd taken such an interest in it that he'd involved some fake psychic. Christ, he didn't even like Ari! Why was he messing with her head!?

Valentine fell back to her old routine—she escaped to the Club Room. Air canons shot confetti into the air at her entrance, scaring the shit out of her. Everyone clapped and cheered, and she was surprised with a performance by a local dance squad. After they were done, women with champagne bottles lined up on either side of the room and popped the corks, sending sprays of bubbly flying into the crowds.

The joint went nuts after that; all her favorite songs were played, and Valentine danced to all of them. Old clients and new clients, co-workers from past and present, everyone came out to dance with her, and she was surprised to find herself feeling so emotional. She'd felt so alone over the months, and now she felt guilty for doing so. She had a huge family, right here. It was weird and it was fucked up and it had way too much nudity going on at any given point in time.

But they were her family. And that night, she loved each and every one of them.

So why do I still feel alone?

Around two o'clock in the morning, she was ready to take a break. She was trying to sneak up a back set of stairs to the break room, but Del caught her.

"No, no, no, my little nincompoop," he laughed, grabbing her by the hips and forcing her back down the stairs. "The night is still young! I have one last surprise for you!"

"If it's anything like your first surprise, I don't want it," Val warned him.

"Hey, hand to god, swear on my mother, I had nothing to do with that. That bitch must be the real deal," Del said, moving to walk next to her and shuddering. "If I had known, I wouldn't have hired her."

"Really?"

"Of course not! Last thing I need is some broad being able to see into my cooked books with her third eye, or whatever. I've seen the Long Island Medium, I know how this shit works."

Valentine burst out laughing as they walked back into the Club Room. The party was still raging, but Del lifted his hands in the air, waving them up and down. The music faded out, causing everyone to groan in protest.

"Alright, alright, shut the fuck up!" Del barked, shouting to be heard as he pushed his way through the crowd, dragging Valentine behind him. "We got one last surprise—one last *gift*—before we bid this saint farewell!"

At the center of the dance floor was a wide, circular go-go podium, with a stripper pool extending between it and the ceiling. Del jumped onto the podium, then helped Valentine up to stand next to him.

"Now, you all know her, you all love her. Our very own Saint Valentine. She hasn't worked here very long, but she's become a cornerstone of Caché. Her infamy will live on for years, and though I'm so fucking happy for her I could cry, it breaks my heart to see her go. Valentine, you're a peach. One of the best. If I'd ever had a daughter,

I'd have wanted her to be like you," Del said, turning to look down at her. She smiled up at him, sniffling to keep the tears at bay.

"Awww, that's sweet, Del."

"Well, you know, like you, but maybe doesn't dress so slutty."

The crowd burst out laughing. She punched him in the arm, but she was laughing, too.

"Alright, alright, enough of the mush! A month ago, Valentine here pulled in the biggest bid we've ever had at one of our St. Patrick's Day auctions, but I recently found out her bidder broke the rules of the contract! So that bid is null and void. I propose that right here, right now, we start the bidding again!"

While the crowd cheered, Valentine frowned and started yanking on Del's jacket.

"Del!" she hissed. "No! This is my last night, I'm not gonna spend a week working for one of your regulars!"

"Don't be so selfish," Del hissed back. "I lost twenty-five grand because of you! Had to give St. Jude's their cut out of my own pocket! Let me get at least some of it back!"

Ari had gotten his money back? Jesus, how? Del would fight a starving child over a nickel. Ari must have gone through his credit card company or bank, disputed the charge.

What kind of jerk does that? Just because I broke up with him? I've been moping—yes, I admit it, moping—at home, praying for him to come to his senses and call me. And all he cared about was his money. About being in control of a situation. Stupid dick. God, I hate him.

While Del went over the rules of the impromptu auction, Valentine delicately wiped tears away from the corners of her eyes. It didn't matter. Ari Sharapov didn't matter to her. He could be as big of an asshole as he wanted—it didn't affect her life, not one little bit. She squared her shoulders and took a deep breath, then smiled brilliantly when Del set the starting bid at two thousand dollars.

"Two thousand!?" she gasped melodramatically. "Have you *looked* at me? C'mon, people, let's start at five!"

A famous local rapper kicked it off with five, and was followed by one of the basketball players who'd been there the other week; he immediately raised it to eight. She didn't expect to get as high a bid as Ari's, of course, or anything even close to it. People planned and saved for the St. Patrick's Day event. So it was flattering knowing that on the spur of the moment, people were still willing to drop a couple thousand dollars just to spend time with her.

Yeah, super duper flattering. Same ol' story. This night cannot end soon enough.

"C'mon, people? Twelve? We're stalling at twelve? I'm fucking embarrassed! This is Valentine, and this is your last chance to win her!" Del shouted, looking over the crowd angrily. Val was a little taken aback by how seriously he was taking the whole thing. "Do you hear me? Your absolute *last fucking chance* to win her!"

There was a murmur in the crowd, people seemed a little confused. Valentine was a little embarrassed. One guy started to raise his hand, thankfully, but then a voice from the back of the crowd called out a bid.

"Zero dollars!"

There was a collective gasp, of which Valentine was a part of.

"Who said that!?" Del demanded, shielding his eyes from the bright spotlight shining down on them. People started to sway and move as someone shoved their way through.

"Zero dollars," the bidder called again. "And not a penny more."

Valentine couldn't honestly say she was shocked when Ari stepped out of the crowd. Anger, embarrassment, humiliation, confusion, hurt, all of those emotions were there. But she wasn't shocked.

"You saying my little Saint Valentine here ain't worth nothing?" Del asked, jerking his thumb in her direction. A couple people in the house booed. "You saying you think she's worth *nothing*?"

Valentine stared down the length of her nose at Ari, hoping he could feel all the disgust for him that was raging inside of her.

WHAT WE DO IN THE LIGHT

"I'm saying," he spoke slowly, never taking his eyes off of her. "That she's *priceless.*"

I hate when he does that. Here I am, ready to hate him all over again, and he has to ruin it by saying something so unlike him and so amazing, it blows all the anger right out of my brains.

16

The whole scene, tt was corny, and it was cheesy, and it was so perfect, half the women in the audience let out audible *awwws* at Ari's statement.

Valentine didn't say anything.

Del snorted.

"Words ain't worth shit—your contract was voided," he snapped. Ari still didn't look away from her.

"By you," he countered. "Your saint stopped doing her job. She still owes me two days."

"Is this true?" Del gasped, and for the first time, Val realized he was in on the whole thing. "My little Vally-wally reneged on one of my deals? I don't believe it! Unacceptable!"

And then he was abruptly grabbing her arm, forcing them both to jump down off the podium. Before she knew what was happening, she was standing in front of Ari.

"Sorry, folks! Looks like the last bidder came to claim his prize after all! Now you have your choice, kind sir. You can take her back for those days, or you can ask for straight payment. What will it be?"

Ari pretended to think for a moment.

"I choose the payment."

"A wise choice, sir, a wise choice."

Before Valentine could ask what kind of payment—cash? Credit?

Her heart?—Ari was kissing her, both his hands spearing into the hairdo she'd worked so hard on. This time, the whole crowd awwwed for her. Then Del was shouting for the music to come back on, and as the beats started rocking again, the crowd surged around them.

"What do you think you're doing!?" Val asked when she'd managed to shove Ari away.

"Slaying my very last dragon, I hope," he said.

"Fuck your dragons!" she hissed. "I am not some … conquest for you! Not some object you can fuck around with whenever you're feeling bored, or lonely!"

"I don't think—"

"Not some *whore* you can just bid on!"

"Let's go over this one last time," he said, pointing his finger in her face. "And then never, ever again. As I've tried to tell you, I didn't really call you a whore, I don't think of you that way. I only said it because my father—"

"'*My father, my father,*'" she mocked him. "You're a thirty year old man, Ari. Grow some fucking balls."

He covered the scant remaining distance between them, and they were now so close together, her chest was pressed against him. But she refused to step back.

"The incredible amount of patience I've had while dealing with *you* shows what kind of balls I have," he replied in a low voice.

"Easy to be ballsy around a *whore*. Daddy, though, that would take a real man."

"You wanna know what the *real* problem is?" he spoke slowly. "It's not that I called you a whore. It's not even that you think I actually think that about you. The *real* problem is *you* think you're a whore, and you're mad because I actually said it out loud."

She slapped him across the face.

"*Fuck you.* Why are you here? You're not wanted."

"I highly fucking doubt that," he laughed darkly, rubbing at where she'd hit him. "Why so eager to get rid of me? Is Caché not big enough for both of us? Am I cramping your style? It is your last night—am I keeping you from some hot client? I'd hate to keep some guy waiting for a ride with the incredible Saint Valentine."

She slapped him again.

"I dance and flirt with guys for money—I don't fuck them," she reminded him. "That was only you. Everyone's entitled to one big mistake in their life."

"Oh, I seriously doubt I'm your only mistake."

Her third slap, she really put some torque on her swing. When Ari's eyes met hers again, there was a fire behind them.

"Maybe not, but you're definitely the biggest," she said in a quiet voice.

That gave him pause, so Valentine took the chance to escape. She scurried around him and headed for the back stairs once again. There were just too many people, though, and he caught up to her in the Music Room. He matched her step for step as she moved into a shadowy hallway.

"This is not how I planned this going," he said, standing close behind her while she entered in the code to open the door to the employee-only area.

"*Obviously,*" she snapped, yanking open the door and stomping up the stairs to the first floor. "And I don't give two fucks about your two days, Ari. I'm not going back to that office building."

"There wouldn't be much for you there," he retorted. "And this wasn't about that—I just needed a way in, I thought you would get it."

"Oh, I got it, alright. Loud and clear. You're the one who doesn't get anything—it's *over*," she reminded him. "It's been over."

They were heading for the back door, but before they could reach it, Ari grabbed her arm and spun her around to face him.

"Don't you get it, Valentine? *This,*" he said, gesturing between them, "hasn't *ever* been over. Not since the first time we saw each other."

"Well, it's over now."

She yanked her arm free of him and burst out the back door. Angel was sitting on the steps, smoking a joint, and she let out a startled shout as the door slammed open behind her. Then she started choking and hacking on a cloud of smoke. Valentine ignored it all and practically ran down the steps. Didn't matter much, though. Ari's long legs were able to easily keep up with her.

"No, it's not. Valentine, I quit."

"Good, I quit, too," she panted, striding down the alley towards the street. "I quit my job, and I quit you. Now go away."

Once again he was grabbing her arm, yanking her to a stop.

"*I quit my job.*"

That finally got through her haze of anger. Her jaw dropped and she stared up at him.

"Wait … you … *what?* You quit?" she gasped. He nodded his head, his mouth grim as he looked down at her.

"Quite spectacularly. In front of everyone. You would've loved it."

Valentine would have. She *did*. But she was still confused.

"But … why? Why now?" she asked. "Why would you do that?"

"I did it for you," he answered simply.

She let out a frustrated shriek and shoved at his chest.

"You're such an idiot!" she shouted. "I didn't want you to quit your fucking job!"

"What!?" he asked, grabbing at her flailing arms. "Are you fucking joking?"

"Not for me," she gasped, struggling against him. "For *you*. I wanted you to do what *you* wanted!"

"Oh, Valentine," he started laughing, and that just made her angrier. "We're both idiots."

And then he was reeling her in, his grip on her wrists firm as he forced her arms around his waist. She wiggled and pulled against him, trying to create space.

"I'm not an idiot," she growled.

"You are," he sighed into her hair. "Valentine, I quit because someone wise once told me they believed I could be anything I wanted to be, with or without my father. And I quit because some idiot told me that having confidence in myself was more important than having confidence in the things I could accomplish. But mostly, I quit because I fucking hated my life. It just took me thirty years to realize it."

Valentine had long since stopped struggling. She had her face pressed against his chest, panting into his expensive shirt. She absorbed everything he said, then lifted her head.

"You hate your life?" she asked. He shrugged.

"I was chasing the approval of a man I didn't even like. Trying to achieve a goal I didn't even set for myself, all for dreams I'd never once dreamt. I'm sorry it took me so long to realize that—it's a hard concept to wrap your brain around when it's all you've known since birth."

Valentine squeezed him tightly around the waist, and he finally let go of her wrists.

"I'm so happy for you," she breathed. She hesitated a second before continuing. "And I'm *so* proud of you."

"Me, too," he chuckled. "Let's see how you feel in a couple months when I can't afford to take you out to fancy dinners anymore."

She went still.

"Who said I'll be around you a couple months from now?"

"Me," he said, squeezing her back. "I've rented an office space downtown, and I've already got one client booked—my specialty is corporate law, it'll have to do until I get more training in other areas. I've got an assistant who left my dad's firm to come with me."

"That's amazing," Valentine said, finally stepping back from him. He nodded.

"I know. It's kinda terrifying, but also really fucking exciting."

"Sounds like you're doing pretty okay," she pointed out, and he nodded again.

"I am. For the first time in my life, I'm in control of it. Of everything. I don't need anyone else's help for once," he said. Valentine managed to hold onto her smile, even though his statement cut through her like a knife.

"That's … good, Ari. That's amazing. I wish you nothing but the best."

"Thank you," he said. "I'm sure I'll get it, too. I tend to get what I want, I'm very persistent."

She couldn't help it, she had to laugh.

"And modest, too. Don't forget modest."

"But I don't *want* any of it."

Her laughter died away.

"Um … what?" she blurted out articulately.

"I don't want any of it without you," he clarified. "I quit because it was the right thing to do for me. And I'll keep practicing law because it's what I'm best at. But the only thing I really want, the only thing I *need*, is you. I can do all this on my own. May have taken me a while to figure that out, but I get it. I really do. I can do it. I've already done it. But for the first time ever, I actually *want* someone to help me. And want that someone to be you."

Valentine's heart swelled, but then sputtered.

"What, like as in a receptionist?" she asked cautiously. He rolled his eyes.

"I already have one of those. I was thinking more along the lines of trophy girlfriend," he said. "You know, someone who will dress up sexy to make potential clients jealous of me, and then will fuck my brains out on top of my desk any time I have to work late."

"Sounds like a tough job," Valentine chuckled, but she quickly lost her smile and decided to tackle the elephant in the conversation. "How is your father taking all this?"

"Not well," Ari shrugged. "But that's his choice. He'll either come around, or he won't. But I think he will. I'm his only son. He can write me out of the will, but he can't change my DNA."

"And if he does come around … how will he feel about your

trophy girlfriend?" Valentine asked. She'd seen first hand how strong the senior Sharapov's influence was over Ari. Attachments like that didn't go away over night. Not even over weeks. It would probably take months, or even years.

"Hmmm," Ari murmured, then he rested his hand on her hip, pulling her in close to him again. "He'll probably feel … jealous."

"Jealous?"

"Mmm hmmm. His estranged son will be dating one of the sexiest women in the entire city—who wouldn't be jealous?"

Valentine glowered up at him.

"You know, I haven't accepted the job yet."

"You will."

"Maybe," she countered. "On one condition."

"What is with you women and your conditions?" he groaned. "Fine. What?"

"I don't want to be your trophy girlfriend," she said. He made a face at her.

"Well, you're not gonna be my fucking receptionist, I'll tell you that for free."

"If I'm going to be involved in this, I want to be your partner," she explained. He snorted.

"That's silly, you don't know the first thing about law."

She laughed and swatted at his shoulder.

"Stop it! You know what I mean. I was Caché's arm candy for half a year—I never want that job again. Like I told you the other week, this girl in the dress? That's not me," she insisted, but he shook his head.

"Yes it is," he said. She wanted to argue, but he held up his hand. "She's a part of you. Just like I'll always be *Aaron*, Donald Sharapov's son. That'll never go away. But it doesn't have be *all* that I am. *You* taught me that—why don't you ever give yourself the same respect you give to everyone around you?"

She blinked her eyes rapidly in surprise.

"I ... didn't realize I didn't," she finally responded. "And Bailey said the same thing, that I could be both."

"You already are," he sighed, leaning close. "Saint Valentine isn't such a bad person to be. Sexy, daring, bold. I like Saint Valentine."

"Me, too," she said, biting into her bottom lip. "But like you said, she isn't all of me."

"Oh no, there's also Val. Silly, playful, *gorgeous.*"

"Maybe you could learn to like her, too," she suggested. Ari chuckled, the sound low and thrilling in her ear.

"I'll let you in on a secret," he whispered.

"What?"

"I *love* Val," he growled.

I hate it when he says all the right things.

She was kissing him like she needed him for oxygen. Like she needed him to breathe for her. His hands were instantly on her ass, hauling her up against him.

"Why?" she moaned, raking her nails across his scalp. "Why did it take you so long to figure this shit out!?"

"Hey, my brain's too busy solving multimillion dollar legal issues—*sue me.*"

They stayed attached to each other, pawing and groping and kissing, until Ari was able to hail a taxi. When they fell into the back seat, she didn't care about the driver. She climbed on top of Ari, straddling his lap.

"This is a bad idea," she whispered against his lips.

"How can you keep saying that?" he groaned, dragging his nails up her back. "Are you not feeling what I'm feeling?"

"There's more to it than this," Valentine countered. "We come from different backgrounds, different worlds. Your father will *never* accept me."

"Funny that you also keep saying that."

"Why is it funny?"

"Because you're the one who can't seem to accept *me* because of *my* background," he said, and she honestly didn't have a response for that, mostly because he was completely right. "Just let it go, Valentine. We're in this moment right now. We'll worry about the next one when we get to it. You were brave enough to move to Chicago all on your own, and you were brave enough to take care of your grandmother all by yourself. Now be brave enough to try and make this work with me. That's all I'm asking for—just be brave."

Valentine sighed and smoothed her hands down his chest.

"Easy for you to say."

"Why?"

"You don't have to deal with *you*. You're asking for *a lot* of bravery."

He laughed, slapped her sharply on the ass, and then they were kissing again.

She hadn't heard Ari give an address, but when the taxi rolled up to his building, she wasn't too surprised. They stumbled through the security door and tripped down the hallway, but when they got to the elevator, he didn't stop.

"Where are we going?" she breathed, batting at his hands when he tried to pull down her top.

"My apartment's too far away," he replied, his breath hot against her neck. "Yours is much closer."

"Mine? I don't—"

"You talk too much."

His tongue darted into her mouth, caressing her own, all while his hand fumbled around his pockets. They pressed up against a door, and after a couple moments and few rattles from some keys, it fell open behind them.

Valentine would've fallen if his arm hadn't been around her. As it was, they tripped across the dark living room, landing hard against what felt like a table. She gasped and put her hands behind her, propping herself upright as he pulled away. The door was kicked shut, leaving them in total darkness for a moment, and then the overhead light was switched on. She glanced around the room.

"You furnished it?"

They were in his empty spare apartment. Or at least, it had been empty the one and only time she'd been inside it. Now it was full of stuff, done in a similar style to his own apartment.

"I thought I was going to have to actually rent it out," he explained, shrugging out of his jacket and letting it drop to the floor. "I figured it would be easier if it was furnished."

"It's gorgeous," she said, getting off the table while he kicked off his shoes.

"Thank you, I have excellent taste."

She laughed and turned to watch as he yanked off his tie. When he started undoing his belt, she started snickering all over again.

"Someone's a little eager."

"Valentine, in the past month, I've had sex a grand total of two times," he reminded her, untucking his shirt and deftly unbuttoning it. "That must be some kind of personal record for me—I'm practically a goddamn monk. I'm fucking you within the next thirty seconds. It's up to you to decide whether or not it happens in your dress."

"Wow, I don't think I've ever seen this side of you. I wonder if I could use it to my advantage, maybe get you to—"

"Twenty seconds, Valentine."

She hopped towards the master bedroom on one foot, yanking off her boot as she went. She barely got the second one off before he grabbed her from behind, shoving her through the door into the room. She fell forward, planting her hands on the bed to keep herself from falling. Before she could push herself upright, Ari was up against her, pushing the stretchy fabric of her dress up over her butt.

"No fair, that wasn't anywhere near twenty seconds," she panted. He slapped her on the ass, startling a squeak out of her, then continued pushing on the material. Valentine stood upright, slowly spinning to face him while he pulled the dress over her head and away from her body.

"Twenty seconds was too long to wait for this," he breathed, running his hands over the cups of her strapless bra, fingering the lace work. "Goddamn, Valentine, I've never met another woman who dresses as sexy as you do."

"It's not the clothing, it's the attitude," she informed him. "I've never met a man who looks as good in a suit as you, and I've met a lot of men who wear suits."

"It's not the clothing, it's just that I'm really good looking."

She burst out laughing, but it didn't last long. Ari hadn't been joking about being hard up. One second he was peeling her bra off, and the next she was being tossed into the center of the mattress. Before she'd even settled into place, he was covering her with his body.

"You're naked," she whispered, smoothing her feet up the backs of his bare calves.

"I know," he whispered back. "But you're not."

He worked his way down her body, teeth skimming against her sensitive skin. When he got to her underwear, he bit down, dragging the lace down her legs. When she was able to kick the material away on her own, he moved back up, kissing along her hip bone.

"You're awfully wet, Valentine," he commented as one of his fingers found its way inside her body. "Must have been a fun night at Caché. New client?"

"An old one actually," she replied, then gasped when a second finger abruptly joined the first.

"You met up with an old client tonight?" he growled, pumping his fingers in and out. She moaned and rubbed her lips together, barely managing to nod.

"I did," she said, nodding her head. "He's this massive jerk. Always says the wrong thing. Doesn't know the first thing about women. But he's *amazing* in bed."

"Sounds like a catch. Better not let him get away," he whispered, and then his mouth was where his hand had been, and she was arching off the bed, letting out a loud cry.

Before her spine hit the mattress again, he was moving, his tongue cutting a path up the center of her body. While he moved so his body was between her legs, he kissed her hard, possessing her mouth. Reclaiming it.

"I wanted tonight to be special," he breathed, his left hand skimming up her body to cup her breast.

"It has been," she assured him.

"Romantic, even. You deserve romance."

"I *want* you."

"I had speeches I practiced, things I wanted to say," he kept speaking, though she didn't know why. She could feel him all hot and hard against her thigh, and she didn't care about anything else in that moment. She wanted him inside her, where he belonged.

"You said a lot of things," she told him, kissing her way down his neck.

"But then I fucked it all up, and then you slapped me, and goddamn, that pissed me off. Don't ever fucking hit me again."

"I won't," she promised. "And you didn't fuck anything up."

"There should be rose petals or candles or music, or something," he sighed, dipping his head down to her breast and nibbling at her nipple. "But I'm just not that kind of guy."

"So what kind of guy are you?" she moaned, scratching her nails across his shoulders, willing him to take things further.

"The kind of guy who wants to fuck you as hard and as fast as he can," he growled. "You deserve to be worshiped, Valentine, but I just don't think that's going to happen tonight. I want all of you, and I want it *now.*"

"Jesus, thank god, finally, we agree on something," she groaned. "Because if you take any longer, I'm going to fuck myself."

He roughly grabbed the back of her knee, forcing her leg high up against his side. She slid her hand between their bodies, gripping onto the base of his cock and guiding him inside of her. They both groaned as she expanded and contracted around him, welcoming him.

"You promised hard and fast," she panted. "A verbal contract is binding, someone once told me."

"Hey, legal talk is only sexy when I do it," he grunted, holding himself still above her.

"It's not sexy when anybody does it, Ari."

He pulled his hips back, slowly withdrawing his whole length. She gasped, then moaned as he slid back in. He did this several more times, pumping in and out at an excruciatingly slow speed. Then he slammed in tight, as deep as he could, startling a shout out of her, and grabbed her leg, lifting it so her calf was against his shoulder.

"Did you miss this?" he asked, beginning to fuck her in earnest.

"Always," she replied, dragging her nails down his chest.

"God, the things I'm going to do to you," he panted, his hips moving faster and faster, slamming into her harder and harder. "To make up for lost time. You have *no idea.*"

"Yes, please, so much lost time," she moaned, pumping her hips back against him, wanting every millimeter he had to give.

"I'm going to tie you to my fucking bed, not let you leave for a week," he growled.

"Yes, yes, I want that. I want that, too."

"Fuck you until you can't walk," he threatened. "Spank you until you can't sit."

"All of that, and then more," she nodded in agreement, her hands squeezing and kneading her breasts.

"God, I love how you let me treat you," he whispered, and she felt his teeth against her ankle, biting down hard.

"You can treat me any way you want, if this is the reward," she chuckled darkly.

"You don't deserve a reward," he hissed, shoving her leg to the side and falling on top of her, crushing her to the mattress while his hips jackhammered against hers. She began whimpering in time to his thrusts. "Making me wait for something as good as this."

"If I had known this would be the result, I would've tried it sooner," she said, throwing her head back as a tremor ripped through her body.

"Fuck, Valentine," he groaned. "I'm inside you, and I'm already thinking about the next time I'm going to be inside you. All the time. I want to be like this all the time."

"We will," she babbled. "We will. Fuck, Ari, I'm gonna come. So soon."

"Yes," he breathed. "My favorite. Seeing you under me, out of control and out of your mind. Owning that part of you."

"Ari," she panted, struggling to breathe. "Ari, you … you …"

"What, Valentine!?" he demanded, moving one of his legs up so his knee was right behind her thigh, allowing him to thrust his pelvis at an angle, hitting a spot inside her that actually made her see spots.

"You own all parts of me."

Valentine screamed when she came, loud and long. She briefly wondered how thick the walls were, then forgot all about it when the second wave of her orgasm hit, capsizing all her senses. She locked her limbs around him, holding him tight to her while his hips picked up speed. She shook and she trembled and cried, and when she sank her teeth into his shoulder, it was too much for him. He slammed into her so hard, it drove her up the bed a couple inches, almost ramming her into the headboard. Then he was coming, and his mouth was against her shoulder, and soon enough, she had a bite mark to match the one she'd just left on him.

"That was insane," he was panting against her skin. "You just killed me. My dick is now broken, and I'm dead."

Valentine managed one laugh, but was breathing too hard to do any more. Ari collapsed off to her side, his torso forcing her thighs wide apart.

When the cool air turned their skin clammy, they finally slid apart and Ari pulled the sheet up over their bodies. Once it was settled into place, he laid down on his side close to her, wrapped his arm around her waist, and pulled her into his chest.

"Careful," she breathed. "Apparently you've got a broken dick."

He chuckled, his face nuzzled into her hair.

"I may have been exaggerating."

"I don't know, you seemed touch and go there."

"Give me fifteen minutes, and I'll show you 'touch and go'," he threatened, and judging by what she could feel against her leg, he wasn't lying. She rolled onto her side and faced him.

"What are we doing, Ari," she whispered, pressing her hand against the side of his face.

"Enjoying playful banter before I fuck you again," he said.

"Ari."

"Excuse me, before I 'make love' to you again."

Valentine swallowed thickly.

"You said you loved me," she reminded him. "Outside the club. You said you loved Val. Did you mean it? Or was that just part of your ... grand gesture?"

Ari sighed and closed his eyes, then pulled her close again, so his chin was resting on top of her head and her nose was brushing his clavicle.

"It's been a very eye opening couple of months," he spoke softly. "I went from thinking my life revolved around my father's footsteps— not just thinking it, but believing it—to starting completely from scratch."

"You said you already had a client," Valentine interrupted, just re-membering that fact. He laughed, the sound a deep rumble in her ear.

"We have a fairy godmother," he chuckled. "She cusses like a sailor and owns a lot of dirty businesses—and thank god, because it means I'll always have a job."

"Del!?" Valentine gasped, craning her head back to look up at him. "You got DelVecchio to be your client?"

"I already knew about all his legal problems, and shockingly enough, he didn't have a lawyer on retainer," he explained. "And as bi-zarre as it may seem, we actually get along pretty well."

"It's not bizarre at all, Del gets along with everybody. He just acts like he doesn't."

"Well, he's now the sole client of the Me, Myself, and I law firm. Good thing he can afford my fees."

"Okay, so you're starting your life anew by branching out on your own," Valentine paraphrased as she settled in back under his chin. "What other changes are you planning on making?"

"Apparently I've acquired a sex slave, so that's a pretty big change."

"Ari."

"What? Just a couple minutes ago, you said I could do anything—"

"*Ari.*"

"I plan on learning what being in a real relationship is like," he whispered. "Let's the hope the girl gives me a big learning curve, because I've already fucked up a lot. I'm going to fuck up some more."

"She's fucked up pretty big herself, so I'm sure she'll give it to you," she whispered back.

"I'm going to *make love* to her as often as she'll let me," he continued, and she giggled at his word choice. "And I'm going spend every free moment I have making her believe that she's every bit as beautiful inside and out as I think she is."

"That's a pretty good plan," Valentine sniffled.

"You were right, Valentine. I'm a jerk. An asshole. And that's probably not going to change," he warned her. She shook her head.

"I wouldn't want you to, I love those sides of you."

"I don't know what I'm doing with you," he whispered. "But I know I want to figure it out."

"Me, too."

"When we first met, I liked Saint Valentine from the first moment I saw her," he kept whispering, and she held her breath so she wouldn't miss a word. "And as I got to see more of her, I liked Valentine O'Dell just as much. And when I got to know them as the same person, that's when I liked her the most."

There was a long pause, and she finally let out her breath.

"… but?" she guessed. He sighed.

"I don't know anything about love, Valentine," he said. "I barely remember my mother, and respecting someone and loving someone are two different things—I'm not sure if I love my father. So I don't even really know what love is; but I do know I want to find out with you."

"With me?" she echoed.

"Only you," he nodded. She paused for a long time, struggling with what to say in return. Then her grandmother's voice floated through her mind, from that last conversation.

"If you like him, and he likes you, then there's no harm in trying. What have you got to lose?"

"After my grandmother died," she started speaking low and fast. "I knew I loved you. I mean, I felt it before then. I think I felt it back when we first started sleeping together. But I knew it for sure after Gam-Gam passed. You answered the phone, and you came, and you were the white knight every girl dreams of; you saved me. You took care of everything. I could've done it, you know. I would've pulled myself together and taken care of it myself. But for the first time in a long time, I didn't have to, and that made me fall so in love with you, I knew I wouldn't ever fall back out."

"Jesus, Valentine, then why did you try to end it?"

"Because I didn't want to be with someone who couldn't love me back," she whispered. "I took care of my grandmother because she was sick, but also because I loved her and she loved me."

"And being with me would've meant taking care of me while I went through all my bullshit with my father," he connected the dots. "It would've been the same thing, only for a person you thought wouldn't love you back."

"Exactly. I was in love with you, and I was exhausted. I didn't have any strength left to fight your battles. And when you walked away and you didn't call and you didn't come back, I thought that was it. That I'd lost the only man I'd ever loved, and you'd just lost that girl you used to sleep with."

"Valentine," he sighed. "You are so wonderfully ridiculous."

"Didn't feel so wonderful at the time," she breathed.

"I'll let you in on another secret," he whispered back.

"What's that?"

"I'm even more ridiculous than you," he said. "Because I was in love with you, and I didn't even know it. Didn't even know how to articulate it. I liked your body and I liked your attitude and I liked your personality, and before I knew it, I was in love with all of that, and you were gone, and I was too stupid to realize any of it."

Valentine squeezed her eyes shut tight, letting a couple hot tears fall down her cheeks.

Then she chuckled.

Then she outright laughed.

"What's so funny?" he asked.

"You," she gasped for air. "You are stupid. So stupid."

"Thank you," he grunted.

"You were in love with me, and you let me walk away twice," she cackled.

"Yeah, but I also got you back twice, so at least I'm good at something.

"Maybe, or maybe I'm just even more stupid than you."

"If being in love with me makes you stupid, then I pray you never get smart," he said with a snort.

"I want to meet your dad," she said when her laughter finally subsided.

"Why the fuck would you want to do that?"

"Because he was the most important person in your life," she said. "And now I am."

"Bold assessment of yourself, Valentine."

"And I want to help you at your work. I need a job, anyway."

"I'm not hiring you."

"Why not!?"

"Because working with the person you're living with is a bad idea."

"I'm not moving in with you, Ari."

"Why not!?"

"Because," she laughed as their conversation moved in a circle. "We barely just got back together. Who knows how soon it'll be before one us makes another boneheaded mistake. It's like you said, baby steps. I'll move in here, and we'll pretend we're a normal couple."

"What is a 'normal' couple?" Ari asked, as if "normal" were a foreign word to him.

"I don't know, people who go on dates or whatever."

"Fine. But I get to sleep over whenever I want."

"Deal. Can I work for you now?"

"No," he said. "You'd hate it, Valentine. You hated it after the auction, and you'd hate it even more if your paycheck actually depended on it."

She frowned, but she knew he was right.

"I won't let you pay for everything," she sighed. "I need a job. I waitressed in New York once, maybe I could do that."

"Valentine."

"What?"

"Go back to Caché."

"What!?"

"Honestly, I was shocked when Del said you'd put in your notice. You love that fucking place," he told her. "It's your home. But for whatever reason, maybe because you were ashamed of what you were doing, I don't know what, you convinced yourself it was a bad place. A fun place, sure, and a good time, yeah, but ultimately bad. But it's not. Del is a good guy, and he takes great care of all of you."

Valentine was absolutely gobsmacked.

"You want me to be an escort," she tried to clarify.

"Are you fucking high? Of course I don't want that. Even having to just watch those guys bid on you made me want to commit murder," he growled, and the sentiment made her feel warm. "But there are other jobs. You were great with the people there, find a different niche. I'm sure Del would be ecstatic if you didn't leave."

Valentine let the idea roll around in her mind. She hadn't wanted to escort anymore, so even though she loved being at the club, the obvious choice had been to quit.

It hadn't occurred to her to ask for a different position.

"It's not the worst idea," she mumbled.

"Of course not. I came up with it."

The arm around her waist moved, his hand gently rubbing up and down the length of her back. Over her butt and then back up, his fingers trailing along sensitive areas.

"This is real," she whispered, lightly scratching her nails in circles against his chest.

"This is the realest," he agreed, his lips against her cheek.

"This is really happening."

"This has already happened."

His mouth was against her ear, his teeth biting down on her ear lobe. When he rolled into her, she moved with him, laying on her back. His hands immediately went to her breasts.

"You love me," she said it, even though the words terrified her.

"And you love me," he was nodding, his thick hair brushing against her face.

"This is the first good thing that's happened to me in a long time," she was whispering again, and her legs fell open when one his hands found its way between them. "So just … take it easy on me, okay?"

"Oh, Valentine," he chuckled darkly, and then he was gently pushing her again, forcing her onto her stomach. "'Taking it easy on you' is something I have no intention of doing."

She laughed, then groaned when she felt him moving over her legs, his hard-on brushing against her bare ass.

"Did I say 'good'?" she mumbled, stretching her arms out above her head as he began to massage her shoulders.

"You did."

"I meant 'best thing ever'."

"That's what I thought—now be quiet, and let me show you how much better still it can be."

*Nothing. Nothing could be better than this right here. This best ending for a not so great romance. Oh my god, Bailey was right ... cut to two hours later, and here we are, attempting to live happily every after, and **that's** the best ending **ever**.*

Epilogue

"Valentine!"

Val leaned back in her chair, looking out her office door at the stairs.

"What!?" she hollered back.

"Get your saintly ass down here, *now!*"

She rolled her eyes, but did as she was bidden. She skipped her saintly ass down the stairs.

"What's the problem?" she asked, twiddling a pen between her fingers as she walked down a hall and emerged in a large room.

"This!" Marco DelVecchio yelled, holding his arms out wide, gesturing to the scene in front of them. "*This* is my fucking problem!"

A veritable mountain of presents dominated the room. All different shapes and sizes, they filled every corner, and reached the ceiling. It wouldn't be too long before they reached the edges of the room. Valentine would have to find somewhere else to store them when that happened.

It had been her idea—donate a toy for a tot for Christmas, get a free "private tour" of Caché with the lady of your choice. All the female workers volunteered for the gigs, no one was forced, and the members leapt at the chance. What usually cost them a couple hundred dollars was suddenly free with the purchase of a beanie baby—the gifts *poured* in. The more presents a member brought, the more intimate the tour.

At the rate they were going, Caché was going to singlehandedly put gifts under the trees of all the needy kids in Chicago.

"You're like Santa, Del," she laughed. "We should get you a red jacket and white beard."

"Ha ha, fucking, ha. Meanwhile, I'm down two whole rooms!" he snapped.

"*Meanwhile* this is going to be a massive tax write off for you," she reminded him. "Not to mention it will put you in good standing with the community."

"Yeah, yeah, so you keep saying. How many days until Christmas?"

"Five days, Del. You can tough it out."

"Whatever. No more of these crazy ideas. Get back to work," he sighed, playfully shoving her out of the room.

Valentine had quit Caché on a Friday. She had spent the following Saturday and Sunday in bed with Ari. And then on the following Monday, she'd gone back to Caché to apply for a job.

She'd barely spoken a word before Del had said *"you're hired"*.

Between the two of them, they'd come up with a whole new position for her—event liaison. Del always planned the big events, like for holidays, or for when celebrities showed up, but he hated dealing with members. So Val became the go-between. She gave tours of the spaces, price quotes, estimates. She began keeping a binder full of all their past events, so people could pick and choose from them.

After a couple months, her job role expanded. She realized that while Del had plenty to offer for his VIP clients, he'd never shown any interest in the smaller—but still lucrative—side business of party planning. Frat parties, bachelor/bachelorette parties, birthdays, and her personal favorite, newly-divorced parties. Sure, they weren't as big a spenders as the rappers and basketball players of the world, but they more than made up for the difference in quantity.

Instead of maybe just one large party a month, Valentine started taking on one small party a month. One small room in the house dedicated to the party's needs—raunchy games for the hen party, or beer pong for the frat bros, whatever. Included in the fee for the parties were one-night passes to the entire club, which about fifty percent of the time led to people buying full memberships. After eight months, Valentine had a team working under her, coordinating the events they were now hosting twice a weekend.

She was making more money for Del than she ever had as a hostess, and she was actually proud of what she did. She enjoyed it. She still got to dress up, still got to play the part of Saint Valentine, but it was also still her. Still Val.

She loved it, just like Ari had thought she would.

"Oh, shit!" she hissed, glancing at her watch. She'd completely forgotten she had somewhere to be that night.

She raced up to her office—actually Del's old office, he'd moved into a bigger space he'd renovated. She threw all her stuff into her bag, then quickly locked the door behind her before flying back down the stairs.

"There a fire, baby girl?" Serge asked as she almost bowled him over.

"No, I was just supposed to be somewhere ten minutes ago," she explained, trying to catch her breath.

"Ah. Gotcha. How is fucko doing, anyway?" he asked.

"*Ari* is fine," she chuckled. "You still coming over for Christmas?"

"We'll see. Charice usually likes to keep me tied up outside of work hours," he said, winking at her. She made a gagging noise.

"There are some things that are best left to the imagination. Goodbye, Serge."

Once outside, she quickly climbed into Ari's Audi. She drove it more often than he did anymore—she'd ridden her bike all through the summer, but when it had started snowing again, he'd insisted on her driving. The roads were icy and dangerous, he'd constantly warned her. She'd insisted she'd be fine, she'd ridden all through last winter.

But then she'd taken a nasty fall one night, cutting a six inch gash into the back of her head. She'd been fine, but when Ari had shown up in the ER, she'd almost thought he was going to hurt somebody, he'd been so angry. He'd threatened to sue the city of Chicago for not salting enough, for not plowing enough, for not making their curbs softer.

It had been very sweet.

After that, he'd bought a second car for himself, claiming he didn't like the Audi very much. She knew it was really because he wanted her to drive it, so she did.

"Love you," she whispered, kissing her finger tips and then pressing them to the rosary hanging from the rear view mirror. It was her grandmother's. They'd spread her ashes in Lake Michigan, and then the very next day, Valentine had found the rosary mixed up with all her stuff. It was strange, considering her grandmother hadn't been to church in a long time, and she hadn't noticed it in the old house. So she'd taken it as a sign, and had kept it near her ever since.

There was no time to go home and change, so they would have to just deal with her in her club clothes. The silver sequins were a little dramatic for dinner in a nice restaurant, and she was pretty sure the cropped top was against any dress codes, but when the maître d' saw the names of the people she'd be joining, they wouldn't care what she was wearing.

They never did.

She pulled to an abrupt stop in the valet line, thankful there was a small back up of cars. She crawled up onto her knees and leaned into the backseat, looking through all the shit back there. Satin and rhinestones and nylon were everywhere, but she was looking for shoes. She finally found a sparkly silver pair of heels buried under a lime green mini skirt.

"Yes!" she shouted in triumph, then she shrieked when someone knocked on her window.

"Uh, ma'am? Valet?" a young kid asked, his eyes glued to her chest. She rolled her eyes and opened the door.

"Yes, thank you," she grumbled, hopping into her shoes before grabbing her purse. He handed her the ticket, and then she hurried around the car.

She'd never been to this restaurant before, but it looked nice. It sat right on the water, spectacular views from all three sides. She patted her hand over her hair, hoping she looked half good enough to be there.

"May I help you?" a snooty looking man asked before she could enter the restaurant proper. She gave him a big smile while she straightened out her skirt. No amount of tugging could change its length, though, so she gave up.

"Yes, I'm meeting some people, they have reservations," she started.

"Of course. It's very chilly this evening, perhaps madam would like to put on a jacket?" he asked, his eyes moving up and down her body, the disdain evident in his eyes.

"Madam is fine," she assured him, putting her hand on her hip. "And the reservation is for Sharapov."

His eyebrows shot up.

"I'm sorry, did you just say—"

"*Ari Sharapov.*"

They both turned their heads to see the owner of the name approaching them, and it was all Valentine could do not to swoon.

Eight months. It had been eight months since Ari had bid zero dollars on her and she had slapped him and they had fallen irreversibly in love with each other. And still to this day, every time she saw him, her heart did jumping jacks. She hoped she always felt that way, like she was just noticing him across the room for the first time.

"Mr. Sharapov," the maître d' sputtered. "Yes, sir, your third party member has arrived."

"I can see that," Ari said, his eyes doing their own perusal of Valentine's body, and without an ounce of disdain.

He wrapped his arm around her waist, setting off sparks against her skin, and guided her onto the restaurant floor.

"I'm sorry," she whispered.

"You're late," he replied.

"I know. Hence why I'm saying I'm sorry."

"This dinner was your idea, Valentine."

"I know."

"*Your idea*, and you're late."

"I know. Repeating it over and over again isn't gonna change it," she said. "When I realized I forgot, I raced over here as fast as possible."

"I know."

"You do?" she asked, glancing up at him. He smirked down at her.

"You drove over in your sneakers," he commented. She glanced down at her feet, double checking that she did, in fact, have on a pair of glittery silver heels.

"How did you know that?" she asked, looking back at him.

"Because you had to dig those heels out of the backseat."

"How did you know I—*oh my god,* you saw me," she groaned, smacking herself in the forehead. They stopped at the end of the bar and Ari stood in front of her, blocking her from the room.

"I'm pretty sure everyone saw *all* of you," he replied. "Nice panties, by the way. I'm glad my birthday gift is being put to use."

"What can I say? It's a short skirt," she sighed. "Did I show my entire ass?"

"Pretty much. I think I heard someone's pacemaker short out," he said, then he reached behind her and took a martini from the bartender.

"Glad I could liven the joint up. I'm sorry, I didn't have time to change. Do you think—"

"Everyone saw, Valentine. *Everyone.*"

"Oh god," she moaned, dropping her forehead to his chest. "I'm so, so sorry. I screwed this up."

Ari gently pushed her upright, then handed her the stiff drink. She sucked down two huge gulps before he pulled it away.

"You didn't screw anything up, you're perfect. Authentically you, which is the best. If he doesn't like you like this, then he's not worth any more of our time," Ari assured her. She smiled up at him.

"You're pretty wonderful sometimes, you know that, Mr. Sharapov?"

"Yes, I do. Now kiss me, Ms. O'Dell, and let's get this over with."

She stood on her toes and pressed her lips to his and kissed him in a way that she hoped would short out another pacemaker or two.

Their eight months together had certainly been *interesting*. Full of fights and makeup sex and regular sex and learning about each other and kinky sex and a couple more fights, and so much love, sometimes she thought she was going to die from happiness.

She'd moved into the apartment he'd bought, just like he'd wanted her to do. She and Bailey lived there happily—the younger girl continuing her online romance, growing a real relationship with her online boyfriend, Devlin Daniels. He flew out to meet her not long after they moved into the apartment, and two weeks after that, she flew to New York to visit him. They kept it up after that, taking turns visiting each other.

Valentine had spent her days at school, which had gotten much easier after Harper Kittering had been expelled. It turned out Ari hadn't stopped slaying dragons when he'd quit his job. He'd decided to make good on all his threats, and he—anonymously—exposed deputy mayor Kittering for bribing college admissions officers to admit his daughter. Multiple people lost their jobs, from teachers to administrators, including his honorable self, Roy Kittering.

Harper turned the whole thing into her own personal soap opera, claiming she'd had no idea, crying to every news outlet she could find. She became somewhat of a walking meme, but she also gained a lot of followers on social media because of it. Last Valentine had heard of her, Harper was attempting to be some sort of lifestyle blogger, taking lots of shitty pictures of her apartment and telling people how they could have it all, too!

After school, Valentine had spent her evenings at Caché, working in her office or hosting parties. *Hosting*—not escorting. A big difference, though she did run into a few of her old regulars. They were all gracious and polite; she'd always had a good eye for good men.

One guy she regularly ran into hadn't been a regular of hers at all—Evans Daniels was still a night owl. He came to the club almost every weekend, and often times she, Ari, and Evans would find themselves sharing a drink and closing the place down. She always found it hilarious that for two guys who had started out having a lot of animosity for each other, they'd grown into a pretty inseparable duo. Spending half of their weeknights together at Caché, and all of their weekdays together at their new firm.

Sharapov & Daniels had officially come into existence barely a month after Ari had quit his father's law firm. Turned out the elder Sharapov had been wrong—Ari's talents had superceded his father, and when he walked, several of his clients walked with him. When Evans found out Ari was on his own, he'd approached him with the idea of going into business together. They were both in corporate law, so it made sense. They could share their case loads, which would make it easier for Ari to study and practice other types of law. It was perfect. They dazzled their clients together during the day, then celebrated with cocktails in the evenings.

Her nights, though, had all been spent with Ari. Every single one of them. At her place, at his place, on his office desk just like he'd fantasized about—they couldn't get enough of each other. She wanted to be with him always, all the time, as much as she could.

When July rolled around, Bailey made the big decision to move to New York to be with Devlin. It had been hard to see her go, but Valentine had been happy for her. Bailey was a great girl, who deserved all the best life had to offer. She could only hope that Evans' little brother would be able to give it to her best friend.

After that, it had seemed pointless staying in the downstairs apartment by herself. All of her free time was spent with Ari, anyway. So they'd spent a day traipsing up and down the stairs of the building, ferrying her belongings up to his apartment, and then they'd spent an evening in the tub he'd had installed just for her, massaging each others' sore muscles.

And that had been it. Perfection achieved.

He was still a jerk. He still put his foot in his mouth, and sometimes he forgot who he was talking to and treated her like an employee.

And sometimes she still overreacted, or misjudged something he said and then slammed a door in his face.

But after two painful break ups, they'd learned their lesson. The foot never stayed in his mouth long, and she never locked the door. They always talked it out with each other. They always came back to each other.

And she was beginning to think they always would.

Alright, Ari. You slayed a bunch of dragons for me. Now it's my turn.

"Okay," she said, pulling away from him and shaking the tension out of her shoulders. "I'm ready."

Ari made a face at her.

"You look like you're about to faint."

"Really?"

"Or shit yourself."

"Thanks, cheers for that," she grumbled, then she snatched the martini back and polished it off.

"We don't have to do this," he reminded her. "Just because he calls, doesn't mean we have to answer. I haven't seen him in eight months, I'm fine with not seeing him for eight more. Or eight more years. Or eighty."

Valentine held up her hands.

"No. Because then there will always be that doubt in our mind, always be that 'what if'? If I'm going to cut somebody out of my life, I'm not giving them the chance to say 'she didn't even try'. We're not going to give him that kind of satisfaction."

"Okay," Ari nodded, and he gripped her hand tightly in his before placing them both over his heart. "So long as you know this isn't about him, or his approval. This is about us. This is about you and me, because nobody else matters."

Valentine melted inside.

"Nobody else," she agreed.

"Good girl. Just remember, nobody loves you like I do, Saint Valentine."

"And nobody loves you like I do, Aaron Sharapov."

He leaned forward and kissed her on the forehead.

"Alright then. Let's go meet my father."

He turned away, but kept ahold of her hand, and she followed in his wake. She knew his father was only a few feet away. Knew he most likely wouldn't approve of her, and knew this dinner was most likely a mistake, and she even knew it was most likely the first of many to come.

Mr. Sharapov only had one son, and no matter what he said, he wanted to be a part of Ari's life. Ari had made it clear that Valentine was a part of that life. It was going to be a battle getting Mr. Sharapov to understand that, and to accept it. But Valentine was ready. After eight months at Ari's side, she was ready to go to war for him.

Because I believe in him, and I believe in us, and ultimately, that's all that matters.

ALSO FROM THE AUTHOR

THE KANE SERIES

"… thanks to Stylo for getting me lost, breaking the rules, and "going there". This was fresh and dark …"—**Penelope Douglas, NY Times and USA Today Bestselling author of the Fall Away series and Corrupt**

Degradation
Separation
Reparation
Completion
Reception

STANDALONES

"I could not fault one moment of this story, I devoured every word and every beautiful depraved page. Days later I am still thinking about it and I know that it will be one of those books that will be etched into my soul, I honestly loved it that much."—**I Love Book Love blog**

The Bad Ones

My Time in the Affair

Just a Little Junk

Muscle Memory

While I Was Away

CHURCH. duet

Church., Book One
Preach., Book Two

THE MERCENARIES

Best Laid Plans
Out of Plans
The Mercenaries: Boxset

TWIN ESTATES NOVELS

"… only one author I know continues to blow my ever-loving mind with the sheer gutsiness and uniqueness of her stories … Stylo Fantôme continues to write with such intelligence and verve … once again, she delivers with a book that is hot sexy escapism at its finest."—**Natasha is a Book Junkie**

Neighbors
The Neighborhood
Block Party
Neighborhood Watch

ACKNOWLEDGEMENTS

This is going to be short and sweet.

The summer of 2019 was one of the worst for me.

Nothing particularly bad happened, I just fell into a spiral of bad luck, which led to feeling a certain way and I just couldn't get out of it. So much pressure to write and produce and come up with something, anything, JESUS SOMETHING!, and it finally happened—creator burn out. I thought I'd experienced it before, but I'd had no idea.

So basically, I had a minor mental breakdown, and I decided to do what I see everyone posting about all the time. I decided to back down and take care of my mental health. I pushed back the release date of this book, and I pretty much went dark on social media, for SIX WEEKS.

But amazing things still came out of it. My readers supported me, as did my friends. People I barely knew checked up on me, and no one got angry about the release date being moved. No one said anything nasty. It was really nice, and kind of changed my view of this industry a little.

SO!

This book would FOR REALS, LEGIT not exist if it weren't for a few certain people—Rebecca Nebel, checking in on me and gently encouraging me and sending me any typos she found. She read it as I sent it to her, and it will forever be known as our CHUNK story.

It wouldn't exist if it weren't for Christine Hendrickson, reading at a lightening quick pace, even though she didn't have to, and sending me screenshots of errors and typos, which she also didn't have to do, but it helped tremendously and I was very grateful for it.

And it would not exist if it weren't for author Alice K. Wayne, sprinting with me and understanding me and being my twinsie. Knowing the ins and outs of this crazy pressure, and letting me vent, and venting to me, and making me feel less alone in this endeavor.

Because make no mistake—we may have a million people in our heads, but being an author can be a lonely, lonely job. Eventually that loneliness starts to eat at you from the outside, and the pressure starts to work at you from the inside, and sometimes it just feels like there's nothing left to give.

There aren't words enough to express my eternal gratitude to Kylie and Give Me Books. I always joke that I'm a horrible client, but this time I really lived up to that title. I lost thousands of words at one point, my computer crashed, my gmail started going haywire—I swear to christ, this fucking book is cursed—AS I TYPE THIS, THE AMAZON PAGE REFUSES TO LOAD THE COVER. See? Cursed.

I kept pushing back deadlines and pushing back dates, and they never EVER once made me feel bad about it. They went out of their way to make me feel GOOD. To make sure I was OKAY. That's not in their job description—they're just awesome frickin' people who deserve the utmost respect, because it's easy to just write someone off. It takes a lot of thought and effort to keep them in mind, to check on them, and to help them. I hope they stay in this business a long time, because everyone deserves people like them in their corner.

Lastly, to Mr. F—I think this was a scary time for you. It was for me, too. But you handled it all with a smile. You never, ever once pressured me to work, to get back in the chair, to do anything stressful, even though you more than anybody knew how much was riding on me finishing this. You always had a joke to make me feel better, and you always had time to spend with me. Thank you for being by my side.

THERE. It's DONE. And I'm actually really fucking proud of it, and everything I went through to get it done.

So now I'm going to sleep for a year. Call me in 2020.

AVAILABLE NOW

My Time in the Affair

~*Mischa*~

How much I wanted him took me by surprise. I didn't want to feel that way—I'd been telling the truth. I wasn't looking for another relationship. Clearly, I wasn't good at relationships, and had no business entering into an already-fucked-up-relationship without ending my last totally-fucked-up-relationship.

But it was like he understood me. I could say anything to him, literally anything, and he just got it. He didn't think I was a horrible human being for cheating on my husband. He didn't care that I was married. Didn't care that I was emotionally stunted most of the time, and physically inhibited some of the time. All he cared about was being with me. Everything else, that was just background noise.

I hadn't ever known that kind of freedom, to just be myself, one hundred percent. Say whatever I want, do whatever I want, in all situations. You just can't be like that with most people, there's always a filter that needs to be in place. But not with Tal.

Not in *any* situations.

I was drunk on him. High on him. I wanted to swallow him down, inhale him, inject him. I wanted him to live under my skin and change my DNA. I wanted to live in his air and breathe his passion.

I thought maybe, just maybe, I could overdose on him. If I could just take him one more time, and shut my eyes, and it would be the last time, with anyone, with anything, that would be alright. Guilt would be gone. Hurt would be gone. Confusion would be gone. Oppression would be gone.

Obsession would be gone.

AVAILABLE NOW

The Bad Ones

"Constantine!?"

Dulcie groaned. *Frannie*. Since Con had come back, she hadn't seen the other woman. She'd begun to think maybe it was a sign, that her luck was changing. Con was her dark little rainbow, spreading peace over her world. But no. Apparently not.

"Hi, Frannie," he said politely, his politician's-smile making an appearance. No hint of the big bad wolf in that grin.

"It's been so long! How are you? *Move*, Dulcie, jesus, I'm trying to talk to my old friend," Frannie demanded, shoving her out of the way. The ice cream fell out of her hand and smacked into the floor.

"It's been a while," Con agreed, ignoring the incident between the girls. "How've you been? You look great."

Dulcie stared at their interaction, dumbfounded.

"Oh, stop. I don't. Do I? Well, not as good as *you*. You look *incredible*," Frannie gushed. His smile got bigger and Dulcie watched as Frannie fell a little more in love with him.

"Thanks."

"Enough about me. What are you doing here? And god, is Dulcie bothering you? Townies, I swear. C'mon, there's a great coffee shop next door, it just opened. Let me get you a cup," Frannie offered, then linked her arm though his and began dragging him away.

"A coffee shop? Wow, Fuller's almost like a real town," he laughed, and she cackled right along with him as they walked out the door together. He didn't look back, not even once.

What. The fuck.

Dulcie stomped the whole way home. She bypassed her elevator and took the stairs, wanting to burn off some energy. When she got into her apartment, she slammed the door shut behind her and locked it. The knob and the bolt, even put on the chain. Something she rarely ever did; she pitied anyone who would be stupid enough to try and rob her. But that afternoon, she wasn't in the mood for anyone to come inside.

She felt like she was going to explode, she had to do something with all the tension that was threatening to blow her apart, so she tore around the apartment. The bed was a mess, blankets scattered everywhere—they'd stayed the night at her place, but hadn't slept much. So she changed the sheets and made the bed, then tidied up other parts of the room. There was a wash basin set up on a counter top, so she cleaned the meager amount of dishes she had and left them out to dry. She was rinsing off a chef's knife when she heard what she'd been waiting for—scratching, on the other side of her door.

"Fuck off, I'm not in the mood for you right now!" she yelled. Deep laughter rolled straight through the wood and brick, almost filling her apartment.

"That's a lie, and you know it."

She frowned and turned so her back was against the wall between the counter top and the door.

"I don't want you to come in."

"I wasn't asking. Open the door, or I'll open it myself."

She held the knife up, touching the tip of the blade with her index finger.

"Go ahead."

The building was old, she didn't expect the door to put up much of a fight. She turned back to her wash station and went about drying the knife. There was silence for a solid minute after her dare, and she paused in her movements. Then the door almost exploded off its hinges as Con rammed through it, and she went back to drying.

"You can't honestly be mad at me," he said simply, brushing his shoulder off as he moved to stand next to her.

"You didn't think that was possible? I spent three years being mad at you. I'm really good at it," she informed him. He chuckled and put his hands flat on the counter top, leaning down so he was at her level.

"Dulcie, you couldn't be mad at me if you tried. *You're scared.* What are you so scared of, little girl?"

I'll show him scared.

She let out a yell as she stabbed the knife down in front of him. The blade lodged in the wood right between his index and middle fingers, and had gone so deep, it stood upright on its own. Con didn't even flinch.

"*Not her,*" Dulcie hissed. "You can do whatever you want, but don't *ever* play your little pretend act with her. *Got it!?*"

Almost stabbing him was fine, but telling him what do do? That was just going too far. His hand was around her jaw, his fingernails cutting into her skin, and he literally dragged her across the room. She cried out as he slammed her up against a window, the back of her head breaking out a pane of glass.

"If you're actually threatened by a girl like her, then I'm insulted. Then you're fucking stupid, and what's going on here between us isn't what I thought. Don't you ever fucking talk to me like that again," he snapped, baring his teeth against the side of her face. She held onto his wrist, trying to relieve some of the pressure he was putting on her jaw.

"While you were off playing pretend for those three years, I was stuck here listening to her voice. Dealing with her insults, her jabs, her digs. Watching as she sucked the life out of her husband. A guy whose only mistake in life was dating me, yet she won't stop punishing him for it. I've had to listen as she spread rumors about me, about you. Had to deal with not getting hired in places because she had her father forbid it. So you know what? *Fuck you,* Constantine. I'll talk to you any way I fucking want."

He was silent for a moment, his eyes wandering over her face. She knew he was attracted to her, obviously, but she often wondered if he found her half as beautiful as she found him to be. His blue eyes dipped lower, tracing over the outline of her lips, watching as she gasped for air.

"You are the most amazing thing I've ever seen," he said, reading her thoughts. She struggled to take in air and stumbled a little; his hand was still on her jaw, holding her up so she was forced onto her toes. His forearm was resting on her chest, making it hard to breathe. Yet she let go of his wrist. Let him push almost his full weight against her, and against the glass behind them.

"We're going to kill each other, aren't we?" she whispered.

ABOUT THE AUTHOR

Crazy woman living in an undisclosed location in Alaska (where the need for a creative mind is a necessity!), I have been writing since ..., forever? Yeah, that sounds about right. I have been told that I remind people of Lucille Ball - I also see shades of Jennifer Saunders, and Denis Leary. So basically, I laugh a lot, I'm clumsy a lot, and I say the F-word A LOT.

I like dogs more than I like most people, and I don't trust anyone who doesn't drink. No, I do not live in an igloo, and no, the sun does not set for six months out of the year, there's your Alaska lesson for the day. I have mermaid hair - both a curse and a blessing - and most of the time I talk so fast, even I can't understand me.

Yeah. I think that about sums me up.

CPSIA information can be obtained
at www.ICGtesting.com
Printed in the USA
BVHW030216231219
567560BV00001B/16/P